'Original, surprising and romantic.'
Woman & Home

'Full of wonder and heart.'
Emma Jane Unsworth, author of *Animals*

'An incredibly imaginative debut.'
Sunday Mirror

'A tense fight for survival with an unexpected ending.' ****
Sun

'Superbly realized . . .
packed with surprises that overturn all expectations.'
S Magazine

'This book made me ugly cry . . .
it breaks your heart then kicks it again for good
measure in the most beautiful way possible.'
The Pool

'A beautiful, moving, truly original tale.
I loved this book for taking me by surprise.'
Anna McPartlin, author of *The Last Days of Rabbit Hayes*

'Beautifully, frustratingly, heart-breaking.'
Maggie Harcourt, author of *Unconventional*

Also by Katie Khan

HOLD BACK THE STARS

and published by Black Swan

The Light Between Us

KATIE KHAN

BLACK SWAN

TRANSWORLD PUBLISHERS
61–63 Uxbridge Road, London W5 5SA
www.penguin.co.uk

Transworld is part of the Penguin Random House group of companies
whose addresses can be found at global.penguinrandomhouse.com

Penguin
Random House
UK

First published in Great Britain in 2018 by Doubleday
an imprint of Transworld Publishers
Black Swan edition published 2018

A CIP catalogue record for this book
is available from the British Library.

ISBN 9781784161781

Typeset in 11.16/13.9pt Dante MT Std by Jouve (UK), Milton Keynes.
Printed and bound in Great Britain by Clays Ltd, Elcograf S.p.A.

Penguin Random House is committed to a sustainable future
for our business, our readers and our planet. This book is made
from Forest Stewardship Council® certified paper.

MIX
Paper from
responsible sources
FSC
www.fsc.org   FSC® C018179

1 3 5 7 9 10 8 6 4 2

For Katy,
who showed me true friendship
can feel like falling in love.

An Alignment at Dusk

Oxford, October 2010

The planets were moving towards each other in the night sky when Isaac and Thea first met. It was a rare conjunction, the type that happens only once a decade – and, at St Catherine's College, Oxford, the Astronomy Club was meeting to observe the curious celestial event.

Their numbers were bolstered that night by random observers hoping to snatch a quick glimpse through the telescopes. Not many understood exactly what they were looking at, but they'd been told Mercury, Venus, Jupiter, Saturn and Mars would align, tracing an arc across the sky shortly after twilight. It was a sight rarer than an eclipse and there was a hum of excitement out on the grass as students and professors mingled, huddling in groups for warmth as they waited with a tangible expectation they could almost taste on the cold wind.

It wouldn't be too much longer.

Those who knew what they were doing moved around fixing telescopes trained upwards, spaced out across grass glistening with dew. Thea Colman recognized many students conscripted in from the Philosophy Department; compulsory attendance, they'd been told. Thea was sure they were only asked to attend because looking out at the universe will make any human feel improbably small.

Hands stuffed into coat pockets, her chestnut hair tucked

into her scarf, neck straining to look up at the sky, Thea's attention was fixed on the pale pools of light pouring towards her, strengthening each minute.

'Here –' a student Thea hadn't met before pushed a hot drink in a red plastic cup at her – 'take one. It'll warm you up.'

'Thanks,' she said, taking her hand from her pocket to hold the cup against her, absorbing its heat. Around them, various people peered into the lenses of telescopes, while those waiting stamped their feet against the cold, similarly clutching steaming red cups.

'I hate these cups,' she murmured.

'Oh?' the same person said, still near her. He was tall with a shock of dark hair brushed away from his forehead; waves that threatened to explode into all-out curls at any moment. 'Why's that?'

Thea swirled her hot toddy, gazing into it as though she could read tealeaves. 'Well, who brought them here? Almost certainly an undergrad who's spent time in the States, gorging on American culture, who has *very* misguidedly thought the Oxford Astronomy Club would be the right place to cultivate a derivative fraternity vibe.'

'Is that right?' he said, starting to laugh.

'I mean, are we supposed to play a game of beer pong, right here on the grass . . . ?'

'Oh, good!' came a voice. The Philosophy professor stood behind them, beaming. 'You've met. Two of my "half" students who, lamentably, I only get to teach for half the time. The rest of the time you're corrupted by other subjects, and other professors.'

Thea smiled politely, as did the person next to her.

'You're both looking rather contemplative,' said the tutor. 'Pondering the otherworldly light from the heavens?'

'Something like that,' Thea said.

'And what do you think light is?' he enquired. 'Colman?'

She raised her eyebrows: the question was too easy. 'An electric field, tied up with a magnetic field, blasting through space at great speed.'

The tutor smiled. 'You like that definition. I can see it in your eyes.' He tilted his head. 'What about you, Mendelsohn – what do you think light is?'

She watched the curly-haired student next to her consider before he spoke. 'Well . . .' His gaze flicked towards Thea, not quite meeting hers before snapping back to the professor. ' "A certain slant of light" is poetry. A spectrum of seven rainbow colours is a symbol of pride . . . And I suppose when we, as humans, look in a mirror – we can find our own truth, within that reflection made from light.'

'Do you see?' the professor said, sadly. 'How your other studies corrupt you. Though that was very lyrical, Mendelsohn – what a shame I don't get you in my Philosophy class full-time.' He brightened. 'Perhaps you'll be a good influence on Thea, here. Get her out of her scientific ways of thinking.'

The student took a leisurely sip from his red cup. 'I'm more inclined to think someone that logical will be a good influence on *me*.'

She regarded him briefly; that secret moment when you instinctively like someone you've just met and must consider whether it's admiration or attraction.

Or both.

'You were saying something about hating the red cups?' he said, turning to her as their professor made his excuses and moved away.

She smiled. 'I don't think we've met before, have we?'

'I've been abroad,' he said. 'I spent a year studying in the States.'

'How did you like America?'

'I loved it.' Around them, people began to *ooh* as the remaining daylight dispersed and the planets became more visible in the dark. He pointed to Mercury, closest to the horizon, and Venus with its whiteish light sitting just above the moon, the three entities forming the beginnings of a curved line. In only a few minutes those brightly coloured dots would be joined by three more, arching in the sky above them, a line-of-sight trick making them look impossibly close.

'I stayed with a fraternity in Princeton,' he continued. Then, when Thea didn't say anything: 'You could say I *gorged* on American culture.'

'Oh.' She looked at him soberly. 'You brought the cups.'

He grinned. 'I'm Isaac,' he said, holding out his hand, waiting as she jostled her red cup to the other hand so she could shake his.

'I'm sorry. I said something rude. I tend to lack—'

'A filter? That's not a bad thing.' He smiled. 'So you're Thea. The scientific one.'

'And you're Isaac,' she said, as their gaze returned to the skies. 'The poetic one.'

It was nearly time.

She could see his profile in the corner of her vision, but when their eyes met they both quickly turned their attention to the emerging conjunction of the planets. They only looked like they were close together because of where they were standing; their viewpoint on Earth tonight would deceive their eyes, and though, for a brief moment, the planets would appear near to one another in the solar system, they were still distinct and far apart – lone lights in the dark.

Thea turned something over and over in her pocket, feeling the shiny, hard surface of glass against her palm as she contemplated the starlight.

Above them, faintly, shone brownish Saturn and pinkish Mars, and far out to the left was yellowish Jupiter. The sound of the groups became louder, as though someone had turned up the volume. 'Do you see it?' People around them began to murmur excitedly.

'The syzygy,' Thea said, and she saw Isaac glance at her as he drank from the blasted red cup.

'That's right,' the Astronomy tutor said warmly. 'Three or more celestial bodies, all in a line. And this syzygy is special, because the curved line the five planets fall on is the . . . ?'

Thea stopped herself answering, remembering to let other people have their turn, and instead took a sip from her cup. But when nobody spoke, she bit her lip.

'It's the ecliptic,' she said, tracing the line of lights in the sky with her hand. 'An imaginary line that marks the path of the sun.' More quietly, she continued: 'It's what makes it look as though we're standing on the edge of the universe. As though we could wave, and the other planets might see.'

Isaac wore a look of surprise, and as the group chattered and the professors posited further questions, moving among the crowd, he turned to her. 'You're into astronomy?'

'I'm studying Physics and Philosophy.'

'Suddenly it makes sense.' He raised his cup in cheers. 'I'm Psychology, Philosophy and Linguistics, myself.'

'Keeping busy.' Thea grinned.

'I spend more time in the library than is entirely good for the soul – there's a hell of a lot of research.' He grimaced. 'Hard science has always been my Kryptonite.'

She took a sip of her drink, smiling into the cup. 'Better not let me tell you my idea for a PhD, then.'

'In Philosophy?'

'No – God, no.' She wrinkled her nose. 'Physics.'

They stood together, staring at the moon ringed aglow, the planets like bright map pins they could reach up and unfasten from the sky.

'When you see the solar system laid out in front of us like this,' Isaac started, 'when you can really see the other planets . . . it makes me think there's no one else out there, in the universe, but us.'

She knew she'd met someone she'd want to talk more with, when he said that.

'Would I be able to follow it?' he said. 'Your PhD idea.'

And whereas Thea would usually reach for every principle under the sun, every technical word to prove her intelligence through the great wealth of fact and theory she'd stored up over the years, she didn't want to lose her new friend's attention – and she didn't want to make him feel bad, if he couldn't grasp it. 'Yes,' she said. She reached into her pocket, feeling for the comfort of the multifaceted glass that dug into her hand. She brought it out and he looked at it, bemused.

'A crystal?' he said.

'Nothing quite so woo-woo,' she said. 'This is a glass prism.'

Isaac eyed her speculatively. 'And what are you going to do with this prism, during your complicated PhD research project I haven't a hope of understanding?'

Thea twinkled. The ecliptic stretched out overhead, a curved line of the solar system's major players, the rarely beheld formation making an imaginary line real to the naked eye once every ten years. 'It's about light,' she said, forcing herself to sound casual. 'The theory is, if you were to travel faster than the speed of light, you could – technically speaking – arrive somewhere before you left.'

Isaac raised an eyebrow. 'Is that so?'

'It's a theory.'

'But isn't the speed of light inordinately fast?'

'It is.' Thea twisted the prism so it caught the moonlight, throwing beams and spectrums across the ground. 'But not if you were to slow it down. Trap it, somehow.'

Isaac looked to the glass prism, and back at his new friend. 'You could arrive somewhere before you left.'

She gave him a conspiratorial smile. 'I'm going to prove that time travel is possible.'

I

The Glass House

One

EIGHT YEARS LATER

Thea watches the light of the day wash away. Golden hour comes and goes; she watches from the window as the amateur photographers of Oxford lift their camera phones to capture the sandy stone of college towers, basking in the milky daylight that makes their images softer and their hearts a little warmer.

She watches.

And she waits.

The golden light dilutes down to dusk. From her window, Thea observes the figures on the street outside hurrying as the warmth dissipates, twilight's blue tinge announcing the coming dark. She turns the glass prism over and over in her hand, her thumb bearing a mark from all the years she's held it – a callus on her skin caused as much by the imprint of her determination as by the hard surface of the glass.

Still she waits.

The lampposts outside flicker on in the gloom. The evening is swollen with anticipation: tonight's the night . . . and it's been a long time coming. Tonight Thea will break the rules.

The University said no to her time travel proposal, firmly directing Thea's PhD studies towards more academic, more

3

'suitable' research. Which she accepted, at first. But after a while the professors' unwillingness to even *listen* made her angry . . . the way they threw Einstein and Hawking in her face, as though someone like Thea would never be able to match them. Yes, the best men that science had to offer established infamous equations and theories about light and time, but their satisfied faces, and the idea there was nothing more to say on the matter, simply *urged* young scientists like her to prove them wrong. So she's going to.

The professors have forced her hand, in a way. Because Thea knows in her gut that she is right – and tonight, with or without permission, she'll prove it. The University Physics Department has something she needs, so tonight she's going to borrow it.

As darkness finally crawls across the city, Thea starts work. In size order, she packs a large holdall with three small industrial-looking photographic lamps and three tripods, a camera, and a battery pack for her phone. She picks up an artist's portfolio case and puts it by the door, her arm tensing a little at the weight. Then she returns to her desk by the window, overlooking the dark street.

The phone in her hand chirrups three times and she blinks from the artificial brightness of the screen. Without thinking, she hopes it will be a message from Isaac, but then she remembers he's in the States and they haven't spoken in a year. She could have done with having him around tonight.

He's lived in New York for the five years since he graduated, and at first they'd spoken daily – after all, a friendship stretched across an ocean is still a friendship. But when Thea finished her Masters, then returned to Oxford for her PhD, and her anger grew as the professors and college didn't listen to her, she knew he'd tired of her battle.

Single-minded, he'd called her, the last time they talked.

Small-minded, she'd called him in retort.

She regrets it most days, the recoiling hurt she'd seen flash across his face on Skype before she'd slammed the laptop shut, disconnecting them for good.

And though they aren't close at the moment, it's only right that, before she does this thing, she speaks to Isaac. He'd want to know, she thinks. She wants him to know.

She taps a message then reads it back, deleting the last character – a full stop – and retyping it three times while she considers if she really wants to send this text to him at all.

She hits send. She doesn't expect a response – he's five hours behind in New York, and probably at work.

Maybe she should have added a smiley face at the end, to help with tone.

Thea nearly jumps out of her skin as the phone buzzes in her hand with a video call from Isaac Mendelsohn. A photo of his smiling face from years ago fills her screen as it vibrates. She hates video calls and the artificial closeness they engender: you're either with someone in the same room, on the same side of the world, or you're not. The inventor of the video call would have been better off focusing their intelligence on the invention of a tele-porter. She wipes away the tiredness from her eyes; the three rings on her left hand flash in the light as she answers. 'Hello, Isaac.'

'What do you mean, "Tonight's the night"? You're really doing this?'

'Yes.' She pauses for a moment. 'I have to.' His hair looks darker on the screen, almost black. He looks like he's been working hard – and probably eating too much New York pizza. 'You've been eating too much pizza,' she says, unthinking.

He doesn't even blink. 'This is crazy,' he says. 'It's too dangerous.'

'I'll be fine. I need it to test the theory—'

'That's the problem,' he says, his eyes hard. 'You're so obsessed by the theory you've forgotten to evaluate everything else. That is terrible science, Thea. You're a terrible scientist for doing this.'

She blinks, wounded. 'I shouldn't have messaged you,' she says, her voice hollow. 'I *mistakenly* thought you'd want to know.'

'Know that you're risking everything? Thea, they could throw you off your course.'

'I don't care,' she says.

'Getting your PhD at Oxford . . . wasn't that your dream?'

'It is. It was.'

Isaac leans forward. 'Wasn't it your parents' dream?'

'Don't bring them into this,' she warns. 'They just wanted their little girl to go to Oxford – tick. Job done. *My* dream is time travel.'

'Your dream is to be right,' Isaac says. 'This is typical Thea-logic. What if you get caught? What if they involve the police?'

'I have to go now.'

He nods, resigned to her stubbornness. 'Most friends call to say hello. But you got in touch to say goodbye.'

She flashes a sarcastic smile. 'Then it's a good job we've never been like most friends.' She looks at Isaac, bathed in daylight, surrounded by skyscrapers on the other side of the world. Then she hangs up and tucks her phone away – because if she's going to break the rules, she's going to do it alone.

At five past nine exactly, Great Tom – the bell at Christ Church College – begins sounding its nightly chimes, ringing exactly one hundred and one times. Thea silently counts each one, certain the college chaplains will one day miss a strike – or rebel, thinking no one is listening, that no one would notice. But she is listening. Thea always counts, finding solace in the routine, excusing the folly of the bell ringing at five past the hour no matter how frustratingly . . . off, that is. Maybe, if she gets caught tonight, that could be her defence. *I'm sorry, Professor,* she will say, *I was merely upholding the University's love of rule-breaking.* She smiles, for just a moment, a sense of peace falling in the aftermath of Great Tom's final toll as she returns her gaze to the street.

Focus.

Lamps are blinking on in the ramshackle houses along Turn Again Lane, while above, small pinpricks of light mar the smooth blackness of a cloudless sky. Other than a few students laughing and calling to one another as they head out for the night, the atmosphere is calm.

At five past eleven exactly – observing Oxford Time, five minutes behind Greenwich Mean Time – Thea picks up her holdall and the portfolio case, and turns out the light. She flicks it on and then off again, for luck. Three is her lucky number, and she could do with a bit of luck tonight.

It's time.

She must be quiet. Thea pads down the stairs of her shared house, just outside the college grounds. On a whim she grabs the old-fashioned egg timer from the kitchen, an hourglass full of blue sand. She soundlessly tucks it into the bag and steps outside.

She pulls the front door to, catching the weight. She leans the artist's portfolio against her leg as she puts the key in the lock so it will close without a clunk. Slowly, she takes the key from its groove and stands on the pavement. The tiny houses don't have front gardens in this tumbledown enclave. She exhales, feeling the chill of the air in her lungs. She has been silent, she thinks; the first hurdle has been jumped successfully. She bends to pick up the portfolio, the night around her still—

'Hey, Thea.'

She startles at the sound of her name. 'Visha,' she breathes, sucking in the air through her teeth. 'You scared me half to death.'

Urvisha Malik, her housemate and fellow DPhil – Oxford's word for what the rest of the world calls a PhD – stands in the middle of the lane, examining her nails. Despite her relaxed demeanour, Thea knows there's a lot happening beneath the surface: Urvisha's intelligence is tightly wound, a predatory bird aware of its surroundings, ready to swoop and snatch the prey between its teeth. 'Nice night for it,' Urvisha says.

Thea nods, slowly. 'I suppose.'

'Beautiful light.'

'Is it? I hadn't noticed.'

'Oh, come on.' Urvisha's face is pitying as she flicks her fingers against the gel of her varnish. 'You didn't really think you would do this without us?'

Thea's surprised. 'Us?'

Urvisha turns towards the entrance to the small lane, where a figure stands guard beneath the first streetlamp. 'Hi, darling,' the woman calls quietly.

'Rosy.' Thea sighs.

It's a three-way standoff:

Urvisha, arms crossed like a stern matron, her expression unyielding.

8

Rosalind, illuminated by the lamppost, a question behind her eyes.

And Thea, making a *what-the-fuck?* face at her two friends. 'What are you doing?'

'Did you think you could cut us out?' Urvisha accuses from her spot in the road. 'We're coming with you.'

'Why are you both wearing black?' Thea picks up the port-folio case. 'What are you, my coven?'

'We're your friends,' Rosalind says, walking towards them, 'and we're coming with you.'

Thea shakes her head. 'I can't let you. Not tonight.'

'Let us? You can't stop us,' Urvisha says.

'We've already talked about this,' Thea says, agitated. 'Mul-tiple times.'

'What can I say? We changed our minds.'

'Not all of you,' Thea says quietly, looking around. 'Where's Ayo?'

Rosalind steps forward, rangy and athletic, a walking juxta-position of haughty breeding and innate warmth. She puts a hand gently on Thea's arm. 'Ayo has a small child; she didn't feel she could put herself in the path of any . . . potential danger.'

'But you two are happy to break the law?'

'We're only going to borrow it, right?' Urvisha says, shrug-ging her shoulders. 'It's not *that* illegal.'

Rosalind's hand still lies on Thea's forearm. 'I've learned the hard way that when you're sticking your neck out – and I mean *really* sticking your head above the parapet – you need like-minded people beside you.'

'When did you learn that, Rosy?' Urvisha says, curious. 'Being captain of the Upper Fifth lacrosse team? During your Duke of Edinburgh Gold Award? Skiing in Zermatt?'

Rosalind cuts Urvisha off with an eye-roll. 'Thea, you need us with you tonight. I know I'm not a scientist, but I'm here to help. I believe in you. And you need a team.'

'No.' Thea shakes her head.

'Stop trying to leave us behind, will you?' Urvisha says. 'Or do you want all the glory for yourself?'

Thea sighs. After the confrontation with Isaac, she can't face another. At least Rosy and Visha are trying to support her. 'It's not like that at all. At the very least, what I'm about to do could get us in serious trouble with the college.'

'The college who ignored you,' Rosalind says, her voice almost maternal. 'It's criminal how they overlooked your proposal.'

'They didn't overlook it,' Thea shrugs, 'so much as forbid me to explore any aspect of what they deem an embarrassing nonsense. But it doesn't matter.' She starts down the street. 'I'm going to prove them wrong.'

Urvisha mirrors the shrug. 'And we're going to do it with you.'

Rosalind nods. 'All of us. We're here for you.'

'I can't—'

'Will you stop protesting? They won't kick us out.' Urvisha smirks. 'Not when we succeed.'

Urvisha nods to Rosalind, who parries left then feints right next to Thea, grasping the portfolio and swinging it off down the street before Thea even notices it's out of her hand. 'Come on, girls! We've got some rules to break.'

'Never thought I'd appreciate lacrosse skills,' Urvisha murmurs.

'Please . . .' But Thea sees it's fruitless as the two women cajole her down the lane.

'I don't know what's worse,' Urvisha says, bringing up the rear, 'being called "girls", or the fact Head Girl over there is the one successfully leading the charge.'

'It's Thea's project,' Rosy says like a true Head Girl as they walk towards the college campus, 'therefore Thea's leading the charge. So, Thea: what's the plan?'

They decamp to the building adjacent to the University of Oxford's brand-new, state-of-the-art Beecroft Building for Theoretical and Experimental Physics, which they can just glimpse across the campus. The Beecroft is the glittering jewel of Oxford's Science Departments, a strikingly contemporary building of glass and copper, nestled amid Grade I listed collegiate buildings and ancient treelines. Hard to miss, the Beecroft provides Oxford with a world-class research centre – with all the security measures expected of such an expensive and sensitive scientific facility.

'The Beecroft has seven storeys: five levels above ground, and two below,' Thea says. 'We need to get to the basement laboratories. They're temperature-controlled, low-vibration, totally secure black boxes.'

'Oh, good.' Urvisha yawns. It's approaching midnight, and they've all been up studying since seven. 'This is sounding more like *Mission: Impossible* every minute.'

Rosy perks up. 'Do I need to abseil down through the atrium? Because we could.'

'Not quite,' Thea says with a smirk. 'We need the laser in Basement Lab 3.' They're currently borrowing an unused study room for PhD students, a cramped space featuring an ancient orange sofa with springs breaking free of the arms, a huge bookshelf teetering under textbooks, and the desks of some other – thankfully absent – students. 'We tried the time travel experiment using normal light, and nothing happened. Tonight I want to try it with the Beecroft laser.'

'Yes, fine,' Urvisha says restlessly from where she's sitting at somebody's desk, trying not to disturb the mountain of papers. 'So what's the plan? How are we getting in?'

Both sets of eyes turn to Thea.

'I was planning to charm Tony. The night guard.'

Urvisha's eyes nearly pop out of her head. 'Thea Colman was going to set a *honeytrap*?'

Rosy, laughing, stops suddenly. 'Isn't that – Is that quite a good idea, actually?'

'No.' Thea is firm. 'I was going to tell him I left the form from Professor Schmidt at home, but I have permission to check on an experiment—'

'Are you kidding?'

'I'm sure he'd let me. Tony's always friendly.'

'Thea, that's ridiculous,' Urvisha says drily. 'I can't believe this is your plan. You're usually so thorough.'

'Is there any way into the building without going past the security desk?' Rosy asks, while Thea stays quiet.

Urvisha opens the laptop she carries everywhere with her, and pulls up the Beecroft Building details on the Oxford website.

'Maybe if we—'

'It won't work,' Thea says, her voice a pin drop. 'I need Tony to let me in.'

'Oh?' Visha says.

'Security controls the power to the lab. When they grant you access, they grant you power. We won't be able to use the Beecroft laser without it.'

'Ah,' Rosy says thoughtfully, from next to the bookshelf.

'Tony has to let you in,' Urvisha echoes. 'You don't have the form, and if he checks the online system . . .'

'He'll see there's no permission from Professor Schmidt, nor any experiment running at all,' Thea finishes.

'We need him distracted when you go in there. I mean, *really* distracted.' Urvisha scans the Beecroft site.

'Maybe some sort of diversion outside?' Rosy suggests.

'Maybe. Or . . .' She looks at Thea, eyeing her up and down.

Thea narrows her eyes. 'Whatever you're thinking – it's a hard no.'

'Yes,' Rosy says.

'Yes,' Urvisha agrees.

'No.' Thea looks between them. 'Absolutely not.' She pauses, cocking her head. 'Actually, if we had time . . .'

'See? Told you it was a good idea,' Rosalind says, her tone smug.

'Not like you're thinking.' Thea rubs her temple. 'Tony's into online dating – you can always see dating sites open on his monitor as you exit the labs. If we had time, we could've hacked his profile.'

Urvisha Malik, studying for a DPhil in Computer Science at the end of a hard-fought and expensive education, shrugs. 'I can do that.' Under her breath, she mutters: 'Because of course my cross-disciplinary research in Quantum Computing and doctoral training in Cyber Security is all so I can hack some guy's Tinder.'

'Very funny,' Thea says, offhand, as she considers the idea, turning it over in her mind. 'How long would it take? One of the professor's undergrad classes is running a lab experiment tomorrow for the next few weeks. We need to get into Lab 3 tonight.'

But Urvisha's already typing fast, her fingers a blur on the keys. It takes just over a minute for her to pull up Tony's search history and generate a profile for Tony's perfect woman, scraping the internet for suitable images and populating the account with enough updates and comments to lend it credibility.

'What are you doing, Visha?' Thea asks.

'I'm writing – quite quickly, I might add – an Autonomous Intelligent Machine and System,' Urvisha says. 'An AIMS – also known as a bot.'

Rosalind looks blank. 'I'm a historian,' she complains. 'In English, please?'

'You know – a bot. An automated program that will engage with Tony, responding with a range of tantalizing answers, keeping him distracted just long enough to serve our purpose,' Urvisha concludes.

'Gosh,' Rosy says, looking suitably impressed. 'You *are* clever.'

Urvisha finishes creating the fake profile for Tony's dream woman, and Thea starts laughing as Visha populates the siren's bio with the line 'Looking for a dreambot.'

Urvisha completes the coding and sits back, satisfied. 'Shall I set it live?' she asks.

'Yes,' Thea says.

Rosy watches, clearly fascinated – despite herself – by the technology. 'This is a bit much, isn't it?' she says. 'I wouldn't have swiped The Boy left on this.'

Thea sucks in her lips, trying not to laugh, as Urvisha types furiously into her laptop, mouthing 'The Boy'. 'You're both enjoying this way too much,' Urvisha says as she hits enter.

'So we know Tony will be distracted. But how are we going to get into the building after you've slipped past him?' Rosalind says more seriously. 'And how do we stop him coming to check on us?'

Thea flicks off the lights in the study, eyeing the glowing Beecroft Building across the darkened walkway. 'I think we've got a few more tricks up our sleeves, tonight.'

Two

As Thea walks up to the security desk of the Beecroft Building, she feels the flutter of adrenalin sitting uncomfortably in her chest. Fight or flight: she knows adrenalin will either make you feel empowered, or terrified.

Terror, she notes with disappointment. She'd so hoped she'd feel braver.

The glass building is ultramodern: behind the security desk Thea can see meeting spaces and offices designed for the discussion of theoretical physics, and a multi-storey glass atrium with skylights looking up to the stars. It's the below-ground levels that have been designed for experimental physics, which is where they need to get to.

It's time for stage one of the plan.

'Hi, Tony.' She forces herself to beam at the guard behind the huge desk, a bank of security monitors in front of him. The University of Oxford spent more than £40 million on the Beecroft, and it's manned twenty-four hours a day.

'Hi there, Thea. You're late today.' Tony looks up only briefly from where he sits, busily tapping on his phone. Their voices are loud against the hush of midnight, and bounce off the shiny surfaces of the cavernous hall.

She crosses and uncrosses her fingers behind her back three times. 'I've got permission from Professor Schmidt to check on a night experiment we're running in Basement Lab 3.'

Tony chortles, amused by something on his screen – presumably a message from Urvisha's dreambot.

Thea starts rummaging in her bag. 'I've got some paper-work here, somewhere, if you need it—'

'Professor Schmidt said it's okay?' Tony smiles, not looking up.

'Yep.' The flutter grows, as she feels her heart begin to patter against her ribcage. 'We're running an overnight experiment.'

'In Lab 3?'

Thea continues to fish around in her bag, her eyes doggedly watching the air just above the security desk. 'Yes. It requires a refresh.'

'And you drew the short straw?' Tony says, so Thea automatically makes a regretful face, wishing she hadn't given up amateur dramatics class at the age of eleven, disinclined to pursue something at which she displayed no skill.

'Yes.' *Poor little me*, she auditions mentally, but as she hears the line she knows self-pity would be overkill to a man like Tony. Who, she reasons, works nights all the time. This isn't even late for him – he's just making conversation. She adjusts her next response accordingly. 'Someone's got to do it, huh? Someone's got to stay up.'

'That's right,' he says, only half listening. 'It always comes down to the people like us. Well, I'm sure you want to crack on.' He presses the release for the security gate, still holding on to his phone.

'Thanks,' she says, remaining where she is, still half-heartedly searching through her bag for the non-existent paperwork as Urvisha, crouched beneath the desk, accelerates with a burst of speed, staying low. She clears the open security gate and disappears round the corner towards the flight of stairs, just as Tony looks up.

He waves Thea towards the gate. 'Head on down, the power's on. I know you won't be causing any trouble.'

'Thanks, Tony,' she says with some over-acted relief, her voice too loud in the echoing reception. She walks to the entrance but, exactly as she had expected, the gateway doesn't give – because Urvisha's already gone through on the single release.

'Tony? Do you mind opening the gate? It won't let me through.'

Tapping away to Urvisha's dreambot, Tony nods and again presses the release without putting down his phone. 'There you go.'

She heads through the gate and towards the steps that lead down to the labs. From the top of the stairs she can see Urvisha crouched low next to a panel in the wall, the laptop on her knees hardwired into the building's system, typing furiously. Thea tries to meet Urvisha's eyes, to share in their success, when—

'Hey!' comes the shout.

It's Tony.

'Thea?'

Her adrenalin spikes again; she almost grimaces with the physical pain. Tony is looking straight at her, and she forces herself to turn slowly and smile. Urvisha is perched on the step only yards beneath where Thea stands; if Tony leaned forward a little more he could probably see her, and he'd surely realize they're hacking into the Beecroft's systems . . .

'Don't work too hard.' Tony smiles at Thea before looking back down as the phone beeps, answering the siren call of a smartphone *ping*.

The architects spared no expense installing the most complex technological systems in Oxford's newest science building.

18

The entire exterior is covered with fins of lightweight metal that move, depending on the time of day, to shield the glass building from the sun, thereby maintaining a consistent temperature to preserve the conditions of the many experiments taking place inside.

This is the next stage of the plan.

Urvisha, sitting on the steps, leans back, meeting Thea's eyes. They both nod, and once more she hits enter.

There's a whirring noise from the shell of the building, and the light inside begins to change. The streetlamps lining the pathways outside start to disappear, and the glow through the foyer from the well-lit college quad and neighbouring campus buildings dims as the steel shutters shift and align in response to Urvisha's new coding. She's programmed them to take up their noon positions; at the Beecroft, at midnight, it's now midday.

'What the . . . ?' comes the surprised murmur from reception as Tony, roused from his dreambot slumber by the falling light across his security desk, lumbers to the main entrance, looking up in horror as the intelligent shutter system becomes . . . not so intelligent. 'Stupid bloody thing!' He picks up speed, hitching up his belt as he runs outside to examine the bizarre movement of the fins.

Perfect.

Rosy's blonde head appears from the opposite direction as she sprints elegantly across the foyer, lifting her feet in the ideal silent run. Without missing a step she fence-hops the security gate, slowing to a walk at the top of the stairs. 'Fancy seeing you here,' she says on the staircase above them.

'Keep it down, will you?' Urvisha says, though she isn't angry. 'It's time for the final stage.' Hardwired into the building, Urvisha purposely crashes the system controlling the metal shutters. Confused, they whir and grind outside, before the system begins to reboot itself. The shutters move to the start-up position – entirely closed – locking Tony outside.

'There.' Urvisha checks on Tony's dreambot one last time before deactivating it. 'He sure likes emojis.'

'What does the aubergine mean?' Rosy asks, and Urvisha bursts out laughing, shutting her laptop decisively. She looks up at the others, who are standing watching her.

'Haven't we got somewhere we need to be?'

The lights blink on as they enter the basement laboratory: first Thea, carrying her bag with the tripods and industrial lamps; then Urvisha, carrying her laptop; and Rosy behind them, carrying the artist's portfolio, gazing around at their surroundings, her face curious. 'I've barely been in one of these things since school,' she says.

Distracted, Urvisha smirks. 'Well, Rosy, this is a *science lab* —' but Thea quickly interrupts.

'Let's be quick.' Thea drops her bag and walks straight over to a workstation in front of a steel grey box, activating the controls. With a satisfying *oooom* the control panel lights up, and Thea starts punching in numbers.

'That's the laser?' Rosy asks.

Urvisha nods while Thea types. 'It's one of a kind—'

'Not for long.' Thea shrugs. 'I've been working on a portable version as part of my DPhil. Ayo's been helping me build a duplicate – it's a shame she's not here.' She pauses for a moment, thinking about the reasons why Ayo has chosen not to join them.

'You're building a laser?' Rosy interrupts Thea's thoughts. 'Wow.'

'My version is nearly there; I'm just waiting for the last parts to arrive –' Thea has the grace to blush – 'from Amazon.' She types fast into the control panel, changing the laser's default settings. 'If this does anything tonight, having my own mini version might prove incredibly useful.'

'And what exactly are we here to test?' Rosy asks.

'A laser is an amplified source of light that stimulates electron energy levels.' Thea sees the lost expression on Rosalind's face. 'It's powerful as hell. I want to see how the light of the laser interacts with the glass house.'

'The glass house?' Rosy repeats, putting the portfolio down on the floor next to Thea's holdall. 'What's that?'

Thea smiles without stopping what she's doing. 'Something else I've been working on. Please will you open the portfolio and start setting up what's inside?' she says to Rosy.

'Absolutely.' Given a task and intent upon executing it with efficiency, Rosy briskly undoes the zip.

'It's prismatic glass,' Thea says. 'Very lightweight.' The glass has geometric lines and grooves etched into its surface, catching the light and giving off an almost otherworldly opalescent glow.

'How does it – Ah yes, I see.' Rosy arranges the beginnings of a cube, flipping open a hinge and clicking it in place to make it double-height. 'That makes it just about tall enough for a person. Is there a lid? Or is it a roof?'

'Simply folds over and should sit on top.' Thea sets up the three industrial photographic lamps as Rosy clicks the final panel into place.

'What is it?' Rosy asks, opening and closing one of the tall panels like a door, running her fingers over a small hole in the centre. The whole thing is about the size of a magician's box, the type a person will step into and wave at the audience, before they fall through a trapdoor and disappear for ever. But the iridescent, prismatic glass gives it an ethereal feel, and Rosy taps it curiously. 'Is it a booth of some kind?'

'Something like that.'

'A phone box? A photo booth?'

'Closer than you think,' Thea says with a quick smile, distributing a pair of the lab's professional-grade safety goggles to each member of the team. 'I told you – I call it the glass house.'

'Like a greenhouse for one.'

'Exactly.' Thea grins. 'Visha, can you look after the reportage?'

'Hmfph,' is all she says, clearly annoyed not to have a more technical role, but Urvisha takes the camera from Thea's bag and turns the setting to record video, pointing towards the glass house.

Thea looks around at the setup, satisfied. 'We need to capture everything. I want to be able to see how the prismatic glass interacts with the Beecroft laser . . . We're going to try to trap the light in the glass house.' She pauses. 'It might get a little crazy in here.'

'Plus,' Urvisha adds, 'we're going to need proof if we pull it off.'

The team step back. The glass house is set up in front of the Beecroft laser, the recording equipment filming the entire experiment at a forty-five-degree angle. Surrounding the glass house on three sides are the three photographic lamps, illuminating the booth like stage lighting. The effect is dramatic.

'I'm keeping the three lamps from last time,' Thea explains quickly to the others, 'even though we're trying the laser as our main source of light, because I don't want to change too many things at once. We won't know what made it work, otherwise.' Thea glances at her watch – they can't take too long; this is an illicit experiment, after all – but it would be nice to start the process at a clean round time if they can (or even five past the hour).

'What are you expecting to happen, Thea?' Rosy says.

Thea considers. 'Remember when I told you that if you could travel faster than the speed of light, you would arrive somewhere before you left?'

Rosy nods, and Urvisha bounces impatiently on the workbench stool, the explanation too simple for her Quantum Mechanics-trained mind.

'We're going to try and harness it,' Thea says. 'Trap the light in the prism and, by extension, the glass house. So it might get a little warm.' She looks around, conscious they've broken in and need to hurry the hell up. 'Everyone set?'

'Err,' Rosy says again, 'what's this for?' She holds up the blue sand hourglass, and Thea kicks herself for forgetting.

'Damn. We need to turn it over the second we fire the laser.'

'I see.' Rosalind looks baffled, but places it down on the workbench. 'I can do that.'

'Thea,' Urvisha starts. 'If you don't want to change too much from the last time we tried this, back at the house . . .'

'Go on,' Thea says.

'Last time you made Rosy sit behind a pane of glass and those photographic lamps.'

'Like an ant beneath a magnifier,' Rosy says cheerfully.

'You need to put someone behind the glass.' Urvisha shrugs.

Thea looks at each element of her setup. 'You might be right,' she concedes. *I would never have been able to do this alone.* 'I'm glad you're here,' she says, and Urvisha and Rosy's eyes meet.

'You're welcome. Now, Rosy – do you mind?' Urvisha gestures at the glass house, and Rosy lifts an eyebrow.

'Do I have to sit in that? I'm the tallest here.'

'If Ayo was here it would be easy,' Thea says gently, 'because she could look after the laser, but as she isn't . . . I think I need to do that. Which means—'

'You can't go in the booth,' Rosy finishes.

'I'll do it,' Urvisha says quickly.

Thea bites her lip. 'We need you to run the other systems,' she says apologetically, nodding at Urvisha's laptop and recording devices.

'But—'

'I'm sorry, we need you out here,' Thea says.

Urvisha's eyes spark. 'I want to—'

'I'll go in the booth.'

Thea and Urvisha both turn to Rosalind.

'Are you sure?' Thea says. 'We don't know for certain what will happen.'

Urvisha is quiet as Rosy nods, then walks with Thea towards the glass house.

'It's fine,' Rosy says. 'Like you said, we should keep as many things the same as possible.'

'Thank you,' Thea breathes.

'And if it works? There's probably no one better to attempt time travel than a historian.'

'She makes a good case,' Urvisha admits.

'Every time-travelling team needs a historian,' Thea says brightly. 'Now, you're sure?' She takes Rosy's hands in hers. 'The theory is sound, but . . .'

'I'm sure.' Rosy pats Thea's hand. 'I believe in this. I believe in you.'

'That's twice you've said that, tonight.' Thea smiles.

'Then it must be true.'

Thea pulls a glass prism from her pocket and walks to the glass house, turning the prism over and over in her hand. She wipes it down with a velvet cloth, the type you get with a pair of spectacles, and carefully slots the prism into a small hole in the glass house door. It fits perfectly. 'We're ready. Shall we do a launch status check like they do at NASA?'

'Yes. Everyone say "Go" if you're ready. Or "No go" if you're not.' Urvisha confirms the recording devices are live, then verifies that all the doors to the laboratory are clear and nobody is around. 'Go.'

'Go,' Thea says, setting the hourglass down next to the laser control panel. 'Rosy?'

'Let's pray for no "Houston, we have a problem."' Rosy takes a breath and opens the door of the glass house, then closes it gently behind her and settles in. 'Go,' she says.

Thea shifts behind the laser control panel. 'Safety goggles on, please.' All three pull the eyewear down onto their faces, and Thea nods. 'Go. We are cleared for – launch?' she says, for want of a better word. 'After three.'

'Three, two . . . one.'

Thea flicks the largest switch on the laser, and the light is blinding. All she can see is white. Her vision of the lab, and of her friends, is bleached in the moment, violently drained of colour.

She feels the thrill of excitement – her skin tingles with the power of the laser, magnified by the glass house; the hairs on her arms stand up and she can't help but smile.

Is it working? There's the smell of electricity in the room, and a sound of crackling, underpinned by a thrumming hum. It must be working – she knew it would. She was right all along.

She hopes Rosy's all right in the glass house, and that it's not too warm. She should check on her.

Thea shields her eyes with her arm, peering towards the glass house where, inside, Rosy should be standing – is she there? It's too bright to see. Thea moves gingerly towards the cubicle, protecting herself from the light, when—

'Fuck!'

A blinding colourless brightness, then the power goes out with a *womp* as the lab falls into total darkness.

'Oh, hell.'

They stand at the centre of it all, surrounded by the black.

'I think we did something bad.'

Thea blinks against the sudden dark; the plunge from shiny white to deepest black is all-encompassing. 'Is it just in here,' she says, her voice betraying some urgency, 'or is it dark outside?'

Urvisha moves quickly to the laboratory door, her hands out in front of her, feeling her way. She peers up through the winding corridors towards the offices and meeting spaces, then left and right at the other laboratories on their floor. 'The power's gone from the whole building,' she hisses back into the lab.

'Check the other buildings,' Thea says, as Urvisha moves cautiously up the stairs.

'Come and look!' she calls.

Thea lifts her feet to run quickly to the window, stumbling as her eyes adjust too slowly, still blinded by the pulse of white light. 'Oh, hell.'

Urvisha looks at Thea impassively.

The University of Oxford is going dark.

Three

As they stand in the glass atrium, looking out across the city, Thea and Urvisha can see the lights clicking off at the neighbouring colleges. The blackout spreads as though contagious, a ruthlessly efficient virus moving towards the edge of the collegiate grounds – *womp, womp, womp* – before finally all of the university buildings are in shadow.

'Where's Rosy?' Thea turns to Urvisha suddenly. 'Rosy?' she calls. 'Are you there?'

'Rosy?' Urvisha jogs back to the glass house, opening the door. 'She's gone!'

'How long since we started the laser?' Thea asks.

The emergency lighting sputters around them as the Beecroft's backup generator kicks in, and Thea blinks in the dim glow of greenish artificial light. She moves fast across the lab, lifting her goggles up onto her forehead to check the hourglass on the workbench, the few final grains of sand dripping through from the top compartment to the bottom.

'Four minutes,' she says, answering her own question. 'And how long since the blackout started?'

Urvisha looks around wildly, spotting her camera plugged into the mains. She pulls it towards her, squinting in the low green lighting. The camera bears the same flashing numbers as microwave ovens and alarm clocks in the accommodation across the campus, marking the moment time had been reset: 00:02.

'Two minutes since the blackout,' she confirms, as the camera clock flashes over to 00:03. 'Three.'

Thea's mind is racing. The power would have to be diverted to avoid a power cut next time—

'Thea, Rosy's gone. What do we do?' Urvisha asks.

The temperature of the prism and the glass house, the density, perhaps—

'Thea!' When she doesn't get a response, Urvisha pulls out her phone and moves to the corridor to find enough signal to call Rosy.

Thea takes a moment to think. Her mind is racing a relay, passing the baton synapse to synapse. If the baton's an idea, she can't quite grasp it; she needs time alone to slow down her brain, a moment to figure out what went wrong – and what went right.

'Voicemail,' Urvisha says from the doorway, lowering her phone. 'Rosy's phone didn't even ring.'

'Right.'

If Rosy is gone . . .

'Are you listening to me?' Urvisha snaps. 'Earth to Thea Colman!'

They look at each other, holding back their excitement, then when they spot the reflected feeling within each other they let their fervour begin to show. 'Do you think . . . ?'

'I don't know.'

'Maybe Rosy's gone back in time—'

'Maybe.' Thea's excitement suddenly drops as her adrenalin cools, and fear begins to set in. 'Oh God, I hope she's all right.'

Their eyes meet.

'With that blackout, they're going to be looking for the source. We need to pack up and get out of here, then work out where she's gone.' Thea puts her hands to her temples, running her fingers into her hair and back. She has baby hair on this part of her head; she can't remember if she started doing this because the hair is soft here, or if the hair is soft here because of the repeated gesture. 'Save the video,' Thea says. 'We'll need to watch it back.'

'No problem –' Urvisha moves to her laptop – 'I'll send it to your online drive over mobile signal now.'

'Good. Make sure everything is transferred across. Then we'll pack up the glass house.'

While Urvisha drags and drops the video files, Thea shuts down the laser control panel, worrying about Rosy.

'Thea?' Urvisha says.

Thea tucks everything back into the bag – no time to do it in size order – as they work fast under the green backup lighting, gathering everything they can.

'Thea Colman,' Urvisha repeats.

She looks up.

Rosy is marching into the laboratory, and the catching breath of relief they feel at seeing her fine and well is chased away when they realize at precisely the same moment that, if she's here, now, they didn't send her back in time. It didn't work.

'Are you all right?' Thea says quickly.

But following swiftly behind Rosy is Tony the security guard, along with Tony's boss, Jim – Head of Campus Security – and Professor Schmidt, Departmental Head of Physics.

'What in heaven's name,' Professor Schmidt says, 'is going on here?' Anger makes the question staccato, his words paired in a short rhythm bursting with fury.

Thea winces. 'Professor—'

'Don't tell me, Thea Colman, that this unsanctioned experiment – which I'm sure is something the department expressly *forbade* – is the reason the entire campus is currently in the dark.'

Tony's eyes look to Thea, wounded. She hopes he knows it's not personal.

'I just—'

'Tell me, Colman, how you decided breaking and entering would be the best way to pursue your own personal interests at this college.'

'I—'

'What was that?' he snaps. 'Speak up.'

'It's not breaking and entering,' she says. 'Or at least, not *breaking*.'

They jump slightly as the main power comes back on with another *womp*. 'I assure you, hacking into building systems is considered breaking and entering by both the University and Oxford police.'

Thea sees Urvisha stiffen.

'Needless to say, by cutting the power to this building you've ruined my team's research experiment in Lab 1. Six weeks of work. And who are you?' He looks around at the other culprits. 'I know you,' he says, looking at Urvisha. 'I taught you undergrad Quantum Theory. Malik, isn't it? Who is your overseeing tutor?'

'Professor Kelly, Computer Science.' Urvisha surreptitiously steps in front of her laptop, though it won't take much for them to work out who in the room's been manipulating the building systems.

'She'll be horrified to hear about your part in this.'

Urvisha bows her head. Behind their backs, Thea gently touches her palm to Urvisha's shaking hand.

'Well.' The professor turns to Rosy, who is skulking by the door. 'I don't know *you*.'

'Rosy.' She clears her throat, a cough wrapping itself around her full name. 'Rosalind de Glanville.'

Even Professor Schmidt looks taken aback. 'Lady de Glanville. I must say, this is an unexpected honour.'

'Dishonour, more like,' Tony's boss leers, but Professor Schmidt silences him with a look.

'And what research are you undertaking with the University . . . ?'

'I'm researching my DPhil thesis in History of Art at the Bodleian,' she says by way of explanation, downcast at being told off like a schoolgirl rather than the twenty-seven-year-old woman she is. Authority figures usually *like* her, Thea thinks – the mature Head Girl routine tends to make them feel safe.

Jim sneers. 'Don't tell us – your family paid for half this building.'

Rosy shuts her eyes, apparently expecting more barbs, but Thea is relieved to hear Professor Schmidt dispatch the security guards to check the ramifications of the blackout. 'This is a departmental matter,' he says, his voice stern. 'Please notify the police that we have found the reason for our power cut and the threat is contained.'

The two burly men head back to the security desk, visibly disappointed at being dismissed, and Professor Schmidt closes the laboratory door behind them quite precisely. 'Now then,' he says, his voice a low hum. 'I want to know what you were doing, why you were doing it, and – most of all – which individual is responsible.'

The room is silent. Thea sets the hourglass back down on the workbench, watching the sand begin to trickle through.

Rosy takes a breath. 'Umm, Professor Schmidt, if I may,' she says delicately, 'my family did invest some money in this building, perhaps even in this laboratory, and I was curious how it worked. I asked for a tour . . . My apologies—'

Professor Schmidt sighs. 'I know what you're doing.'

But Thea isn't really listening. She's looking at Rosy.

Rosy, who wasn't here a minute ago. Who disappeared for five minutes.

Five minutes.

Professor Schmidt raises his voice. 'I'm afraid you are trespassing and there is very real evidence here to ensure the removal of all of you from your relevant DPhil studies.' He looks stern. 'I would think very, very carefully about what you say next.'

But Thea can't concentrate on his words.

Rosy disappeared.

She glances up – all of them are staring at her. She sees how tired her friends look; she notices how Urvisha has lost all of her predatory keenness, the mention of the police playing on her mind. Cyber crime carries huge penalties. She can't afford to fail: not financially, not morally.

Thea looks at Rosy, so frequently seen only as a toff. But Lady Rosalind de Glanville is so much more. She's kind – almost *too* kind – and Thea knows without a flicker of a doubt that Rosy will not hesitate to take the fall, knowing her family name will help protect her – and them.

'Professor,' Thea says slowly, and Urvisha's face betrays her relief. 'You know the theory I've been working on?'

'Not your magic crystals again.'

'It's not magic.' *Rosy disappeared. What happened to her? What does that mean?* Think, *Thea. Not Thea-logic. Time for actual logic.* 'I wanted to explore if it was possible to break the speed of light—'

'Which Einstein stated is impossible—'

'Not if we slow it down.' The words come out in a rush.

'Professor, we both know a crystal is capable of breaking symmetry and trapping light inside, and I know something can be done with time if we find the precise moment when the light wave slows and interacts with matter, and then harness it—'

'Colman, you have willingly ploughed ahead with an expressly banned project and a frankly ludicrous obsession with the mystical, rather than the rational.'

'But Professor, tonight—'

'Tonight you triggered a university-wide blackout and destroyed the results of more than six weeks of experiments for an entire class of students.'

Thea is silent.

'What's more, you dragged innocent friends here to break the law. You brought those without lab training or security clearance into a highly controlled laboratory space and you put everyone at risk.' He eyes Rosalind uneasily. 'I'm disappointed, Colman. And not only about tonight. Do your cohorts here know that you're nine months behind on your DPhil research?'

The two women look at Thea, shocked. She's the hardest worker they know: always at her desk by 6 a.m., typing furiously; scrawling notes by hand over lunch; an entire wall of her room liberally covered with equations worked on late into the night. And everywhere, everything interspersed with the same incessant doodle she draws when she's thinking: an interlocking pattern of diamond and prism shapes, like the lines etched on the glass house.

'Your work is languishing; you've become obsessed with this ridiculous theory about time travel. This, I'm afraid, is the last straw.

'Criminal activity.

'The coercing of fellow students.

'The breaking of health and safety.

'Misuse of departmental property.

'The hacking of university systems.

'But most sadly, for me: the negligence of your studies.'

Rosy disappeared.

Thea shuffles through her thoughts, turning each one over slowly.

She almost laughs out loud when the realization comes to her, the idea forming whole in her mind. Pop culture has it wrong: the eureka moment is not a light bulb going off above your head. It's a light beam.

She's only half listening as Professor Schmidt lays down the price of tonight's misadventure.

'I will be telling the Vice-Chancellor precisely who is responsible, and I will be forced to assure him that the individual in question is no longer with us at the Department of Physics as of tonight. Either that or I will be filing criminal damage charges against all three of you, and you can each take your chances with your respective colleges and the Oxford police.'

Thea's attention snaps back.

She can't let anyone else take the blame, no matter how hard they're trying not to land her in trouble. She can't risk their futures, as well as her own.

The tap dancing in her ribcage tells her it's that time again: fight or flight.

She turns to face the professor who has never supported her, not even at the beginning; not when she gained her undergraduate scholarship, not when she graduated with double honours in Physics and Philosophy. And certainly not when she'd taken her theory of time travel to him, and been denied permission to spend three to four years studying it for a DPhil.

'So,' he says expectantly.

'It was me, Professor,' she says, her voice floating. 'The others had nothing to do with it. I told them it was all above board and that I had permission from you to run tonight's experiment.'

Professor Schmidt sighs, satisfied but disappointed.

'I misled them. I misled you. And –' she stumbles on this one – 'I'm sorry.' She turns instead to her friends, who glance at each other in shock at the turn this is taking. 'I truly am sorry,' she says, genuinely this time, 'to have lied to you. To have got you into this, when I have clearly been working on it for six months with no input from you whatsoever, entirely on my own.'

Professor Schmidt holds up a hand. 'Fine, Colman. Fine, I get it.'

Rosalind takes a step forward. 'Professor—'

'No, Rosy,' Thea says with some grit, urging her to listen to what she is saying. 'I'll take my belongings and leave.'

'What a shame,' Professor Schmidt says to himself, with a shake of his head, but it's hard to know if he genuinely feels sadness or is just saying what a university lecturer must when a promising pupil comes adrift of the rails. 'It's not often I have to unceremoniously remove someone from the most prestigious research qualification in the country.'

'I'll leave the college tonight,' Thea says, then places a bet: 'and the rest of you should go home.'

'Yes. Please vacate my laboratory immediately,' Professor Schmidt says sternly, particularly eyeing Rosy, who probably has, in truth, more claim to the laboratory than he does.

Heads lowered like handmaids, Rosy and Urvisha begin to file out of the laboratory, but as she reaches the doorway, Rosalind turns back. 'Thea—'

'Don't. Please.' She smiles sadly at her friend. 'It's fine. I shouldn't have dragged everyone else into it.'

'Come on, Colman. Let's go.'

Thea looks to her prismatic glass house, partially folded on the floor, and the camera still set up diagonally to the laser. 'May I gather my things?'

'You certainly may not. We're going straight to the Vice-Chancellor.'

'Oh,' she says.

'I'll have security deliver your . . .' He pauses as he casts a disapproving eye over the equipment. '. . . things. After we've finished.'

Thea sighs, following the professor out of the room into the atrium, the glow of the exterior college lights illuminating his head like a ghostly halo. She snatches a glance out at the place she has lived, worked and dreamed for so many years . . . She can't believe it's come to this. Four years of studying for her degree, a year in industry, then three years (so far) for the DPhil – nearly her entire twenties. All for nothing.

They walk out of the Beecroft Building into the night air, the lighting of the college quads once again restored.

'You know, Colman,' Professor Schmidt starts as they arrive at the darkened Vice-Chancellor's office. She has always hated how the older faculty staff insist on referring to their students by surname. 'I've met people like you before.'

Under the cover of darkness Thea rolls her eyes, expecting a vicious diatribe. She is not disappointed.

Professor Schmidt rings the bell. 'You're the type of person who always had potential, but never did anything with it.'

'With the greatest respect, Sir,' she says, as the door to the Vice-Chancellor's office opens, with absolutely no respect at all, 'I'm going to spend the rest of my life proving you wrong.'

Four

The birds are beginning their dawn song as Thea emerges from the Vice-Chancellor's office, two hours before the full light of sunrise will bring a sharp sobriety to the dream-like state of her night.

Hearing her blood pulsing in her ears, heart thumping, she stands looking at the grounds around her, pondering what to do.

She didn't ever think she would come to rely on something outside her own rationale, but with some surprise, Thea finds she has. She wants to speak to somebody who can calm her.

That person is not Urvisha or Rosy – not yet. They were there, they saw it all – they won't be able to process what she'll say without reliving their own experience, or thinking about how it might affect them. She knows that's brutal, but she wants to speak to an outsider. Somebody who will tell her everything is going to be okay.

Like a parent would.

She thinks about calling Ayo, who – wisely? – chose not to join them tonight in the lab. But she doesn't want an I-told-you-so, so decides otherwise.

It really doesn't leave too many options. Anyone else she'd call would need to be told the story from scratch . . .

She does the only thing she can in this situation: she picks up the phone and calls Isaac.

A clunk, then the muffled sound of people laughing. Music in the background, a gut-thumping bass.

'Hello?'

'Thea?' Another clunk, then some rustling.

'It's a bad time,' she says. 'I'll call you later.'

'No – I'm here.' The thumping music fades as Isaac presumably walks out of whatever Brooklyn loft or bar he's in. 'What's the time there? Is everything all right?'

'Please don't lecture me,' she says before Isaac can continue. 'I've messed up, that's why I'm calling.'

'What happened?'

She takes a deep breath. 'I've ruined everything. The college sent me down.'

The whoosh of cars going past, the angry honking of a horn, followed by Isaac yelling.

'Sorry,' he says, his voice back with her, a million miles away from the profanity he's just shouted at the driver from the sidewalk. 'Down where?'

'They kicked me out.'

There's silence – or at least, Isaac is silent while the sound of hipsters in Williamsburg celebrating their Friday night carry on around him.

'I'm off the course. Out of the college. Booted from my accommodation, too, from tomorrow.' Which is a consideration she hadn't even taken into account – a DPhil failure, *and* homeless. What a night. 'Please don't say I should have listened to you. It's too late.'

'Oh, Thea.' She has his full attention. 'What happened?'

'It didn't work, though something clearly went right: Rosy disappeared for five minutes, so if we make some adjustments I don't see any reason why—'

'Theodora? What happened with the *college* – why did they kick you out?'

'Oh.' She cuts short a laugh, brought back to earth with a bump. 'We broke into the science building to use the Beecroft laser. The experiment triggered a power cut across the whole of the university.'

'Oh, fuck,' Isaac says. 'What happened then?'

'My supervising professor rocked up with campus security, and threatened to remove Rosy and Urvisha from their DPhils, as well as reporting us to the local police.'

'Damn.' She can hear the slight pant in Isaac's voice as he walks through the New York streets, the sound of his shoes hitting the pavestones. It's only just after midnight, Eastern Time, a whole five hours behind – if she could somehow travel to where he is, to his time, none of this would have happened, and she'd still have somewhere to live.

But then she wouldn't have known she was onto something. *Rosy disappeared.*

'Without sounding like a parent—'

'Please don't act like my parents would have,' she says at the same time, and the similarity in their trains of thought breaks the tension for a moment.

Isaac wisely doesn't finish his sentence. 'What are you going to do?'

She finds herself grateful to have her friend back, even momentarily. 'Thank you,' she says. She remembers that he never used to judge her, never called her out for her shortcomings – didn't seem to even notice them, on the whole. She could always get on with telling him the things inside her head without having to craft the least offensive way to say them.

'Is it worth,' Isaac says, as she hears him put his key in the door of his rented apartment, 'speaking to the college? I'm sure the proctors would forgive—'

'The Vice-Chancellor was brutal,' she says.

'Really? That surprises me,' he says. 'Hold on – can we change to a video call now I'm home? This feels too important.'

Thea sighs, hating video calls at the best of times.

Isaac appears on the screen. She might be imagining it, but his expression looks marginally softer towards her than the last few times they've spoken. 'The Vice-Chancellor was really nice when I graduated,' he carries straight on, 'even wrote a letter to the head of the museum . . .'

She sighs again. 'I rather walked in with my back up, determined to prove them wrong.' There's nowhere to hide now that he can see her.

'Oh.'

'I know. I didn't mean to.' Though she did, in a way.

Isaac closes his bedroom door. 'What did you honestly think would happen? That you would do this, and the college would thank you?'

'I guess so. They never listened to me, never let me follow this course of study. I wanted to show them as a gigantic "FU" that I could prove the theory . . .'

'And the college would turn a blind eye to the rule-breaking and share the glory?'

'Wouldn't they?' she says. 'If there's one thing any major research institute in the world loves, it's success.'

'I suppose so. They do say success has many fathers,' Isaac says, his voice wise beyond his twenty-six years.

'Exactly.'

'Or mothers.'

'Quite,' she says, daring a grin.

'One day,' he says gingerly, as he thumps down on the rug and winces at the crack of his spine, so loud she can hear it through the speaker, 'can we have a conversation that doesn't revolve around bloody time travel?' He pauses. 'Or not. Whatever.'

'I'm not sure I know how,' she says. 'It's all I've thought about for years.'

'I know,' Isaac says sadly. 'And I still don't understand it.'

Thea tilts her head. 'I didn't think you wanted to. Not a fan of complicated explanations, if I recall.'

'Since I've been working over here, I *only* seem to come across complicated explanations. I've discovered there are two types of people in this world: those who use big long words to sound clever, and those who break any topic down into its simplest form so anyone can understand. Perhaps,' he says, 'you can break down your theory for me.'

'More than I already have?'

'Yes, more than that.' His face looks sober for a moment. 'My boss at the Guggenheim only likes me because I broke down "soccer" for him. Guaranteed promotion.'

'You don't even like football,' she says, laughing despite herself.

'I know.'

'Don't tell me you used ketchup bottles to explain the offside rule?' She's thoughtful. 'Maybe I can explain the speed of light using salt and pepper pots . . .'

'Of course I didn't.' Then: 'I used invaluable manuscripts, instead. We were in the archive at the time.' He pauses. 'I'm coming back to the UK in two weeks, actually, to renew my visa.'

'Oh,' she says cautiously, unwilling to ask if they can meet.

'Maybe we can meet up,' Isaac says.

'Really?' Thea says. 'Sorry, Isaac. I should have asked how it's been going.'

He waves it away. 'You've got bigger things to worry about than me restoring old documents or fiddling with digital records.'

'I'd better go,' she says, reluctantly. 'Apparently I need to find somewhere to live.'

'Call me whenever you need.'

She nods. 'Thank you.'

'What for?' he says.

'For the lack of lecture.'

'Hey, Thea,' he calls down the phone before she hangs up and, lens to lens, she looks Isaac straight in the eye.

'Yes?'

'Did you know approximately three billion pizzas are consumed in the United States each year?'

She smiles. 'I did not. Did you know that, allegedly, eating pizza once a week can reduce the risk of cancer?'

'As if I needed another reason,' he says. 'I'll bring you back some.'

'Pizza? Across an ocean?'

'Believe me, it's worth it.'

Despite the ridiculousness of his offer, and the largesse of his promise, for the first time since Professor Schmidt told her she was the type of person who would fail to live up to her own potential, Thea feels something like hope.

She packs up her belongings quickly: the cheap high street clothes twisting at the seams from over-washing; drugstore makeup leaking free from its plastic packaging; a variety of chipped novelty mugs. It would pain Thea to acknowledge that nothing she considers significant in her life is found here in her shared house; everything she values seems to have an intangible connection to the world she's just lost – her friends, her theories, and her most prized possessions, which are hopefully still lying on the floor of the Beecroft laboratory.

Her friends. Thea has missed calls from Urvisha and Rosy – even Ayo – but failure brings with it its own special type of embarrassment. She'll speak to them eventually, but not yet.

She takes a moment to check that the video Urvisha uploaded went through without interruption or corruption, flagging a section of the video to watch in detail, frame by frame, later.

After she rings the Beecroft reception desk for something like the third time, Tony's boss, Jim, finally delivers her equipment from the lab. Arms crossed, wearing a sneer like it's his own personal brand, Jim fails to lift a finger as she unfolds the huge hinged sections of the glass house, checking for cracks. She's not beyond sending them a bill, should she find any. When all appears to be in order, despite the security guard's heavy handling, she closes the door without a word.

He'd looked at her like she was nothing.

She has to leave Oxford.

The thoughts terrify her, as she looks out of the window at the city she's known for eight years; across Turn Again Lane towards the college grounds, empty at 6 a.m., the bedroom lights of the keenest students beginning their early-morning study, the athletes heading down to the river for rowing practice. She has to get away from here, to escape the labels she can feel attaching themselves to her.

A failure.

A dropout.

And worst of all – wrong.

43

She loads up the car with her paltry possessions and starts driving out of the city. There is only one place she can go, though there she will have to fend off her crushing sense of failure as it combines with something else.

Something worse.

Dawn finally cracks across the sky as Thea heads north, the yellow sun round against the rose-tinted horizon. The red in the sky won't last long – in fact it's already dissipating as the sun rises – but she eyes the first light with a distracted interest.

Thea approaches the outskirts of a small village on the Yorkshire–Lancashire border. She reluctantly follows a long-held family tradition of waving at the sign bearing the tiny settlement's name: Dunsop Bridge. The word *nostalgia* often has positive connotations, but for Thea, the nostalgia of returning to the place where she grew up is melancholy.

Previously part of the West Riding of Yorkshire, now part of Lancashire, there is little in Dunsop Bridge to write home about – and, more significantly, no one at home to write to. She crosses the bridge, the water of the river low and filled with yellow leaves fallen from the trees, and passes the chequered window of Puddleducks. The village tearoom is lit up for a lunch rush that, out of season, will not come.

There's nothing here, really, other than a special geographical status only the villagers enjoy, which adorns metal keyrings and tea towels in the local shop for sale to tourists who rarely appear in the colder months.

Thea draws a breath in, then out, slow and steady, as she continues past the church of St Hubert's with its neat graveyard outside, elegant headstones bordered with clipped box hedges, before pulling off the road past the church onto a dirt track, into the wood.

There's nobody around.

Thea drives through the trees, passing the vast outbuildings of a farm, black wood barns varying from ramshackle to new – well, new fourteen years ago. Almost fifteen.

She continues past a cylindrical brick dovecote and a cart lodge, pulling up outside the farmhouse. Four hours and seven minutes after she left Oxford – a deeply unsatisfying time with neither roundness nor mathematical significance – she has arrived.

She sits in the car for an additional three minutes, breathing slowly, watching until the clock ticks over.

Four hours and ten.

Come on, then.

She opens the car door, taking a key from under a stone gnome and unlocking the front door.

'Hello?' she calls, but nobody will answer and she knows that. It's a courtesy only, an intruder announcing their arrival. She steps into the hall.

It's exactly as she last left it, though that was some years ago. Nothing has changed, except the musty smell and lack of electricity. She'll have to sort that immediately.

White dustsheets adorn the furniture, and Thea reaches up to pull back the sheet covering the grandfather clock in the hall, causing a beautiful dance of dust motes in the early afternoon light. She steps back, eyeing the antique clock face, listening for its tick.

She frowns – it's quiet. Carefully she opens the mahogany clock door, placing her hand on the side of the pendulum disc. She moves it to the far left, and after a beat she releases, so it swings down to the centre and up to the right.

Thea stares at the grandfather clock, deep in thought,

waiting for the pendulum to settle into an even swing. The tick-tock sound is loud in the empty farmhouse. Her sense of failure is even more acute here – if that's possible. The shadow of familial expectation is long, and returning in her current, fragile state has knocked her more than she ever could have expected.

She hates the idea that she's letting anyone down but herself. She needs to redeem herself, she thinks. And there's only one way to do that.

The motion of the grandfather clock pendulum makes her think about the experiment once more, about how Rosy disappeared for five minutes after she fired the laser at the glass house.

Thea drops down onto the bottom step of the dark wood staircase, watching the pendulum move back and forth. She knows with the itchy feeling of surety that, somehow, the motion is important, but in her current mindset she can't quite piece it together. There's something about the swing she can't grasp . . .

She sighs.

She'd better let somebody know where she is. She takes out her phone and messages one person her location.

Five hours behind, most likely texting while eating breakfast, that person responds.

You went back there? Remember, Thea, they're only ghosts.

She knew Isaac would understand the toll it might take; how it might feel to come back to a house that should be filled with the bustle of family life, with parents saying, 'Back so soon?' and offering to make toast and tea as she moans about Professor Schmidt. But Thea's parents are long gone. Her mother and father are memories and dust, where once they were flesh and warmth.

Ghosts.

The thought haunts her. But she's comforted that somewhere, across time zones, somebody understands.

∞

They had met for the second time at another university event, surrounded not by telescopes and hot toddies but instead by drills and pliers of all shapes and sizes.

Thea was arguing with the course leader when Isaac arrived, and he stood to the side as she talked hurriedly. 'You don't understand,' she said to the wiry man in charge, as he neatly laid out tubs of beads on the wooden workbenches, 'I need to reshape this glass prism—'

'This is a jewellery-making class, madam. If you want to cut glass, wouldn't you be better off in engineering? Or the science labs?'

'I can't do it in the labs, not yet,' she said with gritted teeth. 'You work with precious stones, don't you?'

'Sometimes,' he conceded, 'but today is an introductory session. We'll be working with exquisite glass beads. I implore you—'

He trailed off as Thea marched away, and Isaac slid into the seat next to her as the session began.

'We really must stop meeting like this,' Isaac said, and she frowned. 'What?' he asked.

'I like meeting like this,' she said, still fierce from her run-in. 'It means we have the same interests.'

'Or the same obligations. I'm making a birthday present for my girlfriend, the poor girl.'

Thea felt the drop in her stomach, like the feeling you get when you send an email in error. 'That's nice of you.'

Isaac smiled, his face tentative.

She slammed a pair of pliers down on the bench. 'The idiot running this thing won't let me use the glass-cutting equipment until the sixth week of the course.'

'Then I suppose we'll have a lot of time to get to know one another.' He picked up a coil of thick wire, which he began bending into curls. 'Is this about your glass prisms?'

'What are those meant to be?' she asked, indicating the swirls of wire he was shaping without finesse.

'I don't know – earrings, perhaps?' He held one up to Thea's ear, and made a face. 'My girlfriend is rather fancy, from a *very* respectable family, so I don't know if these are quite her style.'

'If a person already owns everything they could possibly want, making them a gift by hand is the best way to go.'

Isaac beamed. 'That's exactly what I thought.'

'Though,' she said, her eyes again returning to the pile in front of him, 'you're going to have a hell of a time making another earring to match.'

'Who says they have to match?' Isaac said, gleefully bending another coil of wire into a bizarre, cloud-like shape. 'You prize symmetry too highly.'

Thea gazed at him, taken aback. 'Tsung-Dao Lee says symmetry considerations are the backbone of our theoretical formulation of physical laws,' she said, having never been so well measured by a stranger in her life.

Isaac glanced sideways at her. 'I don't know what any of that means, but your Mr Lee, whoever he is, is wrong, so far as I'm concerned. I prefer asymmetry. Flaws are what gives a person their character.'

'He won the Nobel Prize.' She wrinkled her nose. 'You know, in diamonds, they're not called flaws; they're *inclusions*.'

'I like that.' He smiled. 'A person has to have inclusions to be whole. Though I bet those rings on your fingers don't have many flaws.' He gestured at the hand holding the pliers.

'These?' She turned her left hand over so the stones caught the light. 'I inherited them.'

'Lucky,' he said. 'Why do you wear them in that triangle formation?'

'I don't know,' she said, lightly touching her three rings: one on her little finger and one on her forefinger, then one with a glittering diamond worn halfway up her ring finger, sitting just above the joint. 'I always have.'

'It's unusual,' he said.

She turned her hand over once again so the diamond caught the light, earning a frown from the course leader on the other side of the room. 'At least this way it doesn't look like an engagement ring,' she said.

'No frightening, rugby-playing fiancé tucked away, ready to box the ears of your newest, jewellery-making male friend?' He pretended to cower.

'Alas, not.' Thea smiled. 'That doesn't sound quite my type.'

'Well, phew. My girlfriend can be quite intimidating when you first meet her, but once she's on your team, she's the most loyal friend you could have. You should meet – I think you'd really get along.'

'That would be nice.' She helped him twist the wire and cut off the excess, so the earrings formed complete, if uneven, loops.

Isaac sat back to admire the homemade squiggles he'd crafted, his smile slipping as the beaded decoration fell off. 'I'd better get to the shops before they close,' he said ruefully, looking at the clock, 'and find her an actual present. It's Rosy's birthday tomorrow.'

Five

A week after she arrives at the farm, Thea wakes on the floor of one of the outbuildings, a dusty blanket lying over her.

'What the . . . ?' she tries to speak, but her voice cracks, and she rolls over and reaches for her alarm clock – which isn't there, because she isn't in her bed. Christ, she feels awful. Is this flu?

The hourglass lies on the cold floor next to her and Thea picks it up, staring incomprehensibly at the blue sand. Her head is hot, and full. That's the best (and only) way she can describe it. The length of her skin aches as she sits up, the texture of the old blanket rubbing against her sensitive nerve endings. Everything hurts.

She gazes round, taking a second to re-orientate, and when she remembers she's at her childhood home she almost hides back under the blanket, afraid to face her ghosts. But the floor is freezing so she rises stiffly to her feet, once more looking at the setup she's been working on here.

She's out in the barn. She remembers now. It's the large one with the double-height ceiling, and the glass house is here, glimmering in the morning light. Lord, her throat's sore, and her head is throbbing.

Thea sets the hourglass down on the workbench and lifts a rickety old ladder from where it's lying on the floor, leaning it against the barn wall. Everything feels new, strange. She makes her way from the outbuildings, walking gingerly towards the

50

farmhouse, when she hears a bell clanging once, then twice. She blinks in the frosty Lancashire brightness, arms huddled against her chest to ward off the cold, and wonders calmly if she might be hallucinating. She had tonsillitis once, and it made her see things. Hearing tolling bells might be caused by a fever.

But when she hears it for the third time, she realizes it's the doorbell at the farmhouse. That might even have been what woke her, if the sound reaches that far. Pushing through the pain of her aching body and exhaustion, she walks as fast as she can through the gardens, letting herself into the kitchen.

The doorbell clangs again, and from inside the house she can hear the ancient bell knocking against the woodwork of the doorframe. If whoever's there pulls that hard again, it's going to break. 'All right, all right!' she shouts, though her voice is fuzzy, her throat sore. 'I'm coming!'

She yanks back the locks and opens the door, her mouth forming a surprised O.

'Where in holy hell are we?' Urvisha says from the doorstep.

'What are you doing here?'

'What do you think?' Urvisha breezes past her, into the entrance hall.

'Nice to see you, too,' Thea murmurs, then brightens as Rosy walks through the door with a huge bunch of flowers.

'Oh no, are you poorly?' Rosy says, bending over to hug Thea with a gap between them, then resting her hand against Thea's forehead. 'You're rather hot.'

'I'm not feeling great – I spent the night in a barn.'

Rosy widens her eyes. 'That would make anyone catch a chill,' she says.

'How did you find . . .' Thea stops talking as she spots Ayo

51

Adebamowo reversing the car they've rented straight over the turning circle.

Determined, Ayo rolls down the window and makes an apologetic face. 'I'm a bit out of practice,' she says as she gets out of the car, leaving it parked awkwardly. She remembers at the last moment to turn and lock the rental, looking proud to be so conscientious.

'You're here,' Thea says as Ayo walks with her into the house, looking around at the dusty building.

'I am. Strictly in a babysitting capacity.'

'You brought baby Bolu?' Thea asks.

'I meant you.' She smiles. 'Rosy thought you might need some company.'

Thea is glad to see her, understanding partially why she didn't take part at the Beecroft, but her mind whirring with ideas of how to utilize Ayo's scientific skills now she's here. 'Where is your little one?'

'With his father, Lord help them both.' Ayo's smile is withering. As a young Nigerian mother researching a PhD at Oxford, Ayo has made more sacrifices than any of them. *Become a doctor*, her family had urged – the scientific one in a non-scientific family. But that wasn't enough for Ayo; with her DPhil in Particle Physics, she will probably redefine the way future hospitals use technology. Develop the next generation's x-ray or MRI.

'This is quite a place you've got here,' Ayo says, looking round. 'Did you say you spent the night in a barn?'

'I like it!' Rosy calls from the kitchen, where she's divided the bouquet between pint glasses of water and is currently rustling up mugs and looking round for a kettle. 'This house is very Miss Havisham.'

'I tried to take most of these down,' Thea says, pulling the white dustsheet from a huge scrubbed oak table, her nerves aflame, 'but I got a little distracted. I've been working round the clock.' She throws back some painkillers laced with caffeine, and gestures for the others to sit with her.

'Where exactly are we?' Urvisha asks.

'Dunsop Bridge,' Rosy answers unexpectedly, and Thea looks at her in surprise. 'We used to go hiking near here with Daddy.' Rosy puts a rusty coffee pot down on the table, and slowly pours out the black liquid.

'And why are we here . . . ?' Urvisha asks, as Thea pulls a mug towards her and takes a sip, choking on the thick texture, which in turn develops into a coughing fit.

'Because—'

'It's actually the middle point of the country,' Rosy says. 'We're currently at the dead centre of Great Britain.'

'Isn't that a bit misleading?' Urvisha says, also taking a mug. 'We're pretty far north. Makes "the Midlands" a misnomer.'

'Maybe the Midlands are *the middle of the land* if you don't include Scotland,' says Rosy, reasonably.

'Lop it off and let's move this experiment to Birmingham.'

'You know what they say,' Thea steps in: 'Don't discuss money or politics if you want to stay friends.'

'We're colleagues,' Urvisha replies, somewhat stoically, and Thea smiles at a typical Urvisha non-joke.

They sit in companionable silence as Rosy reheats the espresso pot on the stove, though this time the others wisely avoid drinking from it.

'How did you find me?' Thea asks at last, her voice quiet.

'We're so sorry about what happened,' Ayo says. 'I can't believe how the college reacted.'

KATIE KHAN

'Isaac told us where you were,' Rosy says gently, and Thea is surprised.

'Isaac?'

'You know,' Urvisha says, scratching at the coffee pot's rust, 'Rosy's ex-boyfriend.'

Rosy looks uncomfortable. 'He was worried, Thea – he thought you could do with some company.'

There's a second of silence as Thea recalibrates her opinion about her friendship with Isaac being five times stronger than Isaac and Rosy's dalliance six years ago at university, but she avoids saying it out loud. 'It's good to see you all.'

At least two of the group visibly breathe with relief. 'We thought you'd be mad,' Urvisha says. 'Because you took all of the blame.'

Thea cocks her head. The movement makes her muscles ache. 'Of course I did. It was my fault.'

'It wasn't—'

'It was. Anyway, what's done is done,' Thea says. 'I'm sorry you got in trouble, too. How did it go?'

'We're fine. But we thought you'd be sad,' Rosy says delicately, 'because the experiment with the laser didn't work. That's why we're here, for support.'

'We know how you hate failure,' Urvisha says, more bluntly.

'I do. But we didn't fail.'

The other three look at her, and Urvisha leans forward. 'What?'

'The experiment didn't work,' Rosy repeats softly. 'I was there, remember?'

'Didn't it? Were you?' Thea puts down her mug and looks around at her friends. 'Don't you want to know what I've been doing since I left?'

*

Thea pauses in the doorway, looking back at Ayo who is still standing in the kitchen. 'Ayo?' she says kindly. 'Nothing bad will happen just from taking a look.'

Ayo's face is uncertain. 'Just a look? That's all?'

'Of course.'

'Then I'll come with you.'

They wait while Ayo shrugs into a large waxed jacket, arranging it about her shoulders like she's on a country-themed photoshoot.

'Come on, princess,' Urvisha calls, and Rosy smiles, for once not the focus of her teasing.

'More like a queen,' Ayo says haughtily as they tramp out of the farmhouse and across the courtyard, past an overgrown kitchen garden with vegetables so gone to seed it looks like an abandoned garden at the end of the world.

'Gosh,' Rosy mutters, as they step around stinging nettles and rogue cauliflower leaves. 'It's quite wild out here.'

'Haven't had much time to be green-fingered,' Thea sniffs, her nose streaming in the cold air.

'I know a terrific gardener, if you . . .' Rosy trails off as they walk across three large, spaced paving stones – *one, two, three* – past the dovecote, then round the corner to the outbuildings, where she takes in the scale of the barns. 'Wow.'

'This one.' Thea leads the group to the newest barn at the back of the enclosure, two tall storeys of black painted wood, a stack of firewood piled by the double-height door.

She creaks open the door, pulling it all the way out until it rests against the shingling of the barn wall, letting the October light pour into the outbuilding.

Rosy walks in first, the most comfortable of the three in the great outdoors. Urvisha, a city girl through and through, keeps eyeing her loaned wellies with disdain. Ayo is shivering inside her waxed coat, balling her hands inside the sleeves of her wool jumper – the autumn chill bites harder up north.

As they enter the barn, their eyes adjust slowly to the light. 'Oh, my.' Rosy turns round and round, looking at the barn's setup. 'You've built—'

'Your own version of the Beecroft lab,' Urvisha finishes.

Around them, workbenches line the long walls of the barn, while in the middle sits the glass house, three photographic lamps, and a box.

'It's a bit rough and ready,' Thea says, 'and I'm still tweaking the laser.' She points at the box, and Urvisha starts laughing.

'You're mad,' she says, 'completely mad.'

'This is where you spent the night, Thea? No wonder you're poorly.' Rosy runs her hand along one of the makeshift workbenches.

'Long-term I'll need better facilities, but it should do for now. For the next iteration of the experiment.'

The group look at each other.

'That's why you're here, isn't it?' Thea asks seriously.

'I'm here in a supportive capacity only,' Ayo says, holding up her hands. 'But Thea, I feel I must say . . . with such basic equipment . . .' She shrugs. 'Even using the most state-of-the-art laboratory in the country, the experiment triggered a campus-wide blackout.'

'Which Thea predicted would happen.'

Urvisha and Ayo snap their heads over to Rosy, who is leaning against a bench, holding the blue egg timer. 'Didn't you, Thea? Otherwise why would you have brought this hourglass with you to the Beecroft?' Rosy says, waving it around so the sand runs from one chamber to the next, then back again, as she shakes it. 'I can only guess you wanted something ana-logue to keep time, in case the laser knocked the power out.'

Influenza burns with fire in her veins but Thea still smiles, never failing to be impressed by her friends. That's why she's friends with them.

'You knew it would happen!' Urvisha is close to exploding as Ayo puts a hand on her arm.

'I feared it could,' Thea says. 'It was a precaution, a small detail so we could be prepared for any eventuality.'

'You knew the power would cut out.' Urvisha is not one to hide her anger. 'When are you going to trust us?'

Thea has the chagrin to look down. 'Sorry.'

'So, what,' Urvisha says, 'we're going to try, and fail, *again*? Here? In a ramshackle barn?'

'Who said we're going to fail?' Thea asks.

'We failed at the Beecroft, using a world-class laser.' Urvisha is talking fast now. 'What makes you think we're going to fare any better in the middle of goddamn Lancashire using oven gloves and swimming goggles? It's dangerous, Thea. We could get hurt.'

'But we're so close.' Thea doesn't elaborate as she walks across to her laptop, unfolding the screen and waiting for it to boot up. Urvisha makes to explode a few more times, her mouth running away with her, but Thea doesn't rise to it. Very calmly, when the computer is ready, she opens a full-screen video and taps play.

The group are silent.

'What . . . ?' Rosy eventually asks, moving closer to the screen. 'Can you run that again?'

They watch the video again, then loop it back and watch it once more.

'I'm sorry if I haven't told you quite everything.' Thea presses enter again, playing the video without sound over and over. 'Yes, I feared the power might trip at the lab. I was prepared for that possible outcome, and I'm sorry I didn't warn you so that you could be prepared, too.'

All four stare intently at the screen, watching the outline of Rosy standing inside the prismatic glass house, before the picture is whited out with a blinding flash of light, followed by darkness.

'Play it again,' Urvisha says, her voice very, very low.

Thea feels the wooziness kick in – the price of remaining highly functioning while suffering the fast onset of the flu. She taps the button once more, and the group lean forward, watching the short video. 'So no, I don't think the experiment was a failure. Because I watched the tape. And while *we* stayed in the lab, the recording contains a few clues about where Rosy went. Or should I say, where Rosy *travelled*.'

The excitement in the barn isn't palpable so much as at fever pitch. There's the crackle of electricity, the kind produced by humans rather than the National Grid, and the high-pitched frequency of female voices under enthusiastic duress.

'What happened to you?' Ayo begs, and Rosy lifts her shoulders into a shrug.

'I don't know!'

'Where did you go? What did it feel like?'

Rosy holds up her hands, palms out. 'I'm really not sure. I was standing in the glass house, then . . .'

'That's a good idea, actually.' Thea takes out her notebook. 'Run through it step by step.'

'Okay.' Rosy takes a breath. 'I was in the glass house, and we ran all of the checks. First Visha, then me, and finally Thea. We were ready to go.'

Thea nods, jotting it down.

'The laser started, and the light was dazzling. I couldn't see anything. The glass became warm; it got hot in there, almost too hot. Then . . .' She scrunches her eyes, thinking hard. 'I was outside the lab by the atrium.'

'You were gone for five minutes,' Thea says. 'Then you were marched back in by Professor Schmidt and the security guards.'

'Those horrors.' Rosy shudders.

'Here's a question for you,' Thea says casually, though she feels anything but casual. 'When you were out in the atrium, were the lights on?'

Rosy thinks. 'Yes. The lights were on, I could see the whole hall – and the lights of the college outside.'

Thea feels the fizz of triumph alongside the flash of fever.

'That's great,' she says, finishing scrawling in her notebook, the margins filled with her interlocking diamond and prism doodles. 'I think we've got everything we need, here.'

The others look at her in shock. 'What are you talking about?' Urvisha demands. 'Rosy's just getting started.'

'I think I know what Thea means,' Ayo says slowly. 'If I may . . .' She reaches for the laptop, again pressing play on the video of Rosy's disappearance. 'You see, here –' she pauses the tape at the white flash – 'is where Rosy goes, but here –' she nudges the cursor to the next second of the video, which is the moment the lab falls into black – 'is where the power cut is triggered.'

Thea nods. 'But the lights came back on as Professor Schmidt and the security guards were telling us off, remember?'

Rosy's eyes are wide. 'So if the lights were on when I arrived in the atrium . . .'

'Then you arrived before the power cut.' Urvisha smacks the worktop, making them all jump. 'You arrived before you left.'

'Precisely.' Thea smiles. 'You travelled back in time.'

Six

Thea tries to calm the group, to no avail. 'Come on, guys, we can't just plough ahead – we need to plan. Systematic methodology.'

'Bullshit.' Urvisha is blunt. 'We need to do the experiment again, now. Now we know . . .'

'We know we can do it.' Thea nods. 'But if we run it again, and actually succeed—'

Rosy steps forward. 'If we *do* succeed, Thea, then you could show it to the college. You could prove the theory – and they'd have to reinstate you.'

'Oh.' Urvisha looks as though the proverbial light bulb has gone off over her head, too. 'They'd have to take you back, with a breakthrough like that.'

'That's true,' Thea considers, 'though you're not thinking of the bigger picture. If we manage *more* than five minutes; if we make a breakthrough like *that* . . .' She gulps, and after a beat during which they each consider the magnitude of what they're talking about, they laugh. 'It's good you're here, Rosy . . . it looks like we're going to need a historian.'

'Let's do it again!' Urvisha bounces up and down on the spot. 'I want to do it again!'

'I want to tweak the laser.'

'And,' Rosy says sternly, 'you need to take a nap. You look completely washed out.'

It's true: flu has knocked Thea for six, and despite the buzz she gets out of working in a group – this group – she can feel the drag of tiredness on her mind, her thoughts not surfacing quite as quickly as they usually do.

'Ayo, I know you're only here to babysit,' Thea says, 'but perhaps you could take a look at the laser with me? I could really use your skills.' When Ayo nods, Thea continues: 'then we'll aim for a late-night setup again. That way, if we do trigger any power outage, most people will be asleep so they won't notice.'

'Hmm,' Urvisha says. 'I might be able to help with that, actually.' She scowls. 'Now that I know a blackout might be on the cards, I can plan for it. There's something I can run on my laptop.'

'Thank you,' Thea says. 'We should probably keep things as much the same as last time. Rosy, are you happy to go in the hot seat once more?'

'Yes,' Rosy nods. 'Though don't remind me it can get a little warm in there.'

'Don't complain,' Urvisha warns. 'Or I'll get angry.'

'And you wouldn't like her when she's angry,' Thea says. 'We have a plan, then. We'll work through the afternoon, rest until the evening, then bring about the onset of the apocalypse during the night.'

The others stare at her.

'That was just a little joke.'

Their eyes meet, surprised. Bullet points and lists, yes; things organized neatly, yes; jokes . . . almost never.

'That cold-flu bug must have gone to your head,' Rosy murmurs.

The phone rings on Thea's nightstand, waking her from a nap at 9 p.m. She looks at the screen and sees that Isaac is calling.

It buzzes a few times, but when she tries to answer, the line goes funny – so she cancels the call, and rings him back.

'I guess you're mad at me for telling Rosy where you are, and now we're right back to not speaking.' Isaac dives straight in, and Thea sits up in bed, groggy.

'It's fine—'

'I knew you'd be like this. I knew you'd be angry. But I didn't want you to be alone in that house, dealing with this—'

'Isaac? I said it's fine.'

'You don't have to deal with the fallout alone,' he says.

'I know. I'm not.' She yawns. The paracetamol plus some sleep has worked wonders, and she enjoys the brief reprieve from the pressure inside her head. 'They're here – Rosy, Urvisha, even Ayo. They all came.'

'Yeah?'

'Yes.'

'I can't believe you're not mad,' he murmurs, more to himself than to Thea. 'I'd planned everything I was going to say.'

'I'm not mad. But I do have to go shortly – we're going to try something. Tonight.'

There's a pause before Isaac speaks. 'Not the experiment again?'

'No,' she says quickly, 'something else. Something fun! A sleepover. With face packs and pyjamas.' She crosses her fingers.

'That's good,' he says, sounding relieved if a little confused. 'You'd have to be a psychopath to try an experiment like that again.'

'Isaac—' A deafening echo comes on the line, followed by the sound of a loud tannoy. She waits for the triad of tones ending the announcement before she speaks. 'Where are you?'

'At the airport,' he says. 'I'm on my way back to the UK.'

'Can't be.' She stands up, looking out of the window at the dark night sky. 'You're a week early.'

He laughs. 'Surprise! I changed my plans. I'm getting on a plane in about five minutes – I should be around from tomorrow, if you need me.'

I never need you. She stops herself from saying it as she realizes it's not true: it's an echo of what she used to say, of how she'd taunt and push him away, but she never meant it. 'Okay,' she says slowly. 'That sounds . . . good.'

'Good.' He sounds similarly cautious.

'Safe travels.'

'Thea?' The tannoy comes on again, and this time she can hear his gate being called. 'Are you sure you're all right? You sound strange.'

'I caught a chill or something, sleeping out in the barn. It might even be flu.' She grimaces. 'And honestly? We haven't spoken like this for a while . . . It's probably making me overly sentimental.'

'Oh no! Feel better.'

'Thanks.'

'Because if this is you overly sentimental,' he says, 'I'd like to see you positively nostalgic. Perhaps we'll break out the photo albums when I'm back.' Isaac laughs, bidding her farewell as he boards the plane.

She gets dressed quickly and heads downstairs to the kitchen. Ayo has worked a miracle: the countertops are free of dust, the rustic tiles a sunny red and yellow instead of a grubby grey. Rosy's flowers are blooming in their glasses on the scrubbed table, and Rosy is pulling the cottage pie Ayo has made from the oven.

'Our babysitter is enjoying an early night upstairs,' Rosy declares. 'Hasn't she done a brilliant job?'

'Incredible.' Thea sits down on the kitchen bench, looking around. 'I haven't been back here for ages – it was such a state.'

'I'm not surprised.'

'The others – they don't know.'

'No,' Rosy says, sitting down next to Thea, 'I don't suppose they do. But that's okay.' She brightens as Thea takes a bite of warm cottage pie, gravy sliding down her chin. 'Not everybody has to know everything.'

Urvisha slides in. 'Who doesn't know everything? Me?'

'Yah,' Rosy says, somehow playing up to the wide vowels Urvisha teases her for. 'You don't know when to mind your own beeswax, for one.'

'Beeswax? You talk funny sometimes.' Urvisha takes a seat at the table, helping herself to some cottage pie. 'Does this have carrots in? I hate carrots.'

'Pick them out,' Rosy says, not unkindly. 'The meat is halal, at least.'

Thea takes a minute to look at the two women and feels the raw affection of true friendship. They came for her. They're here. And with them by her side, she's invincible.

'What's up with you?' Rosy smiles at Thea warmly. 'Good sleep? You look punch-drunk.'

Thea doesn't want to get emotional with them right now – probably a side effect of being unwell. 'I guess it's the anticipation of what we're going to do.'

Urvisha shakes her head. 'You mean, what we're going to *achieve*. Where's Ayo?'

'Staying way out of this,' Rosy says. 'She's taking advantage of twelve hours' baby-free sleep. And you're not to wake her,' she warns. 'Ayo has her reasons for not wanting to be involved.'

'Even if she's wrong,' Urvisha says, plucking carrots from her plate.

'Cautious,' Rosalind says, more fairly. 'After all, she has a child, and a husband – dependants – unlike any of us.'

'That's true,' Thea agrees. 'Especially after the Beecroft experiment – we're not quite sure what will happen, how far this could go. It's not right for Ayo to risk anything.'

'But it is for us.' Urvisha grins. 'I, for one, cannot wait to be on this winning team. The first people to successfully establish time travel, fully documented. *Everyone* will know our names.'

Thea is quiet.

'I want to see what it's like.' Rosy smiles dreamily. 'If I could travel back . . . Imagine the notes a historian could take. The worlds I could see—'

'The textbooks you could correct,' Thea interjects.

'Quite. I can't wait to see what other historians got wrong.'

Thea nods. 'And we'll be the ones to tell them.'

They demolish Ayo's dinner, then suggest that a bottle of red from the farm's cellar would be a good investment in their success.

'Are you sure?' Ever cautious, Thea doesn't want any slowed or impaired reactions. She's already concerned about suffering with the flu.

'Just a tipple,' Rosy says, pouring much more than a tipple into everyone's tumblers. 'I couldn't find any wine glasses,' she apologizes, but nobody has noticed. 'Here – to being together.'

'To success!' Urvisha clanks her glass against the others'.

At midnight, they pull on wellington boots and thick jackets once more and head out of the warmth of the farmhouse kitchen. 'Here,' Thea says. 'These should make it a little easier.'

'Head torches! It's like being on holiday camp,' Urvisha says, though she's never been on a holiday camp, nor has she ever been camping.

'Jack Frost,' Rosy says, pointing at where the windows have begun icing over as she pulls on her head torch. 'Winter is on its way.'

Urvisha huffs her breath, watching the air she exhales condense to a puff of cloud in the night chill.

They walk across to the barn, three streaks of light against the darkness of the night. Moving past the firewood, Thea opens the door, and Urvisha and Rosy pull off their head torches.

'No,' Thea says, 'keep them on. They might help.' She sets up the three industrial lamps to point at the glass house, illuminating it against the dark wood of the barn, then moves to the controls for the new laser. Urvisha sets up her laptop, a black page of code open on her screen. Rosy stands by the glass house, ready to take her place.

'Thea?' Rosy says quietly, but is interrupted by Urvisha cursing.

'Oh, piss.'

'What's wrong?' Thea says, turning to Urvisha.

'I'm trying to ... *communicate*, shall we say, with the National Grid.' Urvisha indicates the code on her screen. 'To keep the power regulated while we do this, and handle any surges in the local area.'

'Communicate?' Rosy says. 'Or "hack"? She means hack, doesn't she.'

'Hacking is a dialogue,' Urvisha says, tapping at the keys.

'And this host server seems to need a constant stream of dialogue.'

'Like some men I know,' Rosy murmurs, and the others laugh gently.

'Can someone take over the recording and reportage?' Urvisha says distractedly. 'I'm going to need my full attention on talking to the Grid.'

'I will.' Thea turns on the camera and walks back to the laser, leaving the camera rolling. They may as well capture everything, including the setup – plus this way she won't forget to hit record as she fires the laser.

Rosy is running her hand over the variegated and wavy texture Thea has had carved into the prismatic surface of the glass house. It might even be 3D-printed – they know so little about the work Thea has put into this.

'Ready, Rosy?' Thea calls.

'Do you know, I've always felt like I was meant for something like this. *Ad majora natus sum*,' she says, ducking into the prismatic booth. 'Oof! I forgot how cosy this was.'

'It was designed for someone a little shorter than you.'

Thea runs a final check on the camera setup at forty-five degrees to the laser, then places a multifaceted, cut-glass prism in the door of the glass house. 'You might want to wear this.' She throws Rosy a blue striped oven glove, and Rosy barks a laugh.

'You've got to be kidding.'

'In case it gets too warm. We're on a budget.' Thea grins, tossing cheap school lab goggles at Urvisha and Rosy, then pulling her own down awkwardly across the torch on her head.

'I've come prepared,' Urvisha declares, pulling out a roll of kitchen foil and stretching it vertically in front of her, like a shield.

'Smart,' Thea says approvingly. 'Though God only knows where you're going to reflect the laser beam. You'll probably wipe out the entire village. Goodbye, Dunsop Bridge.'

Urvisha smirks, but lowers the foil and pulls out a pair of sunglasses instead. 'What?' she says, seeing their faces. 'I need to be able to see my screen when it gets super-bright in here,' she explains, returning to her simple task of hacking the National Grid.

In a repeat of the routine from the Beecroft, Thea looks around the barn one last time, then says: 'We're ready. Launch status: go or no go?'

Urvisha checks and rechecks her screen, then verifies all the doors to the barn are clear and the farm is deserted. 'Go.'

Thea checks the recording devices are live, and that the ley line between the glass house and her new laser is perfectly set. 'Go.'

'I'm ready.' Rosy waves from behind the glass.

'You have to say "Go."'

Rosy opens the glass door and leans her perfect cream-blonde head out. 'Go!' she bellows, making the others jump.

'Thank you, Rosy. That red wine is clearly working wonders. We are good to go. After three?'

'I'm so excited,' Urvisha says.

'Three.'

'Two.'

'. . . One.'

Thea turns on the laser, and once again the light is blinding. Just like before, all she can see is white. Her vision of the barn, and of the others, is bleached in the moment, violently drained of colour.

Thea doesn't allow herself to become excited this time. Once more she feels the tingling of the laser, the goosebumps rising on her skin. The background smell of the barn is replaced by a metallic tang as the light gets whiter and whiter.

She can hear Urvisha near her, typing furiously, but Thea's eyes are fixed on the faint outline of Rosy.

Urvisha makes a noise, but Thea can't quite hear her over the thrumming and the heat.

'What?' Thea turns towards her.

Urvisha gestures at her laptop, pointing at the screen.

It's so bright in the barn, Thea moves towards the bench slowly, shielding her eyes, looking back every few seconds at the glass house. She doesn't want to miss it, if Rosy makes the leap. That's the key, that will be the fundamental marker: the moment. She takes a step—

And it hits. The blinding flash, followed by the lurch into darkness, then the sound they all dread.

The *womp* as the power cuts out.

'Oh no,' Urvisha says, audible now the thrumming has been silenced. She scrolls through the code, watching as the transformers sitting next to the high-voltage pylons across the country flash a warning. 'Oh no, no, no. This one's a biggie.'

On Urvisha's screen, Thea sees the major arteries of the country lose power. City by city, she watches them fall into darkness. She can see the details in her mind's eye: traffic lights and shop windows blinking off. Bus stops and station signs turning blank. The power is sucked from the National Grid like a blood transfusion.

Thea watches as the power cut spreads down to the limbs of the south coast until, finally, the whole of Great Britain has turned dark.

But just outside the barn, at least, the night remains quiet.

'Oh no.'

At the dead centre of the country, surrounded by the black, Thea feels a remarkable sense of déjà vu.

'I think we did something bad,' she echoes from another time. But there's no emergency lighting to sputter on around them now, no backup generator out in the barn. The three photographic lights are extinguished, so they turn their head torches on, the beams cutting through the dark, shafts of light bobbing and ducking across the walls of the barn.

'Rosy?' Thea calls, feeling her way across the barn as quickly as she can.

'Is she there?' Urvisha says.

'Rosy?' Thea's voice is half excited, half terrified. She yanks open the prismatic glass door. 'She's gone.' She lets the door swing all the way open so Urvisha can see. 'Rosy's gone.'

'That's brilliant!'

Something stirs in the pit of Thea's stomach. *Is it?*

Now the glass house is open, the metallic tang is stronger; if they licked their lips, they'd taste it. Thea pauses, thinking about what to do. 'Can you get the power back up online?'

'For the whole country?' Urvisha cocks her head. 'It's going to take some time. The entire Grid is drained.'

'Hurry. Before they spot where the drain originated from.'

'It's fine –' Urvisha's hands skate across the keys – 'it's untraceable. The benefit,' she says, making an ironic face, 'of being at the central point of the country. Probably the *only* benefit.'

Thea moves quickly to the barn door, craning out into the night towards the village. 'It's dead quiet out there.'

'I'm working on it,' Urvisha says, fingers flying. 'Any sign of her?'

'Not yet.' Thea looks out into the darkness, then back at the hourglass. All of the sand has run out. 'She should be back any minute.'

Urvisha doesn't look up. 'You think . . . ?'

'Any minute now.' Thea is certain. 'Just like at the Beecroft, Rosy will walk back in and tell us precisely where she's been.'

Excited, Thea looks back and forth between the glass house and the path leading back to the farmhouse.

'Why won't she turn up inside the glass house?' Urvisha says.

'She might. I'm only going on what happened before, when she ended up in the atrium.' Thea ponders it. 'Perhaps because the Earth's turning while she's gone, she ends up outside the glass house. I don't know.'

'I can't believe we've done it,' Urvisha says eagerly.

'I know. Let's watch the tape.' Thea moves towards the camera, hurrying to play back what they witnessed simply moments before. But like Thea, Urvisha is still staring at the glass house.

'We know it worked, don't we?' Urvisha says. 'She's gone. We should be celebrating.'

Another *womp* and the lights in the barn flicker gently back into life, the outbuildings and farmhouse beyond lighting up like a chain letter of fluorescent bulbs stretching across the fields. Urvisha smiles, her mouth taut. It's still night outside, the rest of the world not yet awake, and the small Lancashire village they've made their base is deserted.

'Not yet.' Thea speaks softly. 'We'll celebrate when Rosy reappears. Making someone disappear is only half the act. The other half is bringing them back.'

Seven

Fiery clouds splay against the horizon as another pot of coffee percolates, and they down it quickly, black and hot. Dawn is breaking, so they move outside to wait for Rosy's return. Urvisha leans against the barn door, jiggling her leg, while Thea, crouched low, holds a steaming mug of coffee in her hands.

The distant windows of the local village stay dark as Thea throws back painkillers laced with caffeine, eyeing the first light of the sunrise. 'Red sky in the morning . . .' she whispers, noting the worried crease across Urvisha's face, the agitation in her jiggled leg.

'Shepherd's warning,' finishes Urvisha. 'Don't take too many of those.'

'I'm fine.'

'It's 5 a.m. Rosy should be back by now.'

'Last time it was five minutes,' Thea says, 'maybe this time it's five hours.' Her voice belies a rising worry.

'Do you think? I mean, the power cut *was* probably ten times bigger than last time.'

'That's it – she probably jumped back further than we expected.'

But they both find it increasingly hard to be excited when Rosy hasn't yet returned.

Urvisha stands up straight. 'We need to wake Ayo and start a search.'

'We will,' Thea says. 'Soon. Five minutes more. She'll turn up, I know it.'

'Oh,' says Urvisha, her voice suddenly bleak. The exhilaration of ambition has been etched over with reality.

'She'll come back.' Stiff from the cold, Thea gets to her feet and rests her hand on her friend's arm with reassurance. 'She's going to stroll in any second now.'

They leave the barn door open, and beyond that, the door of the glass house is open too. Thea watches the first, tentative shards of daylight filtering through the clouds and streaking the frosted ground, but most of all she notices the heavy absence of their friend. She hadn't foreseen how nerve-racking this would be.

Soon they notice the lights in the farmhouse turning on.

'Ayo's awake. That's early,' Urvisha says.

'She's a mum, isn't she? Ayo's used to seeing the dawn.'

'Let's go and tell her. Maybe she can help.' Urvisha doesn't wait for Thea to agree, striding past the dovecote and stepping stones, back towards the kitchen.

Ayo is unsuccessfully trying to figure out the Aga when they almost fall through the door. 'You startled me!' she says. Then: 'What's wrong?'

'We . . . may have been successful,' Urvisha starts.

Thea speaks at the same time. 'Rosy hasn't come back yet.'

'. . . So we don't know exactly *how* successful.'

'Oh,' Ayo says, her eyes going wide. She drags an old copper kettle on top of the hob. 'But it's the morning. Do you mean to say Rosy has been missing all night?'

Thea slumps down on the floor to remove her boots. 'I don't want to use the word *missing*.'

'Absent,' Urvisha says.

'In transit,' Thea tries out.

'For nearly six hours?' Ayo says.

'Until someone's been gone twenty-four hours, it doesn't qualify as a missing persons case,' Urvisha, an avid watcher of detective shows, states.

Ayo looks frightened. 'A whole day?'

'She'll be back before then,' Thea says. 'I know it.'

'Have you tried calling her?' Ayo asks.

'We both have,' Thea says, pacing around the kitchen. 'Numerous times.'

Ayo picks up her mobile from the table and dials Rosy anyway, getting through to her voicemail. 'Voicemail,' she says unnecessarily, as they can all hear the plummy tones of Rosy's recorded message coming from the handset.

'Maybe phones don't work when somebody's time travelling,' Urvisha reasons. 'Like on an aeroplane.'

Thea's brain lags with the weight of the inference, and she'd like to take a moment to contemplate the science behind Urvisha's suggestion, but she knows the others will be looking to her for direction.

She didn't expect Rosy to be gone so long. She feels nauseous as she hears the grandfather clock strike the hour, marking an extension of the time Rosy has been absent.

'All right,' Thea says, her voice rallying, 'let's make a plan.'

'Yes. Very good,' Ayo says.

'Urvisha and I have been up all night, which isn't helping.' She can already feel the skittishness of exhaustion mixing with the edges of her concern. 'I think we need to get some sleep. Ayo, would you mind waiting for Rosy?'

'Of course.'

'Thank you,' Thea says gratefully, rubbing the heaviness

from her eyes. 'When we're tired we make mistakes. I'm going to take a quick nap, and after that I'm going to go and examine the setup out in the barn, to see if it will provide any clues about why Rosy's been gone so long.'

'It has been a long time,' Ayo says cautiously.

'I know.' Thea looks at them both in turn. 'But Rosy's smart. And kind. She'll turn up here and be *very* upset she's made us this worried.'

Urvisha nods. That does sound like the Rosalind they know.

Thea reaches for their hands. 'And when Rosy comes back – it won't matter that we're catching some sleep upstairs, or examining the barn, instead of waiting on the exact spot for her to return.' Thea gives a tentative smile. 'It's 2018. She'll be able to call us.'

On cue, Thea's phone beeps.

'Jesus Christ.' Ayo jumps, her nerves frayed.

Thea takes out the phone and looks at the screen. 'Sorry. It's Isaac – he just got out of the airport.'

After the whoosh of adrenalin, Ayo's voice is quiet. 'For a minute, I thought it was . . .'

'I think we all did.' Thea switches her phone to silent. 'So we're agreed on the plan? Ayo will wait for Rosy, and Urvisha and I will catch a quick rest.'

Urvisha shrugs. 'And if she doesn't show up?'

'She will.' Her phone vibrates and, looking at it, Thea shakes her head in case they again think it might be Rosy. 'If she's not standing here when we wake up, affectionately holding a bunch of flowers, then I'll eat my words. But she'll be here. She will.'

When Thea wakes, a few hours later, the atmosphere is different. More anxious, and even more concerned. Throughout, the grandfather clock in the hall keeps ticking, marking every passing second in sober fashion.

The truth is settling in.

Rosy is gone, lost in the dark of the night like a locket slipping from a neck into the gutter.

'I feel sick,' Ayo says in the kitchen, and Urvisha agrees.

'Me too. This is all our fault.'

Thea is discovering she had been so focused on whether someone *could* jump back in time, it never crossed her mind that people would be standing here, worrying, waiting for them to return. The aftershock hits her in a fresh wave of anxiety, the dread and guilt rushing over her skin and giving her goose-bumps. 'We'll form a search party,' Thea says as she quickly eats a piece of toast. 'Maybe we sent Rosy back only a tiny amount of time, but a vast amount of space. She's ended up somewhere far away from here – we'll need to spread out to look for her.'

'That's a good point. Maybe she's knackered, somewhere, and has lost her phone,' Urvisha suggests.

'Totally possible.' Thea takes out her pad and scratches down a note to physically pin their phone numbers to the coat of anyone else who jumps, whenever or whoever that may be. 'First thing's first, we'll look for her in all the places that mean something to her: Oxford – the library, her house . . . Where else?'

'Maybe we should contact her family?' Ayo says.

'Rosy's dad is terrifying,' Thea confides.

'Lord de Glanville? Why am I not surprised.' Urvisha makes a face.

'We shouldn't say she's missing,' Ayo says. 'We don't want to alarm anyone just yet. Do we?'

'Absolutely not.'

'Let's just say we heard she was heading home,' Ayo advises.

'Didn't she say she was doing research at the Bodleian? We should check if they've seen her there.' Thea jots down the note. 'Actually, that could also be our cover – we could tell the family she mentioned she might head home to finish her thesis in the de Glanville family library, and we're checking how she's getting on.' Thea tries out the white lie, and find it sounds authentic.

Ayo nods. 'Is she dating anyone?'

Thea frowns. 'Not that I know of – not recently, at least.'

'The night we broke into the Beecroft, she referred to somebody as "The Boy", remember?' Urvisha says to Thea.

'Oh, yes. Let's try and find out who that is.' Thea draws a table with three columns across two pages of her notebook. Quickly she scrawls each of their names at the top. 'Ayo, I'm sure you're anxious to get back to your little one. Would you mind looking for Rosy in Oxford?'

'Of course,' Ayo says. 'I can head back shortly.'

'Thank you.' Thea writes *Oxford* under Ayo's column, then adds *Bodleian*, *Rosy's house* and *Boyfriend?* as subheadings.

'And Urvisha, you'll pay a visit to the de Glanville estate?'

'What could go wrong?' Urvisha murmurs.

Thea dutifully writes *Cotswolds* in Urvisha's column, then adds *Rosy's family – any leads?* beneath.

'And you're going to stay here?' Ayo asks, and Thea nods.

'I'll keep my eyes on the barn and the house, in case she comes back here,' she says. 'And I'll carry on looking into the experiment – see if I can figure out where Rosy might have jumped to.'

Urvisha looks troubled. 'In my opinion we need more than the three of us out searching for her.'

Thea bites her lip. 'Not yet—'

'This could be huge. We should be looking everywhere she's ever been, talking to everyone Rosy knows, asking *everybody* if they've seen her.' Urvisha agitates as she talks.

Ayo considers. 'Perhaps after twenty-four hours. It hasn't been a day, yet – we wouldn't want to make anyone even more worried—'

'And we should consider calling the police and filing a missing persons report.'

'Not yet!' Thea exclaims. 'It's too soon – we've got to give her time to get back to us.'

Even Ayo sets down her tumbler of water on the table. 'And how long is that?'

'I don't know,' Thea says, feeling sick too. 'This is already long past the outliers of any calculations I've made.' She gazes at the chart she's drawn, speaking aloud as the thought comes to her. 'And what do we do if Rosy can't get back to us?'

'What do you mean?'

'What if she's stuck . . . somewhere . . .' *In time*, she doesn't say, but as soon as she starts the sentence she knows they're thinking it too.

'We need help,' Urvisha says again, stubbornly.

'We need to keep this between us, for now.'

'When it gets to twenty-four hours, I'm filing a missing persons report.'

'You're wearing this guilt very heavily, Visha,' Thea says. 'Something on your mind?'

'You have trust issues.' Urvisha stands, her chair scraping behind her and making them jump. 'Rosy is missing and you're so busy worrying about keeping your precious theory secret, you're not focusing on finding her. There has to be somebody else who could help us?'

'That's not true at all. I'm completely focused on finding her.'

'We need more manpower,' Urvisha says. 'People to help look.'

'There's nobody,' Thea says quietly. 'Excluding Rosy, everybody I trust is standing in this room.'

'Then you need more friends,' Urvisha says. 'I—'

She's cut short by the ring of the doorbell, the farm's ancient pull-cord making the clanger hit the bell more times than necessary.

'Rosy?' Urvisha and Ayo say at the same time, as the echoing of the bell peters out.

The three women look at each other for only a fraction of a second before they're almost climbing over each other to get to the front door. Ayo winces as Urvisha barges past, while Thea jogs to the hall, pulling the door open—

'Shit, all the locks are done.'

'Hurry!'

Thea fumbles with the chain, unlatching it quickly, then reaches down to the iron key sticking out of the weathered oak front door. She turns it once clockwise, then anti-clockwise—

'What? You just unlocked and locked it again.'

'Sorry – nervous habit.' She unlocks it once more – three turns, her lucky number – and finally pulls open the door.

'You make quite the welcoming committee,' Isaac says on the doorstep, a box of cold New York pizza balanced in one hand, grease stains marking the crumpled cardboard.

Urvisha groans.

'What? I know it's a bit cold, but I got delayed at Heathrow . . .' He trails off as he takes in their expressions and the palpable tension on the doorstep. 'Surprise,' he says weakly. 'Why do I get the feeling I'm not who you expected?'

'Hi.' Thea takes the pizza from him, handing it without looking to a disgusted Urvisha.

It's been a year since they last saw each other properly, a year in which they've said many things they didn't mean, and some things they did. Without thinking too much about it she steps forward and puts her arms around Isaac, hugging him for a second.

'Hello, friend,' he says into her ear, clearly a little surprised, though he hugs her back.

'Hello.'

He steps back. 'When Rosy called, she said you needed—'

'Rosy?' Urvisha shouts. 'When did you speak to her? What did she say?'

The three gabble at once, a staccato barrage of questions, and Isaac looks concerned.

'Last week,' he says. 'When we spoke about Thea coming out to the farm, Rosy said you'd need a team around you.' He looks at the three standing on the doorstep, and they physically droop at his words.

'Last week,' Ayo repeats, with some sadness.

'Can I come in?' he says. 'I've just got off the redeye, I'm knackered, and it's bloody *freezing* up here.'

'Welcome to Lancashire,' Urvisha says.

'The true middle of the land,' Thea says, as she pulls his suitcase in and shuts the heavy door against the autumnal chill.

'What's going on?' he whispers to Thea, as the others lead the way into the only warm room in the house. 'You guys seem wired. Is everything okay?'

'You'd better sit down,' Thea says, nodding towards a ladder-back kitchen chair, the raffia seat worn but comfortable. 'This is going to take quite some explaining.'

'If it's got anything to do with science, I am going to need coffee. Really strong coffee,' he says, 'the kind that makes your heart tremor. My body clock is running five hours behind and I am *feeling it*.' It takes a moment for it to register he's talking about his flight across the Atlantic: the basic concept of time zones makes every long-haul passenger a time traveller.

Thea watches him look round the oak-beamed kitchen and at its anxious occupants. 'You're starting to scare me. What's up?' He looks around once more. 'Hey, where's Rosy?'

'We should take him out to the barn,' Urvisha says, not looking at the others.

'Why, what's in the barn?' Isaac says. 'Is Rosy out there?'

'Are you sure?' Ayo says, distinctly unsure.

'Maybe he can help.'

'He's—'

'Can you stop talking about me like I'm not here?' He taps his chest, then taps the table. 'I'm here. What's going on? Thea?' When she doesn't answer, he appeals to the others. 'Visha? Ayo? Anyone?'

Thea cuts them all short from answering as she sighs, her loud exhalation joining the bubbling of the coffee pot as it percolates on the hob, steam hissing from the spout. 'We'll explain everything,' she says, speaking over the hiss, her voice full of air. She finally meets his eyes. 'I just have to figure out where to start.'

'Start at the beginning,' Isaac wisely advises, and Urvisha rolls her eyes.

'Oh, brother. The genius is back.'

'Relax, Angry Spice,' he says, taking in Urvisha's face.

'Listen, I can take the piss out of us. But that doesn't mean you can. Got it?'

He nods. 'Got it. No jokes.'

'Wrong,' Urvisha says, connecting the camera to the laptop and preparing to hit play on the video. 'Only *good* jokes.'

'Before you show that, Visha –' Thea indicates the laptop – 'let me tell him a bit more about the theory.' She turns to Isaac. 'So you know what you're watching.'

'Get on with it, will you?'

Thea sighs again. 'I'm going to need you to get the hang of two scientific principles, Isaac. Just two. The first you know about – the speed of light.'

'Right,' he says, 'we're back to your favourite then, are we? The whole "If you were to travel faster than the speed of light, you could theoretically arrive somewhere before you left" bit?'

'A-plus,' Thea says, impressed. 'So you were listening all those times I mentioned it.'

'Being able to parrot something back doesn't imply intelligence,' Urvisha says grumpily.

'I was,' Isaac says, ignoring her and answering Thea. 'So . . . ?'

'I want to slow down the speed of light. It's not that crazy an idea – there are places in the universe where the speed of light varies. Even Einstein was on board with the concept of the variable speed of light.'

'Okay . . .' Isaac says cautiously.

'And the place where I want to slow the speed of light is inside a prism.'

'I'm with you,' he says, accepting a steaming mug of black coffee from Ayo. 'I think.'

'The second scientific principle is borrowed from the theory of time crystals. They're not real crystals, like my prisms; they were – are – a theoretical type of four-dimensional structure that exists in spacetime.'

'Nope. You lost me.' Isaac grimaces. 'Lost at the first sentence . . . this bodes well.'

'No, that's my bad – let's try that again.' She pauses, finding the way back in, taking one of her ubiquitous glass prisms from her pocket. 'If you shine a light through a prism, the light refracts, like a rainbow.'

He nods. 'Oh – like the Pink Floyd album cover.'

Urvisha is surprised. 'Yep, kinda exactly like that.'

'The white light is dispersed into its component colours, and they bend at different angles, which is why you see a rainbow.'

'I'm still with you,' Isaac says.

'The light wave is slowed by the density of the glass,' Thea continues, moving the prism in her hand so it catches the light. 'When light passes through a transparent material, like water or glass, it's slowed slightly, and it bends. Good so far?'

Isaac looks suspicious. 'Why do I get the feeling you're dumbing this down for me?'

'You're not going to want to talk about spontaneous translation symmetry breaking inside time crystals with your jetlag. So I'm finding a way round it.'

'You're doing a good job,' Ayo interjects, her eyes on her watch.

'Thank you. Anyway, if the inside of the glass prism is cut like a crystal – not a woo-woo "magic" crystal; I'm talking about a highly organized solid crystalline structure – then the light wave can be trapped in there for a bit, bouncing around, stuck inside rather than coming out as a refracted rainbow.'

Isaac nods, and Thea can't help but smile as he immediately looks more cheerful – he's seen Thea's collection of crystals and prisms. They seem much easier to understand than a complicated theory, because they're tangible. You can hold them in your hand.

She flicks the prism so Isaac can see the light catching the facets inside. 'The delay is minimal – I'm not talking about the light wave being stuck in there for hours. It's a fraction of a millisecond.'

'Right . . .' Isaac says, blowing over the top of the scalding hot coffee.

'But the longer you trap something, the more powerful it can become. Because light usually travels so fast, it doesn't interact much with matter. The benefit of slow light and trapped rainbows is we can make these interactions stronger.' Thea pulls her notebook towards her, opening it to a complicated page of maths equations. 'This is the part I've borrowed from the theory of time crystals, so bear with me, okay?'

Isaac nods.

'The light wave is momentarily stuck inside that crystalline structure, bouncing back and forth, oscillating like a pendulum. Have you ever looked at a pendulum?'

Isaac looks around at the others. 'Is she kidding?'

'I don't think so,' Urvisha says.

'We could look at the grandfather clock in the hall. Or . . .' Thea examines her friends, searching for something she needs. 'Ayo, can I borrow your necklace for a moment?'

Ayo touches the silver cross with her hand. 'This?'

'Please. Thank you.' She takes the delicate chain in one hand and steadies the cross. Slowly, she starts it swinging, keeping her hand still, so the necklace acts like a pendulum.

'Tick-tock,' Urvisha says pointedly.

'I'm going as fast as I can. Now, Isaac, watch the swing. Do you see how it accelerates as it falls towards the centre, then decelerates as it swings up towards the top?'

Isaac's forehead knits in concentration as he stares at the necklace. 'Yuh huh. I think so.'

Thea waits until her makeshift pendulum is at the slowest part of its swing, then reaches out and snatches it with her other hand. The movement is so sudden it makes Isaac jump.

'Imagine the light wave inside the crystalline prism bouncing back and forth like a pendulum. If you catch it at the precise moment it slows . . .'

'You can slow the speed of light.'

Thea nods appreciatively. 'Basically, yes. You can slow an already decelerating light wave. It was slowed by the density of the prism, remember? We're just slowing it even more. Then we harness it at that speed, and Bob's your uncle, Thea's your aunt.' She smiles, humble. 'And as we know, if you can travel faster than the speed of light . . .'

'You can arrive somewhere before you left.' Urvisha and Ayo finish the sentence by rote.

Isaac sits back. 'Fuck.'

'I know.'

'And that got you kicked out of Oxford? Because right now it sounds like you should be winning the Nobel Prize.'

She swats him, getting up to make another pot of coffee. 'See? I told you it would be easy to understand.'

'Easy to understand for a room full of—'

'Spice Girls?' Urvisha asks.

'DPhils,' Isaac finishes. 'I am but a lowly digital archivist.'

Thea snorts. 'You're not lowly.'

'It's incredible,' Isaac says genuinely. 'So that's why you have so many prisms?'

'Yes,' she nods. 'They all trap light inside in different ways, depending on their inner crystalline structure. I can experiment with speed, refraction, strength . . .'

'Amazing.'

'Thank you,' she says, modestly. 'When I read about the scientists at MIT theorizing a four-dimensional time crystal that exists in spacetime, I was blown away – it opened up so many new ideas about how to piggyback the light.'

'Piggyback?' Isaac looks suspicious.

'It's probably a discussion for another day,' Thea says hurriedly. 'But spacetime is the key. You're familiar with space and time being paired, right? Isaac Newton. Stephen Hawking.' At his nod, she continues. 'Well, four-dimensional spacetime gives rise to the question: if it's happening in *space*, could it be happening in *time*, too?'

Isaac puts down his mug. 'What?'

Urvisha and Ayo catch each other's eyes, both sitting back down.

'This is hard for anyone to get their head around,' Thea says. 'Essentially, in four dimensions, if it's happening in space, it's also happening in time. So theoretically—'

'But how does any of this relate to Rosy?' Isaac says, interrupting her indecipherable flow. 'She's not a scientist.'

Thea doesn't answer straight away, and the others avert their gaze in a way that could only ever seem suspicious: Urvisha looks straight down at her feet; Ayo slides her eyes to the kitchen window and out towards the barn.

'It also doesn't quite answer why you all looked so panicked when I arrived. Unless you were concerned about me bringing banned produce through customs, including that incredible pepperoni, and that I could therefore probably be deported.'

He looks remorsefully at the unopened pizza box, containing an uneaten pizza, then round the kitchen at the three women there with him.

'Thea – where's Rosy?'

Eight

Thea sighs, her heart breaking every time Isaac asks the question. 'Rosy's missing.'

Saying it aloud makes it more real.

'Where is she?'

She wants to run from the room, pull one of the dustsheets over her head and hide until the situation resolves itself. But she can't, because she's responsible.

She knows that when he understands what she's done, his awe at the science will once again make way for anger at her single-mindedness. This cosy reunion they're enjoying is about to turn sour, and there's nothing she can do to stop it.

Thea nods at Urvisha, sitting with her laptop. 'Show him. Show Isaac the video.'

The footage shows the group setting up the barn. Thea, her head out of the frame, walks away from the camera and fiddles with the grey box of the laser. Urvisha is concentrating hard on her laptop, wearing a frown between her brows, and Rosy walks over to the glass house and steps inside. The glass house glows dramatically under the light of the photographic lamps, almost like they're watching a play.

On camera, all three laugh when Rosy bellows 'Go!' Then the screen turns to white.

As the others did when they watched Rosy's first leap at the Beecroft, Isaac leans in to the screen as the image whites out, trying to decipher what his eyes are seeing. 'Show, don't tell,' he says, looping the video, watching it over and over. 'Isn't that what they say? Because fucking hell, you could have shown me this without all that explanation about Pink Floyd and pendulums and whatever the rest of it was. Even a fool could see she disappears.'

'I thought you might like to understand what you're seeing,' Thea says, on the defensive.

'That damned theory,' Isaac says.

'Yes. The principle.'

He replays the video again. 'Are you sure it's not the camera glitching?'

'I'm sure,' Thea says, gritting her teeth.

'Because it might not be that Rosy's disappearing, simply that the video buffered or moved on to a different frame for a second.'

'It's not,' Ayo says.

'Isaac, Rosy is *gone*. Don't you think we'd have noticed if she had been sat in the barn all along? It's not the video buffering.' Thea is contemptuous.

'I don't believe it.'

'I knew he wouldn't,' Urvisha says, frustrated. 'We shouldn't have told him. What a waste of time.'

'Are you sure she wasn't vaporized on the spot?'

'That's not helpful,' Ayo reproves.

It's past midday, and Rosy has been missing for twelve hours. The sun is overhead but far away, its warmth weak in late October.

'If you looked at this without understanding at least that Rosy was carried away on the streak of white light . . . You wouldn't have understood at all.'

'Regardless, I believe you when you say that Rosy is missing. What's the plan? What are we going to do?' Isaac says.

'There is no "we",' Thea says. 'You're not involved. We're handling it.'

'I'm here, aren't I?' Isaac says.

'You're here, but you're judging me again.'

Ayo busies herself at the kitchen counter. Urvisha leans forward, drawn to the building anger.

'If you've risked Rosy's life because of that stupid theory—'

'*That stupid theory*? The one you just said should win the Nobel Prize? The theory I've been working on for what feels like my whole life, Isaac? *That theory*?'

Isaac pushes his mug across the table. 'Yeah, it sounds good on paper, Theodora, but in real life a person is missing. And not just any person: Rosy—'

'That's what this is about, isn't it?' Thea stands up and her chair falls over backwards, cracking loudly on the floor tiles. 'Because it's Rosalind de Glanville. When I rang to tell you I was doing the experiment myself, you weren't bothered in the slightest about *my* fate.'

He pushes his hair aggressively out of his eyes. 'Of course I was. And what I'm worried about right now is you don't seem to have even contemplated that you might be wrong.'

She jolts backwards. 'Of course I have. I'm absolutely *terrified* I am wrong.'

'Then—'

Urvisha comes between them, breaking their locked view of each other. 'Umm, guys? If I may – can you stop being so fucking stupid?'

They both look at her, amazed.

Urvisha slides the notebook over to Isaac, open on the page bearing the three-columned search for Rosalind. 'This is the plan, Isaac. Either add a fourth column with your ideas for where to look, or get out of our way.'

Taken aback, Thea can't believe Urvisha is actually taking her side. 'Well, quite.'

'You can shut up and all. I just couldn't bear hearing your ridiculous lovers' tiff while we're all sitting here. We've got more important things to do.' Urvisha nods at the notebook.

'We're not—' Thea starts.

'Don't be fatuous,' Isaac says flatly.

Urvisha shrugs. 'Whatever. Let's focus, shall we?'

Isaac scans the columns outlining Oxford, Rosy's family and the farm. He walks to the kitchen door, putting on his coat. 'Can someone show me the barn?'

'Yes. Why?'

'It's probably the first place she'd return to, isn't it? The place she left. And anyway,' he says, stepping outside, 'I'd like to see it.'

'I'll take you,' Ayo says, stepping into her wellies and hurrying to catch up with him. 'Thea, why don't you think about making lunch?'

'Umm, sure.' Thea sits back down and watches as Ayo and Isaac pick their way across the overgrown vegetable garden, out towards the paddocks and barns.

Urvisha looks at Thea watching them from the window. 'Thea,' she says, 'while they're gone, tell me honestly – was there really never anything more between you and Isaac?'

'What? No. Why?'

'I want to know what group dynamic I'm getting myself into,' she says.

Thea opens the fridge, full of bits and pieces from Ayo's trip to the village, and ponders what she can combine to make a simple meal – cooking is Ayo's strength, and maybe Rosy's, but not Thea's. She's ashamed to say that at twenty-seven, she still lives like a student. 'We made a mistake once,' she says at last. She chooses beans on toast. 'But we're just friends.'

Urvisha arches an eyebrow. 'A mistake.'

Thea shakes her head. 'I'm not getting into it right now, Visha. Haven't you ever mistaken a friendship for something more?'

'Okay. "Just friends" it is.'

'You asked for honesty; I'm giving it to you. He's my friend – a good one – but I don't feel more than that.'

'Does he?'

Thea closes the kitchen cupboard and it accidentally slams, the noise loud in the quiet house. 'I couldn't say. You'd have to ask Isaac.'

∞

'You make for an unusual team,' Isaac says to Ayo while they cross the overgrown kitchen garden, as though he were chatting about the weather in that typical English way. 'The three – four – of you.'

'A crazy genius, a sarcastic hacker, an upper-class lady, and a Naija queen? Sounds like a good team to me,' Ayo says haughtily as they cross the three stepping stones leading to the barn. 'Diverse. Different. Strong.'

'Until the lady went missing.'

Ayo is quiet. 'Yes, there is that.'

'What does "Naija" mean?'

'Nigerian,' Ayo explains. 'Look it up sometime, the word has an interesting definition.'

'I will. How did you get drawn into this?'

Ayo glances at him. 'Thea and I were lab partners.'

They walk in silence for a minute, as Isaac thinks through everything he's heard since he arrived at the farm. 'You can't possibly believe all this,' he says, shifting gear without even looking at her.

'Believe what: time travel?'

'It's completely and utterly nuts.'

She sighs. 'In the late 1980s two of the most prominent physicists of the time, Kip Thorne and Carl Sagan, concluded there is nothing in the laws of physics – specifically, Einstein's theory of general relativity – that would make time travel impossible.'

'Oh, *come on*,' he says. He'd forgotten she was also a scientist.

'You were utterly on board with the physics when Thea explained the theories involved, Isaac.'

'Yes, but I don't know better.' He stops to tie his shoelace. 'You do.'

'You heard her – she's a genius, combining those principles—'

'Ayo.' Isaac straightens. 'You didn't take part in the experiments in Oxford – there must be something that made you uncomfortable, something that didn't chime well with you.'

She's silent.

'You should be spending every waking moment looking into the experiments they've already run,' he says as they walk past the dovecote, towards the barn. 'You are the only person she will trust to hear sense on the science.'

'Why would I want to—?'

'Because people are getting hurt. Has it occurred to you that Rosy could be dead, incinerated by an unregulated laser?'

Ayo's gait and quickened pace give away her anger, though

whether it's directed at him or herself, Isaac can't tell. 'No. That's not possible.'

'Is it any less probable than Thea managing to successfully establish time travel here in a barn in Dunsop Bridge? Look around –' Isaac waves at the yellow and red leaves dropping to the floor, the wood edging the farm's borders – 'we're pretty far away from Oxford University's Department of Physics.'

'I checked it,' she says in a low voice, though she doesn't slow. 'The laser was sound.' They get to the barn and she wheels the door round. 'Anyway, being far away from Oxford was sort of Thea's point.'

'All I'm saying is it wouldn't hurt to have someone cynical on the team, looking at the facts,' Isaac advises.

'That role's taken.' She flicks on the lights inside the barn. 'By you.'

'Me? You heard Thea – I'm not on the team.' He gazes around at the setup.

'You should be.' She beckons Isaac in, showing him first the laser, then the glass house. 'I'm sure you've got skills we could utilize.' She looks at him. 'What do you do, anyway?'

'I deliver resilient long-term access to digital content and services so there are records of them in the future,' he parrots, chin raised high.

Ayo shrugs.

'I digitize old documents for the Guggenheim. It's all research and databases. So this is where Rosy disappeared?' He tries the glass door, peering inside. 'I have no idea how this booth thing would work.'

'You'd have to ask Thea,' Ayo says, shrugging again. 'She calls it the glass house.'

He steps inside, crouching down to fit. 'What's this?' She

leans in quickly and looks over his shoulder as he pushes against the rear glass wall. It opens like a door into a much smaller antechamber, only a few inches deep. 'What's that for?'

'I've no idea. It's never been mentioned.' Ayo steps into the small booth too, packing them both in tightly – it's comfortable enough for one, constricted with two.

'Thea's a genius,' Isaac says with genuine admiration in his voice, looking at the etched lines of the prismatic glass. 'But that doesn't mean I truly believe she has successfully established time travel.'

Ayo climbs out and walks across to the laser. 'The thing is, if she can't prove she *has* established time travel, then she's up shit creek – please excuse my language. Out of Oxford with few prospects in the world of physics, and worst of all . . .'

'Rosy is missing.'

'Yes.' Ayo examines the laser. 'It's quite the conundrum.'

Isaac hops up onto the workbench, taking a seat. 'That's an interesting choice of word, *conundrum*.'

Ayo is earnest. 'With Rosy missing, it actually makes it *more* probable that we – they – successfully established time travel.'

Isaac sucks in the air as he understands. 'Because if Rosy were here, you'd have failed.'

'Precisely.' Ayo sits next to him. 'If we can *prove* Rosy's gone because she's stuck somewhere back in time, well . . .'

He's dumbstruck. 'What do you mean, if Rosy is stuck somewhere in time?'

They hear a cough and Urvisha stands in the doorway, clearing her throat, illuminated by the daylight outside. 'Any luck?' she says.

'With what?'

'Finding Rosy.' Urvisha is impatient. 'Because if not, Ayo should probably head back to Oxford and start the hunt.'

Focusing on the trees behind Urvisha, Isaac jumps off the workbench, making it shake. 'Let's get Thea,' he says, stepping out of the barn, 'and start searching the woods. We can talk while we look.'

Urvisha looks at him with unveiled cynicism. 'Oh?'

'I might have an idea.'

Leaves crunch underfoot as they wind their way through the yellowing trees. What had looked like a huge forest when they arrived and had loomed, menacing, in the dark, turns out to be a small wood bordering the farm. Beyond that, an open landscape of patchwork green fields with brown fallow is criss-crossed by lanes and roads leading in either direction: towards the village, or towards the hills of Lancashire.

'Pretty,' Ayo concedes as they wander through the trees.

'Why are we searching out here?' Thea asks gently. The cold air is taking its toll on her fragile condition, dosed up to the eyeballs on flu medication.

'You ran a displacement experiment next to a wood,' Isaac says. 'We should definitely search the wood.'

'Displacement,' Thea repeats. 'Interesting.'

'You said Rosy turned up in the atrium right next to where you were? Hence, displacement.'

'Keep looking,' Urvisha says, marching along, her sleek ponytail swinging. 'Rosy could have been *displaced* anywhere round here.'

Isaac treads carefully around bogs and puddles, watching the group; if they were out walking on a happier day, they might pick up handfuls of crunchy orange leaves and throw them at each other, laughing. But the mood today is not care-free. They walk cautiously, looking left and right, talking in hushed tones – though there's no one around to overhear.

The trees give way to the road, and the group begin to walk towards the village. Isaac runs his hand along the top of the low stone wall alongside the road, and his palm catches on the shingle packed into the wall hundreds of years before. He bides his time, waiting for the right moment. 'I think I know a way I can help with the search,' he says finally.

Thea stops to listen, but Urvisha urges her on. 'Come on – walk and talk.'

'How?' Thea says to Isaac, moving next to him.

'We follow the plan you've already outlined.' He gestures at each of the group. 'Thea stays at the farm in case Rosy turns up there. Ayo heads back to Oxford.' A jagged stone tears into his thumb and he retracts his hand from the wall, examining it. 'Urvisha makes contact with Rosy's family in person, to scope them out.'

'So far, so familiar,' is all Urvisha says.

'That should cover our bases. But I keep thinking about something you've each hinted at but don't seem to want to talk about,' he continues. 'That Rosy could be . . . stuck, somewhere, unable to return.'

Ayo's mouth cinches with worry, and Thea kicks a pebble on the road.

'So if you three are covering the search in the here and now,' he says slowly, 'how would you feel if I searched back in time?'

They all stop walking. 'What?'

'That makes no sense.'

'You can't jump back, too—'

Isaac holds up his hands. 'I'm an archivist. I could search through history for any sign of Rosy. I can look for mentions of her, before she could have been known.'

Ayo meets his gaze, and the side of her lip quirks up; on any other day, it would be a full smile. 'And how would you do that?'

'Online. Databases. Research. Archives. I do –' he gives her an imperious look – 'have some skills in this area.'

Urvisha's eyebrows shoot up. 'And here I was, thinking you were just the—'

'Pretty face?'

'Vacuous cheerleader,' she finishes.

'It's only an idea. A group of American scientists ran a jokey study some years ago where they trawled the internet for time travellers – I remember reading about it at the time. They looked for any mentions of big events, like a comet being discovered, or the Pope seceding, before they happened.'

'And you think you could do the same with Rosy?' Thea asks.

'I don't see why not. Those researchers weren't searching for physical time travellers themselves, but traces of information left by them.' He shrugs. 'That sounds right up my street.'

'It's a good idea. Although –' Thea jumps across a small stream as their walk becomes a little more like an autumnal hike – 'non-corporeal informational remnants may not be transmittable or visible to us across spacetime.'

Isaac looks at her blankly.

'We don't know,' she tries again, 'if anything we change in the past shows up in our present. That might violate the laws of physics.'

'I see. So if, hypothetically speaking, I went back and

murdered Hitler . . .' Isaac starts, and despite the tension of their search for Rosy, all three women groan. 'What? We're talking about time travel – all time travel discussions get to Hitler sooner or later.'

'Isaac,' Thea pleads.

'What do we want?' Isaac parodies a rally chant. 'Time travel. *When* do we want it?'

The others look at him, awaiting the punchline with dread.

'It's irrelevant.'

'Oh, brother,' Urvisha mutters.

Thea smiles quietly.

'After what Hitler did to my family during the war,' Isaac says as the sound of running water gets louder, and Thea leads the group down towards the main river, 'he'd deserve it.'

'No one would argue with that.'

Urvisha slips a little on the bank of the River Hodder, and Isaac assists Ayo across a stile.

'You're sure you want to help with this?' Thea says.

'I'm sure.'

'Because you've never really been on board with my time travel project before.'

Isaac sighs. 'No, Thea. I was always on board with the project. What I *wasn't* on board with was you sacrificing everything, including decent conversation, for your single-track-mindedness over this. It was like being friends with an obsession, rather than a person.'

'Anyway,' Urvisha reasons, 'he's doing this to find Rosy.'

Isaac is quiet. 'I just want to help.'

Thea, too, is quiet. 'What do you need,' she says eventually, 'to search through time? What resources?'

'Libraries. Galleries. Museums. Research hubs. I need to head down to London to renew my visa, anyway – I can start work there.'

'And you'll let us know how you get on?'

'Of course.'

'Good. It sounds, then, like we have a plan.'

'Can I check something?' Urvisha asks, as they stroll up from the river into the village and past Puddleducks, deciding to stop in for some scones. 'Isaac's a member of the team now, right?'

'It appears so.' He inclines his head, his tone sombre.

Urvisha ignores him and continues speaking to Ayo and Thea. 'Because him stepping in to help – he's not white knighting, is he?'

'Are you kidding?' he says. 'You're smarter than me, with more knowledge than me, and we're working in a field where the best course of action is to follow your lead. I'm lending a skill to a search party, that's all. Rosy's my friend, too.'

His last words hang over them, the weight of her absence oppressive. They grab some food from the tearoom and head back to the farm, each with their individual task to undertake in the vain hope of finding Rosy, alive and well. Hopefully with a lively tale to tell about where she's been – the alternative is too bleak even to consider.

Nine

Though she has become accustomed to the others' noise and camaraderie, Thea quickly adjusts to living with only the ghosts on the farm again. And it means the others won't witness what she's trying to accomplish.

She has a secret project.

Terrified her kindest friend may never return, despite their extensive search, Thea has decided their plan has a flaw. (A plan split into four, which isn't a number she particularly likes.) Thea knows sometimes the best way to find something is to retrace the steps you took before it was lost.

So she's using the opportunity to revisit the experiment.

The group stay in touch constantly, sharing updates and having catch-up calls after each member has tried to find Rosy in their respective places. To allow them to all speak at once, they try a mix of video calls over the internet, and conference calls which they dial into the old-fashioned, corporate way. On the first video call they join haphazardly, two from mobile phones and two on laptops and desktops, their faces rendered in varying numbers of pixels. Ayo sits at a formal walnut desk, her young child on her lap as he snoozes.

'Did anyone find anything?' Thea asks from her farmhouse bedroom, the internet connection occasionally fragmenting her image. 'Any sign of Rosy?'

Ayo had visited Rosy's accommodation in Oxford, a neat townhouse on the edge of the city that Ayo suspected was owned by the de Glanville family. There was no answer when she rang the bell.

Playing up to the detective role they'd all been assigned, Ayo looked through the letterbox, spying a pile of post on the mat. She peered around Rosy's well-appointed living room: the elegant cream sofas, the Moroccan rug. 'Oh,' Ayo breathed as she spotted a vase filled with lilies on the hall table. The flowers looked fresh . . .

She needed to see them more closely. She scrabbled around on the ground for a pebble to throw, getting ready to sling it through the letterbox. But as she craned back her wrist, she hesitated, not wanting to break the pretty glass vase. What was she thinking?

She looked again at the glass.

There was no water in the base; the vase was totally empty. The flowers were made of silk.

'Damn,' Urvisha says, wrinkling her nose on the video call just as the screen freezes, holding her in that pose for several moments. 'Good thought, though,' she says grudgingly, when her image catches up with time.

'Thank you.' Ayo nods, then looks down as her sleeping child snuffles against her arm. 'I also went to the Bodleian – chatted to a few History of Art types hanging around. Nobody has seen her – though I did find a man who's dating Rosy and believes that she's ghosted him.'

Urvisha takes in a loud breath. 'Oh, my.' Despite herself, she starts laughing.

'I know. Thought I might set him up with your dreambot, Visha.'

'Did I miss something?' Isaac asks. 'Actually – I don't want to know.'

'Sorry, Isaac. Forgot about you and Rosy.'

'That's not what I meant,' he says, somewhat uncomfortably. 'But now it's got a bit awkward, I'm going to go and check on a lead. Great chat, guys. Let's do this again sometime.'

'Capability Brown,' Urvisha declares by way of introduction, when it's her turn to update the group on an audio-only call.

'What?' Thea says, from the barn.

'The de Glanville gardens were landscaped by Capability Brown. Do you know who that is?'

'A . . . gardener?'

'Yes, very good. He was only the gardener to bloody *royalty*,' Urvisha says, her voice dipping in and out as she loses phone reception and regains it. 'I Googled him. He did the gardens at Blenheim Palace and Warwick Castle in the 1700s. *Imagine.*'

'They've probably handed down the family seat for years,' Thea sniffs. She wipes her nose – the flu has subsided somewhat, leaving the remnants of a cold.

'They have tennis courts,' Urvisha says. 'And a huge rangy lurcher dog who kept sniffing my crotch.'

Thea's scoff transforms into a coughing fit, disguising her laugh. 'Any sign of Rosy?'

Urvisha had pulled up at the gates outside the de Glanville family home near Malmesbury in the Cotswolds, marvelling at the warm yellow stone – not unlike the buildings of Oxford. Her voice had cracked as she'd spoken into an intercom box, but the tall iron gates eventually creaked open, allowing her entry into this strange world.

Rosy's father opened the door (she had been sure they'd have a butler) and shook her hand, beckoning her in and proffering tea.

'Thank you,' she said, sitting down hard on a wooden chair she suspected was medieval, or made from the bow of a great ship. The *Mayflower*, perhaps.

'You said you were looking for Rosalind?' Lord de Glanville was kinder than she expected; he met her eyes straight on and his gaze didn't wander the way busy, important people are prone to do – in search of someone more valuable, interesting or worthy of their time.

'I wondered if she was here,' Urvisha said, remembering to add: 'She mentioned some books she needed for her thesis were back home, in your library.'

Oh God, she thought. *Please show me your library*. Her nosiness was well and truly piqued as she sat on the ancient chair, sipping Earl Grey from a bone china cup.

'I hope you haven't travelled far.' He rubbed his greying temple, a ring glinting in the light.

'I was in the area,' she lied, 'on my way back to Oxford, so thought I'd stop in.'

'I'm afraid she isn't here.' He smiled sadly. 'We haven't met many of Rosalind's friends; she doesn't bring anyone home with her.'

Because she'd be judged for it, Urvisha thought – and judged incorrectly. A home like this, family wealth like this, is a leg up in the world, but Rosy's best traits don't come from her family or her heritage. They come entirely from her. 'She's a great friend,' Urvisha said without hesitation. 'If someone's ill, she's the first one there.'

'That's lovely to hear,' the entirely unexpected man sitting opposite her said. 'Will you tell her to ring me, when you see her? I miss my Rosy.'

'So do I.' Urvisha flailed momentarily. 'I mean – I normally see her every day! The last few days have been quite rare. Of course I'll tell her,' she said kindly.

'Thank you. Can I offer you anything else before you head back to Oxford?'

Urvisha shook her head.

'You know,' Lord de Glanville said, standing, 'Rosalind is very close to her brother, Edward. She may well be with him in London.'

'Oh?' Urvisha tried not to show her rising excitement.

'He works at Sotheby's. He was looking into getting her a job there.'

'How lovely,' Urvisha said, trying to look sincere. 'You're probably right – she's probably down in London.' The lurcher crammed its face into her lap and she laughed nervously, pushing the dog away and disguising it with much patting. 'Good boy,' was all she said, working out when she'd be able to get down to Sotheby's to scope it out.

'No news, then, but some news,' Ayo says on the group catch-up, the timbre of her voice tinny as she tries to make the best of it.

'I know,' Urvisha says, 'a mixed bag. This detective lark is hard.'

But they're all feeling the sinking sensation of failure, as they're no closer to finding Rosalind. It's been three days.

'I can save you a trip to London. I'll go and meet with Edward de Glanville at Sotheby's,' Isaac says, his voice unexpectedly loud and booming.

'That would be great,' Thea says. 'How are you getting on?'

'I'll let you know on our next call. Sport, lacrosse and Rosy's hobbies have all been dead ends,' he says. 'I'm moving on to her family history. What you said about Capability Brown and the family seat was interesting – that time period could be a good starting point.'

'Hold on,' Ayo says. 'Wait a minute. Do you think she could have gone back that far?'

'I have to start somewhere,' Isaac says, reasonably.

Urvisha snorts. 'But Isaac, Rosy only went back five minutes during the first jump.'

'Yes, but look at the power outage it caused,' he says. 'Your first attempt was campus-wide; when Rosy disappeared, it was nationwide.'

They let that sink in.

'Thea?' Urvisha says. 'What do you think?'

'I'm only surprised,' she says slowly, 'that Isaac didn't start with the Nazis. You're right,' she says to him, 'you have to start somewhere, and family history is a good shout.'

'Thank you,' Isaac says. 'Because if *I* got stuck somewhere in time, the first thing I would do is track down my relatives.'

There's a noticeable silence on the line as Thea doesn't answer.

'Well, yeah,' Urvisha says, filling the gap. 'Like Thea said – good shout.'

'Let us know how you go,' Ayo says. 'I'm going to head back to yours tomorrow, Thea – if you don't mind. I feel useless in Oxford – I'd like to help you with the science.'

Urvisha huffs. 'We'll make a detective out of you yet.'

Thea is out in the barn, after the call, when Isaac messages her. She checks her phone, wondering if it's a group text – it's not.

Do I need to say sorry? Isaac has written. *Feel like I do.*

What for? she types one-handed with her thumb, shifting the prism into her other hand.

Being blasé, talking about relatives. Didn't mean to be insensitive, he writes back.

She'd felt the familiar freeze when people spoke about their families. She's felt the same when people have talked about Christmas at home, or Mother's Day; that sort of wrongly inclusive chat which presumes everyone is like you, that everybody has the same home life.

I'm not THAT sensitive, she types, dismissing it. *You're fine.*

I'm sorry, Isaac writes anyway, and the lack of emojis and any fun punctuation makes her think his tone might be serious.

I don't have any family, she puts, deleting and retyping the last character three times – causing her to nearly drop the phone. She sets the prism down and grasps the phone properly. *I've confronted my ghosts. There's nothing for you to be sorry for.*

He doesn't reply for a minute. *Want me to come back?*

Here? No – it's fine. I'm fine.

Damn. I wanted to get more of those scones from Puddleducks, he writes, and she sends the pig emoji.

Pig. Do you know Dunsop Bridge isn't even the true centre of the country?

Sacrilege! I bought the tea towel and everything. He sends a photo of him holding up a Dunsop Bridge tea towel, beaming, a foreign kitchen in London gleaming behind him in brilliant gloss white.

She steps inside the glass house, pulling the door shut. *The true centre is Whitendale Hanging Stones, 4 miles away,* she tells him. *Creepy place.*

Standing stones usually are. There's a pause as Isaac types – she may be imagining it, but the pause seems longer than usual. *Like gravestones, aren't they?* he writes eventually.

Perhaps she should build a seat inside the cubicle, out of glass. It could fold out, like a little stool.

They're . . . meditative, she replies, praying she won't be crossing a line for Isaac, as she understands now that he was probably trying not to cross it for her: *Like the Holocaust Memorial.*

Been there, have you? His tone is easy, and she's relieved. *Tourists taking photos, posing on top of those big grey blocks, posting them to Instagram with #culturevultures #holocaust. Not for me.*

We make our own memorials, she writes. *From memories.*

Or out of prismatic glass.

She looks around at the glass house, her life's work, wondering if maybe he's right. *How are you getting on with the great search back through time?* she writes.

Tricky, he types, before a lengthier message, which takes some time to appear on her screen. *It's hard looking for people before they could have been known. Not just the person: cultural markers made by the person.*

Like what?

Tell you more later. I'm off out in a sec – following another lead. Sure you're okay?

She signs off with a thumbs-up, already hating herself for the lazy reliance on a graphic that could never accurately sum up the depth of her feelings.

On the one hand, she's worried Rosy is never coming back. Which would be her fault. She's sick with guilt. And on top of that, she'd have been wrong all this time. The thought makes her numb.

But she's also excited Rosy is missing, because then she'd have been right.

Most of all she feels the conflict between both, a strange sensation that mostly results in a roiling stomach.

'Oh, hell.'

Thea's voice bounces off the glass door opposite her, making a small echo. She steps out, focusing her attention on the array of prisms on the workbench. If Rosy is lost, could it be because Thea didn't use the right prism? And if so, what would the right prism look like?

Ten

Thea is still working in the barn when her phone rings on the workbench, the incessant vibration breaking her concentration and stealing away her thoughts. Irritated at the interruption, she wipes her hands clean and reaches for the infernal device. They've become slaves to the beeping of a phone – more so than usual as the group stays frantically in touch. Being permanently reachable is exhausting.

She looks at the time in the top corner of the screen. Damn, she's late for their group call at seven o'clock – it's 7.09 p.m. She's been working for three hours straight and has five missed calls (at least it's a prime number), all from Isaac.

That's weird, because Ayo was going to connect Thea, and Urvisha was going to connect Isaac. He's not meant to be calling her.

She must have been concentrating really hard not to hear that irritating buzzing. She stretches, her nerves on fire from where she's been hunched over the desk, and calls Isaac back.

'Thea?'

'I'm here. Sorry I missed the group call,' she says, holding the phone to her ear with her shoulder.

'Where are you?' he asks, and his voice sounds odd – a studied casualness, so she immediately knows something's up.

'What's wrong? Did you find Rosy?'

'What are you doing?' he asks again, his voice sounding so

relaxed that to anyone else, he could be lying horizontal. But she knows better.

'I'm in the barn. Did you find something?'

He pauses. 'I might have.'

'Where are the others?' she says. 'We should connect the others.'

'No—'

'Hold on, I'll dial in Ayo—'

'Thea, wait. Can you . . .' He inhales, his breath whistling in the autumnal air, which is how she knows he's outside, somewhere.

'Where are you?' she says.

'I'm in London. Trafalgar Square. Listen, will you meet me here? Tomorrow?'

She's taken aback. 'Rosy's in Trafalgar Square?'

'No – listen – it's not that. Can you meet me?'

'I can't hear the pigeons.' She picks up a piece of firewood, the bark splintering in her hand. 'I would have thought I'd be able to hear the pigeons cooing.' He waits. 'Of course I'll meet you, Isa.'

Isaac pauses at the old pet name. 'You haven't called me that in ages.'

'I probably have, you just didn't hear.'

'Tomorrow?' he says.

'Can you tell me what this is about, at least?' she says.

He finally drops his faux-casual demeanour, his voice sincere. 'I can't tell you, Theodora,' he says in earnest. 'I can only show you.'

'Cryptic,' she sniffs, her nose streaming in the cold air.

'Tomorrow, then. Let's say midday?'

She thinks about her journey down, how she'll drive to Clitheroe and travel by train to Blackburn, then on to Preston, and finally down to London Euston. There are two changes on that route, which she doesn't relish: not a great number. But she supposes it's a three-legged journey, which is better. 'Are you sure you can't tell me what you've found?' she says. 'If it's about your search for Rosy, I think I'm entitled to know.'

'It's only sort of about Rosy.' She waits as he finds the words. 'It's not something that can be explained over the phone, Thea. I really have to show you.'

Thea arrives in a rain-soaked Trafalgar Square just before midday, the unrelenting London traffic stop-starting around the square creating a dogged and perpetual echo.

A busker on the steps plays a guitar, fighting the sound of chugging engines by hitting the strings of the instrument percussively. The dove-grey paving slabs are shiny with wet, and Thea treads carefully to avoid taking a tumble – she only just caught the elbow of an elderly lady losing her footing in front of one of the great lions.

She'd set her right and they'd both gazed up at the lion, into his mouth, and Thea wondered idly who'd put them there. She knows she could Google it. But instant access to information steals the magic of your own imagination. She thinks of some long-dead rich person commissioning four whopping great lions for a square in central London; the poor metalworker forced to make the bloody things, probably for a pittance; and the generations of pigeons who got to sit – and shit – on the shiny monoliths. She laughs to herself as Isaac appears next to her.

'What are you giggling about?' he asks by way of greeting.

'Oh, nothing.' She laughs again, a stutter of a half-laugh, and he looks at her quizzically. 'The pigeons had ancestors that sat on this thing,' she begins to explain, but she can sense tension in his body so she holds off from talking about the passing of time.

'The fourth plinth is a platform – excuse the pun – for artists,' Isaac says as they cross the square together to the National Gallery steps. 'Maybe one day you could put the glass house up there. *Alakazam!* Make people disappear.'

'Less a modern art installation,' Thea says, ducking inside her bright yellow raincoat to shield herself from the rain, 'and more like the magician who sealed himself inside a Perspex box for forty-something days. Without food,' she adds, disgusted.

'An illusionist.'

'What?'

'He doesn't call himself a magician, he's an *illusionist*.' Isaac makes a haughty face.

'Then he's already missed the trick. Isaac, what are we doing here? Did you speak to Rosy's brother – has he seen her?'

'I'm afraid not.'

'Oh.' Thea droops with disappointment. 'I really hoped she'd be with him.'

'You've run the glass house experiment multiple times, haven't you?' he says, leading her up the steps.

She blinks at his sudden seriousness, the lack of preamble. 'Yes.'

'Twice with Rosy—'

'Why are you asking?' The yellow raincoat slides off her chestnut hair slightly and raindrops pool around her fringe, framing her face, as she looks up at him. She blinks away the water that runs towards her eyes and across her cheekbones.

'I found something you need to see.'

He steers her round the impressive portico of the National Gallery, past the street artists drawing in chalk on the paving stones despite the rain, their masterpieces blurring beneath the water. A replica Cézanne; a caricature of the American president; flags from around the world – with a soggy packet of chalk for visitors to add their own country's flag.

'What did you find?'

Isaac snatches a glance at her. 'A reference to somebody before they could have been known.'

Thea is suddenly very awake. 'You found something referring to Rosy?'

'This way,' is all Isaac says.

They walk around St Martin's Place to the more modest entrance of the National Portrait Gallery, set back from the square. The lobby is quiet, and they move through the entrance archways past the donation boxes, ignoring the ticket desk for the paid exhibitions. So it's free, whatever they've come to see, part of the main national collection. Isaac leads them across the patterned mosaic floor to the stairs, worn smooth beneath centuries of eager feet.

On the first floor they pass a modern gallery with photographs of well-known faces, but Isaac doesn't stop there.

As they climb the floors they seem to move back through time. After the contemporary portraits on the first floor, lit against bright white walls, the second floor is darker; they bypass a dim mauve room featuring a pair of full-height statues in the centre, posed as though they're whispering about the marble busts lining the edges.

Thea's trainers squeak and squelch against the unending herringbone of the parquet floor as they continue through the early Stuarts, past students huddling over sketchpads, trying to recreate the alchemy of the paintings hanging on the blue walls.

'Pointless,' Isaac mutters. 'A replica can never capture a fraction of the beauty of the real thing.'

Thea can't help herself. 'What about a photocopy?'

'But the copy is always flat,' Isaac says, weaving past the later Stuarts on pale brown walls, then through the George III gallery with its forest green fleur-de-lis wallpaper. 'It loses the texture, the colour, the individuality – the flaws.'

'I don't like the word *flaws*,' she says quietly.

'Inclusions, then.' He smiles as the natural light diminishes, skylights and windows covered over to protect the older paintings. The rooms darken and darken before they arrive at the Tudors, where Isaac stops.

'Here?' Thea says.

Isaac scans the gallery information wall, reading quickly. Then he takes off, striding through the sombre rooms, and she quickens her pace to keep up.

'What exactly are we here to see?'

He slows, scanning the regal faces in gloss-black frames. 'NPG 1488. Which is just . . . over . . . there.'

Thea's phone vibrates in her pocket and she looks at it, wondering guiltily if it's socially acceptable to answer in a gallery. 'It's Ayo,' she says, then slides her finger across the screen to accept the call. 'Hi,' she says quietly.

'Thea?'

'It's me.' She holds her hand above her mouth to muffle the sound slightly.

'Where are you?' Ayo says.

'I'm in London with Isaac. I can't really talk—'

'I'm back at the farmhouse. Where's the key to the barn?'

Thea keeps her voice the same. 'It's by the kitchen door.'

'I'm going to do some exploratory work on the laser, if you don't mind?'

'Be careful—'

'Urvisha's here, too.'

Thea forces down any possessiveness she feels over the equipment. 'Great,' she says. 'Go for it.'

She glances towards Isaac, who is gazing up at an image of Elizabeth I sitting regally in an ornate frame of swirls topped with a crown, but she knows his attention is on her and the call. 'Everything okay?' he says, and she nods.

'Ayo and Urvisha are back in Dunsop Bridge.'

He looks pleased, almost satisfied, and though suspicion is tickling at the edges of the trust she has for her friends, Thea knows she must overthrow her tendency to work alone, and continue with the task at hand. The reason they are here at the National Portrait Gallery – what was it Isaac said? NPG 1488.

It's time to find Lady Rosalind de Glanville.

The room is filled with antiquated paintings in embellished gold frames; rich colours muted slightly with age, set off beautifully by the dark amethyst walls behind. The paintings are packed in, doubled up – one high, one low – and Thea doesn't know where to look, there are so many faces staring back at her.

'Here?' she says, baffled. She supposes it's the right setting for Rosy – the gallery is full of aristocracy with Roman bone structures and matching alabaster complexions.

'Here. Her.' Isaac raises a hand to point at a modestly sized oil painting: *Portrait of an Unknown Woman.*

Thea peers towards the correlating description, squinting to read the small plaque. 'Formerly known as Lady Margaret Beaufort, Countess of Richmond and Derby. Artist unknown.'

She leans back and looks at Isaac, her upper body forming a question mark. 'Why—?'

'Do you notice anything?' he says. 'Look closer.'

It's just the sort of challenge Isaac adores. An observational test she's afraid she'll fail – and the only thing Thea truly fears is failure.

She focuses on a crest (or flower?) behind the Unknown Woman's head. 'Am I supposed to recognize that symbol? I can't quite see it—'

'Not that. Okay, don't look closer; step back. Take it all in.'

Bewildered, Thea obeys. She steps back and almost crushes a toddler, apologizing to the frazzled father gripping the child's harness.

'You don't see it? I suppose you wouldn't.' Isaac sighs, looking at his best friend. 'It's you, Thea.'

She tilts her head in surprise. But before Thea can question what he means, a crocodile of schoolchildren wearing hi-visibility neon vests over their uniforms traipse in, two-by-two, and drop cross-legged onto the floor. Politely, Thea and Isaac shift out of the way of the class, as the teacher and a curator from the gallery wave at a painting on the next wall showing Henry VIII and Anne Boleyn.

Thea cranes to see the painting Isaac has shown her, but the schoolchildren have blocked her view, separating her from both the painting and Isaac.

'Now, class, how can you tell it's Anne Boleyn?' the curator asks, his tone friendly, and hands shoot up from the floor.

Across the room, Isaac's and Thea's eyes meet.

'By the B necklace!' a small girl answers when called upon, and the curator nods approvingly.

'Very good. And does anyone know how we can tell how

old the painting is?' A few of the children falter, and no hands go up. 'What if I tell you it's painted on the wood of a tree . . .'

Thea is only half listening, as she stares at the *Portrait of an Unknown Woman* on the wall, trying to discern any similarities to her own appearance. Perhaps the bridge of the nose . . .

More hands fly up. 'From the rings of the tree!'

'That's right. That's how we know this painting of Anne Boleyn was made after her death. Because the tree wasn't old enough to have been painted on when she was alive. So what does that mean?'

It's hard for Thea to tell, though. Isaac's painting is small, the oil giving the sitter a soft focus, and with the class taking up the whole floor space of the gallery Thea is forced to look at it from the side. Could it be—?

The curator appeals to the class. 'Remember what we learned with the Stuarts – is this painting of Anne Boleyn a primary source, or secondary?'

The entire group of children answer excitedly in response – they know this one. 'Secondary!'

'Very good. This particular example is actually a copy of an earlier painting, with changes. The next question we need to think about is – Why? What was the artist trying to say with the changes he made? If you come this way, we'll look at a primary and secondary source for Elizabeth I . . .'

Isaac and Thea wait patiently as the children find their pairs, chuntering out of the dimly lit room into the next gallery like a neon caterpillar.

'Gosh,' Thea says, drawing a breath, as Isaac moves back next to her.

He nods at the *Portrait of an Unknown Woman*. 'It's you in the painting.' He lifts his palm in a sweep: 'Look at the three rings she's wearing on her hand.' He points to the image, then down at Thea's left hand hanging limply by her side; one ring on her little finger, another on her forefinger, the third between the joints of her ring finger.

'Why do you wear that particular ring halfway up?' he asks, already knowing the answer because he asked her the same question a long time ago.

'That's just where it fits. And this way it doesn't look like an engagement ring,' she says quietly.

'Have you always done that?'

'I don't know.' She looks from her own hand, with its three rings, up to the painting of the Unknown Woman, formerly known as Lady Margaret Beaufort, Countess of Richmond and Derby. 'I just don't know,' she repeats, a larger statement than her previous one.

Making sure she knows what he's doing so he doesn't take her by surprise, Isaac gently lifts Thea's yellow hood partway up over her hair, looking between the painting and Thea. 'Look at the hair,' he says, 'look at the face. It's your face, Theodora – can you really not see it?'

'I don't know – maybe—'

'It is.' He takes a deep breath. 'You don't remember what's happened, but you will. This is the start of us finding the proof.' When she doesn't say anything, he places a hand on her arm. 'Thea, you did it. *You* travelled back in time.'

II

The Unknown Woman

Eleven

Thea steps back from the painting, disbelief clouding her mind as her faded fever threatens to break back through.

'I don't believe it,' she says, but he's insistent.

'I know it's hard to see. Especially for yourself. But the likeness – it's uncanny. Truly.'

'It's just a painting.'

Isaac smiles, his face bearing that sympathetic look people make when they think they know more than you, and you're trying desperately to catch up. 'It's you.'

Another class of schoolchildren begin snaking into the gallery in their bright yellow vests, and Thea feels a migraine twinge from the loud colour. She wilts against the wall, her forced speedy recovery from the bout of flu and the long journey down mingling uncomfortably. And on top of that there's . . . this. Whatever this is.

'Is this a joke?' Thea says, her voice low as the fluorescent alligator of children files past. 'Did you put my photo into that app, the one that matches you with your museum doppelganger? Because Rosy's missing, Isaac, and I've come to London because I thought you said you had something.'

'I do,' Isaac says gently. 'It's not a joke.'

Thea sighs. 'That app is popular; it must be really common to look like a painting.' Unwittingly Thea's eyes return to the *Portrait of an Unknown Woman*, to the three rings on her hand.

'It is relatively common,' Isaac admits.

'Exactly. I'm a scientist, Isaac. I need more – I'm going to need some hard proof.'

'And we'll get it. This is only the start – I needed you to see this.' He reaches for her, but she pulls back, holding up her hand to compare the painting's trio of rings with her own. 'This is the starting point of our . . . search.'

'You were going to say *quest*, weren't you?' She almost spits the word out in disgust.

'No. Absolutely not.'

'Because I know how you love a challenge like this, Isaac. We don't have time to head off on some ridiculous tangent.' Her face is pleading. 'We have to find Rosy. We have to bring her back.'

'I've been looking.' Isaac sucks in a breath, about to speak, when Thea continues.

'Have you considered that maybe this lady's my great-great-grandmother?' Thea says bluntly, gesturing at the painting. 'Or my great-great-grandmother's sister? Or, perhaps, some-body in my family saw this painting once and thought it might be fun to make me wear my rings in the same triangle forma-tion? I've done it for years. *Years*, Isaac.'

Isaac is silent.

'Three rings is scant proof.' Thea sticks her hand in her pocket, not wanting to admit she's finding them unnerving. 'What else have you got?'

'It's not just the rings. It's the likeness . . . and we'll get the painting's history . . .'

'Because *Rosy*—'

'Thea,' Isaac says, and for once she stops speaking at the firm-ness of his tone. 'When it comes to Rosy, there are no leads.' His eyes meet hers. 'Not a single one. Urvisha's found nothing. Ayo's found nothing. And I've searched everywhere I can think of; every database, archive, social media site, family history, lists of births, deaths, wills – everywhere. There's no sign of a Rosalind de Glanville anywhere else in history but now.'

Thea lets that sink in.

'But you,' he says, '*you've* run the experiment multiple times – you just admitted as much. You've experimented with time travel on numerous occasions and now here you are, on the wall of the National Portrait Gallery.'

She blinks, but when she speaks, her voice is softer, calmer. 'What am I supposed to have done, Isa? Gone back in time, sat for a portrait and then come home?' she says. 'When?'

'I don't know. But it's too much of a coincidence to ignore. We have to piece it together because, right now, this is the only clue we have.'

They step aside as a group of tourists enter the gallery, snapping photos on oversized cameras.

'Oh,' she says finally, dismayed.

'You see?' he says.

'I see. No leads.'

'This is a lead,' he corrects.

'No proof.' Thea eyes the tourists' cameras longingly, wishing for the clean capture of a photograph, rather than a muted oil painting hanging on the wall of a Tudor gallery.

'Shall we get out of here?' Isaac suggests.

'Yes, please.'

'Where do you want to go?'

Thea looks up. 'Somewhere with wine.'

They find a spot in the bar on the top floor of the gallery, taking a seat by the window with far-reaching views across a vaulted glass roof to Nelson's Column and beyond. It's an incredible panorama, a slice of rooftop London filled with icons and landmarks.

But they're not admiring the view.

In his hand Isaac holds a postcard of NPG 1488 bought from the gift shop downstairs, which he turns over and over between his fingers as he orders a flat white from the waiter.

'I'll have a glass of rosé, please,' Thea says. 'Large.'

When the waiter moves away, Isaac leans towards her over the black leather menu. 'You really don't remember when you might have jumped?' he says, his voice no more than a whisper in the busy restaurant and bar.

'Not a thing.'

'When did you—?'

The barman arrives quickly with their order and Thea takes the wineglass gratefully from his hands, downing a large gulp. 'Thanks,' she says. 'I really needed that.'

'You know, I've never heard you say that.'

Her eyes flick up to the right as she thinks. 'You're right. I've not felt like I've ever *needed* a drink, before.' She glances at the postcard on the table between them. 'But it's not every day you're told you time travelled back to a past century and ended up in an oil painting hanging in the National Portrait Gallery.'

He flashes a grin, then begins typing on his phone.

'What are you doing?' Thea murmurs.

'I'm tweeting a curator,' Isaac says.

'Huh?'

'If you use the hashtag #AskACurator, someone from the gallery will answer. I've left my tweet pretty vague, but I thought we could use the help.' Thea would usually boggle at him expressing something so personal, sharing their search online with strangers, but she says nothing. They've argued before about the validity of social media and, while she doesn't see the value in many of the platforms, she can at least appreciate the idea of connecting with experts.

'Okay,' she says, and he looks surprised that she hasn't kicked up more of a fuss.

'Okay,' he repeats, smiling, then returns to looking serious. 'When did you run the experiment alone?'

'When I first got to the farmhouse,' she says honestly. 'And a couple of times since. Nothing happened, though. I woke on the floor of the barn – it was a failure. A double failure, if you consider that I must have knocked myself out. Do *you* remember anything?'

'What do you mean?'

'Was there a power cut?'

This time he does look out over the rooftops of London, the spire of the Houses of Parliament just visible behind the pillar of Nelson's Column. 'No, I don't think so. The first time, you triggered a blackout in Oxford – while I was in New York. Then on Rosy's leap, I got held up at Heathrow Airport after I landed because the power had cut out nationwide overnight. So if you really *did* leap back far enough to appear in a nineteenth-century painting, by rights you should have taken out the power for the whole damn continent of Europe.'

'It wouldn't work like that.'

Isaac looks surprised. 'I was speaking in hyperbole. But it wouldn't?'

'Urvisha showed me how the National Grid works.' She pauses, catching sight of Isaac's eyes glazing over as she warms to her theme of the logistical challenge of distributing high-voltage electricity. 'There's a power flow running from the north of the country to the south,' she says more simply. 'In fact, I should talk to Visha about that. Because of the north-south power loss, we'd actually have better luck running the experiment on the south coast – better generation capacity.'

The waiter bustles back, arranging crockery in front of them. The restaurant is much too fancy; they should have gone outside to a cafe where they'd be left alone, but they're committed now.

'I can't believe you're still looking for ways to improve it,' Isaac says as he takes a sip of coffee. 'You really are incorrigible.'

Thea's eyes have softened from the wine, and she watches him from above the rim as she finishes the rosé from the over-sized glass. 'I'm sorry,' she says. 'I didn't mean to get sidetracked by the theory again.'

'Don't you remember anything?' he says.

'You really want to talk about the experiment?' she asks.

'It would seem pressing.'

She looks at him, her face speculative. 'I didn't tell you I was working on it alone, because you'd have told me not to.'

Isaac leans forward. 'When do I ever tell you what you should do? When would you ever listen?'

'That's true,' she says, putting down the glass. 'You never tell me I shouldn't do something. You just disappear instead.'

He watches her, not rising to meet the fight.

'Sometimes I wish I'd had somebody – anybody – to tell me no. "You can't do that, Thea,"' she says, her voice slurring a fraction. '"Do your homework, Thea. Go to bed, Thea."'

'You always did your homework and went to bed.' He speaks quietly.

'Maybe that's why – I was my own parent. Maybe I'm my own grandmother, too. Could that work? If I went back in time and I . . .' She pauses, and he waits for her to finish, allowing the rant to play out. In all their years at university together, she'd only once mentioned her family.

The splash of cutlery is loud in the restaurant, the rain tapping against the windowpane like an inquisitive stranger.

'I never talk about my family,' she says eventually, her voice almost lost beneath the scrape of plates. 'Mainly because they died when I was a child.'

'You told me that, once.' Isaac's face is sympathetic.

Maudlin, Thea scowls at the wineglass as though it's an enemy, feeling the bottoming-out of emotion alcohol can so often bring. She reaches instead for the water Isaac has poured, sitting quietly for a moment with her thoughts.

Isaac's phone chirrups. 'Would you look at that,' he murmurs, audibly impressed. 'A curator's replied. Isn't technology great?'

'What do they say?'

He pushes back his chair. 'The curator can tell us the history of the painting,' he says. 'Which sounds like a great place to start.'

'No, Isaac.'

'No?'

'We need to be searching for *Rosy*. I'm here, I'm fine. She's not.'

Isaac is adamant. 'It's all related; if we can trace *you* back in time, then we can trace Rosalind de Glanville. I'm sure of it. Right now, this is the only lead we've got. Don't you want to discount it, at least?'

Thea gets to her feet as Isaac indicates to the waiter that they want to pay the bill. She reaches over and downs the rest of Isaac's cooling mug of coffee, with the hope the caffeine will knock the after-effects of her rosé on the head. 'But I came back, Isaac. Why hasn't Rosy?'

Isaac leads the way out of the gallery restaurant, away from the rooftops, back down into the darkened womb of the Tudor gallery. 'That's what I'm hoping to find out.'

Together they make their way through the mauve-walled rooms, past the floor-to-ceiling gold frames, back to the modestly sized oil painting. 'Hello again,' Thea says aloud, as though greeting an old friend, and Isaac hides a smile. He paces in front of NPG 1488, looking at one side of the gilt frame, then the other.

'*Portrait of an Unknown Woman*, formerly known as Lady Margaret Beaufort, Countess of Richmond and Derby,' Thea reads once again, paying more attention this time to the smaller, italicized text at the bottom of the description plaque.

'Hi there,' says a voice, and Thea looks round in surprise.

Isaac shakes the hand of a woman in a smart bottle-green suit holding an iPad, who then stretches out her hand towards Thea.

'This is Helen Claassen,' Isaac says. 'She's a curator here.' At Thea's confusion: 'From the tweet.'

'Oh,' Thea says, 'I see.'

Helen smiles, her mouth set in a professional line. 'You had some questions about this painting, in particular? It's not often we get tweets from people inside the building, so I thought I'd come down and see you.'

'Thank you,' Isaac says smoothly. 'I wondered if you could tell us about its – er – history?'

'Its provenance?' she says, raising her voice as a particularly loud guided tour makes its way past. 'Of course. It's oil on panel, probably wood, and measures –' Helen Claassen takes out a small tape measure from her suit pocket – '445 milli-metres by 318. As you can see, it was painted in the nineteenth century, and at the time was identified as a portrait of Lady Margaret Beaufort, Countess of Richmond and Derby. Do you know much about her?'

Isaac shakes his head, taking his rucksack from his back and pulling out a notepad.

' "Lady Margaret Beaufort, later Countess of Richmond and Derby",' Thea says unexpectedly, reading from the phone screen in her hand in an attempt to hurry up the proceedings. ' "Born 1443, died 1509. A key figure in the Wars of the Roses and an influential matriarch in the House of Tudor, she is credited with the establishment of two prominent Cambridge colleges." ' Thea looks up. 'So if we'd gone to Cambridge—'

'We'd have known the name instantly,' Isaac finishes. 'Bloody Oxford.'

Helen Claassen looks bemused. 'We know quite a few details about Lady Margaret Beaufort – she was a renowned figure. Margaret was only twelve when she married the twenty-four-year-old Edmund Tudor at the beginning of the Wars of the Roses. Her husband was taken prisoner and died in captivity from plague, leaving Margaret a widow at thirteen, seven months pregnant with their child.'

'That's grim,' Isaac says. 'She was a child herself.'

'Lady Margaret gave birth in 1457 to her only child –' Helen Claassen indulges them with a smile – 'Henry Tudor, the future Henry VII of England.'

Isaac drops his rucksack loudly on the floor. '*King* Henry VII?'

Thea blinks.

'Indeed. Lady Margaret was determined her son Henry

would become king. She was quite the formidable woman. In fact, King Henry VII built the Lady Chapel at Westminster Abbey in her honour. She's buried there.'

'Why –' Isaac speaks slowly – 'was *this* particular painting – NPG 1488, an Unknown Woman – originally thought to be Lady Margaret Beaufort?'

Helen Claassen lifts her gallery iPad and quickly taps out the name, pulling up the archive of Lady Margaret Beaufort. She moves to sit down on the studded leather bench in the middle of the room. 'Here, take a seat. This is every portrait of her we have in our collection. They vary from seventeenth-century hand-coloured stipples to the earliest line etchings.' The curator taps the screen, stopping on a pencil drawing. 'In many portraits of Lady Margaret Beaufort you'll see symbols in the background marking the House of Tudor. Then there's the distinctive ring pattern on her fingers, the unusual positioning. There's the covered hair – stylistically, Lady Margaret is almost always represented in the same devoutly religious pose.' She flips from image to image, making her point.

'That's an impressive archive system,' Isaac says, in his element now that they're no longer in laboratories and barns full of scientific equipment. 'Can I have a quick look?'

'Of course.' Helen hands him the iPad, watching as he flicks through the images, magnifying certain details.

Thea remains standing, itching to continue the search for Rosy. But she remembers what Isaac said about this being their strongest lead, so she stays quiet as he sits beside the curator, looking through portraits of the mother of a king.

'You mentioned three rings . . .' Isaac says.

'Yes.' Helen Claassen shows them five different portraits, pointing at the Lady's hand. 'They're unusual.'

Thea leans over, looking at the rings on an ancient stipple engraving. 'They could be folds in the paper,' Thea says cynically, 'or cracks in the canvas.'

'The pattern is too frequent to be a flaw, or coincidence,' Helen says, then gestures back up to the portrait on the wall. 'Like many others, this painting bears those symbols. What's likely, in this case, is that the painter – the artist is unknown – styled the sitter in such a way to *look* like Lady Margaret. Royal homage of this nature was incredibly popular in the latter part of the nineteenth century. Profitable, too. It would have made the picture much more valuable. Perhaps the artist needed to earn as much money as possible from the sale of this painting. Conjecture, of course.' She smiles.

'Wonderful,' Isaac says admiringly. 'You've been so helpful. You really know your stuff.'

She doesn't blush – this is her job. 'The painting was purchased by the gallery in 1908, and relabelled as *Portrait of an Unknown Woman* in the middle of the twentieth century.'

'Would you have,' Isaac says, 'any record of the 1908 sale? A receipt, for example?'

Helen Claassen nods. 'We should do – so long as it wasn't bestowed on the condition the seller remain anonymous. Would you like me to get that information for you?'

'That would be great,' Isaac says, visibly relieved, and as Helen turns back to face the painting he winks at Thea, who shrugs at him.

'It may take some time. Perhaps if you came back next week—'

'I'm only in London for the day,' Thea says, and Isaac blanches.

'I'm so sorry, Helen – may I call you Helen? – but we're only down for a short time. Is there any chance . . . I suppose it would be too hard to get the information today?' Isaac says.

'Well . . .'

'Or perhaps it would be too hard for *most* people to get the information today.'

'I'm sure I could find it for you.'

Thea watches with amazement as curator Helen Claassen melts like warm butter folding around a knife, falling for Isaac's charm.

'We're open late on Thursdays,' she says, 'so perhaps I could make an exception today.' She looks solely at Isaac, ignoring Thea. 'Just this once.'

'That would be so very kind,' Isaac says, smiling broadly. 'I'd be so grateful.'

'Why don't you leave me your number,' she suggests, 'and I can let you know when I have that information for you?'

'Oh, lovely. Thanks ever so much.' Isaac types his number into Helen's iPad.

But Helen isn't looking at Isaac any more. She's looking at Thea, a frown on her face. 'You know, your sister really does bear a striking similarity to this painting,' Helen says.

'I'm not—'

'Doesn't she?' Isaac says lightly. 'That's why we're so keen to learn about the painting's provenance.'

'Of course.' Helen straightens her green jacket. 'We often help families piece together their ancestry. I'll see you later,' she says as they walk back towards the stairs, 'when I have the documentation.'

'I can't thank you enough.' Isaac kicks Thea.

'Yes, he can't thank you enough.'

*

'You really are a piece of work,' Thea says, as they make their way down the two-storey escalator back to the entrance. 'You're a terrible flirt.'

Isaac blinks. 'You think that was flirting?'

Thea smirks. 'Of course.'

'I complimented her at her job.' Isaac turns to face her on the escalator, so he's travelling backwards. 'I challenged her to find what we needed, by saying most people wouldn't be able to. That isn't flirting –' he shrugs – 'that's efficient.'

'Fair enough,' Thea says, wrapping her scarf around her neck.

'We're well on our way,' Isaac says, nodding to himself. 'The search is *on*.'

'I hope so,' she says quietly. 'I really want to find Rosy.'

'Thea, if *you* jumped . . . You wanted hard proof, so we're getting hard proof.' They reach the bottom of the escalator and Isaac puts his bag on the floor to get his coat on, gazing through the main doors at the drizzle coming down outside. 'What did you think of all those portraits of Lady Margaret Beaufort? Your rings keep turning up.'

'It's strange, huh? There's no way she's connected to this.'

Isaac straightens. 'Why not?'

'Because – the Wars of the Roses? That's too far back. There's no way any time travel experiment could involve the Plantagenets. I'm not the mother of a king,' she says sternly, as Isaac opens his lips to speak.

He wisely closes his mouth again. 'You're probably right . . . but aren't you curious, at least?'

Thea lifts her hands in bewilderment. 'The rings – yes, that's odd. But all those portraits? We have no idea what she really looks like. There's no consensus; her appearance changes in every single painting! She's from too old an era.'

'I know what you mean. Like paintings of Shakespeare,' Isaac says, 'the subject changes in every interpretation, by every painter.'

'I wish there was some way to view a photograph of Lady Margaret Beaufort.' She sighs. 'So we could see what she looked like in real life. An undeniable cold, hard likeness.'

Isaac looks thoughtful. He pulls out his phone and stares at the screen, waiting for it to load. 'There might be.'

She's cynical. 'How? She was born in 1443.'

'Remember the curator said Lady Margaret was buried in Westminster Abbey?' He finds what he needs to know and snaps his phone shut, satisfied. 'It's only a fifteen-minute walk from here. And in the interests of being thorough . . .'

'What?' Thea says, uncomprehending. 'Why would we go there?'

'We have another set of three rings worn by a famous woman in history. A woman your painting doppelganger was previously identified as. If you want to do this scientifically—'

'I do—'

'Then we should leave no stone unturned. Let's go to Westminster Abbey and see Lady Margaret Beaufort's tomb.'

'Why?' Thea isn't even exasperated by this point, so much as curious.

'Honestly, it will only take us half an hour, there and back. You want to see what she really looked like? Like a photograph?'

'Yes . . . ?' she says, her voice uncertain. 'I think so?'

'Well, our friend Wikipedia tells me the effigy on Lady Margaret's tomb was cast from her death mask.' Isaac hustles them both out of the door. 'So if we visit her tomb, we'll see her actual face. Let's see if she looks like you.'

Twelve

They step out into the bright grey light of the October afternoon, a brief hiatus in rainfall making the air fresh. Thea winces as a bus slows right next to them, brakes screeching, the sharp sound piercing after the hushed rooms of the Portrait Gallery.

'This way,' Isaac says, starting to walk in the direction of Whitehall. 'Shall we?' He follows Thea's gaze, traffic noise washing over them. 'Oh,' he says, bemused. 'You want to . . .'

'Yep,' she says, striding over to a row of red rental bicycles. 'Let's re-live our uni days. Blow the cobwebs away.'

'Boris bikes,' Isaac says, apprehensive. 'I don't have a helmet.'

Thea shakes a bicycle free from its stand and chucks her bag into the basket on the front. 'Me neither,' she says. 'We'll be really careful. Oh, come on – I've heard it's the best way to see London.'

'It probably is the fastest way to the Abbey,' Isaac concedes, paying at the docking station before pulling a bike free, testing the brakes and looking at the wheels.

'Hurry up,' Thea sighs, pulling her yellow hood up against the wind, 'or don't they have these in New Yoik?' She twangs the city name as she'd heard Isaac do when he'd just moved there.

'I'm a walker,' Isaac says, as she lugs the heavy bike off the pavement and onto the road. 'Everyone walks in New *Yoik*.' They pull off, gasping at the weight of the bikes but relieved when they find that the heaviness makes them sturdy – more tank than bicycle. 'Hey, Thea,' Isaac calls as Thea pulls ahead, but his voice is taken away on the wind, the sound not penetrating the hood of her raincoat. 'Thea!'

She turns, knocking the hood down so he can see the blue and white striped lining inside. 'Yes?'

'Let's take the route by the Thames,' he says, pointing in a different direction. 'It will be less busy.'

'And more scenic.' She grins. 'Good idea. I love the river.' They cycle down past Trafalgar Square, the sky atop the fountains and statuesque lions ominously grey. 'Do you think we'll *really* be able to see her actual face?'

'Lady Margaret? Yes, I think so,' Isaac says, his tone light, as they turn down an enormously wide road filled with grand hotels and embassies. 'Most of those sculptures we passed in the Portrait Gallery would have been cast in death. We had an artist at the Guggenheim a few years ago,' Isaac explains, 'who cast eight sculptures – statues of political figures – but one of his models died before he could take the cast. He managed to convince the relatives to let him do it anyway, and you could barely tell the difference between the sculptures cast from the living and the one from the dead – even the relatives said it looked like him. Only the facial expression was . . . unusual.'

'It will be interesting to see if Lady Margaret looks like the painting. Or even like me.' She takes a breath of cold air, looking at the regal entrances to the Corinthia Hotel as they cycle past, paparazzi camped on the steps to capture candid photographs of any visiting celebrities. 'But we shouldn't take too long.'

'It's worth it. While Helen Claassen pulls the records of the painting sale, we'll rule out Lady Margaret and her three rings. It's a win-win.'

Thea throws a glance at him, trying to keep her eyes on the road. 'You know, if you'd told me we'd be whizzing round London looking at lords and ladies in galleries and churches, I'd have sworn this would be about finding Rosy. Her relatives are so grand – they even have a family crest! Not about poor little me from a farm up north.'

He cocks his head. 'The thing about the nobility is they often trade on the achievements of their ancestors. Everything *you're* doing, whether I think it's a good idea or not, is about making your own way. Even Rosy would know that's admirable.'

They weave past the angry cab drivers by Embankment as the grey clouds finally crack, a deluge of rain almost knocking Isaac off his bike. He puts a foot down on the road for balance, the fractional delay causing the bus driver behind to toot his horn. 'People don't have much patience, do they?' he says, pushing off again, but Thea is quiet as they ride along the riverbank, bridges flanking their left-hand side. She feels the confusion of time, the sense that not everything is in its rightful place – including, possibly, her – and it makes her uncomfortable.

The thought gives her the start of a headache, and she's relieved for a moment that it's raining. So long as you're not cold, a downpour can be refreshing. No, more than that – cleansing. Isolating. Invigorating. She understands the joy in the easy symbolism of baptism, the washing away of sins. But there's something neurophysical in it, Thea's sure: the sensory overload of raindrops touching the skin at random. They wait at traffic lights to turn away from the river, next to Westminster Pier, and Thea takes the minute to tug back her hood, turning her face up to the rain, eyes closed.

In Thursday afternoon traffic in London, in the middle of

an autumn downpour, Isaac catches his breath as she blinks away the rain, wetness turning her lashes into spiders.

She meets his gaze and smiles. 'It's neurophysical,' she says, not even trying to explain her full train of thought, not knowing how to lead someone else along the same track.

'Rebirth,' Isaac says simply, and she thinks how he never fails to surprise her. Of course he'd see what she's left unsaid; he too would observe the clean symbolism of falling water.

'It would be nice to see all this when it's not raining,' Thea says, indicating the pier.

'One day.'

As they near their destination they drop their bikes at the closest docking station, pushing the front wheels into the locks. Thea takes in their surroundings, looking up through the rain towards the Houses of Parliament and the craggy Yorkshire stone of the Elizabeth Tower housing Big Ben.

It's so grand. They weave across Parliament Square, a flash of yellow and navy against the flat wet sky and creamy classical buildings, around the black cabs and red buses towards the pedestrian area in front of the Abbey. She wonders what tourists make of it when they come here – the history, the proud architecture of the place. She finds it a shame modern architecture doesn't revel so much in the details. Nobody nowadays would spend so much time on stonework.

'Ready?' he says kindly.

'Yes.'

'Good, because you're paying for our entry.'

'Am I, now?'

'It's your project, this time travel lark – plus I bought the drinks at the Portrait Gallery.' He beams.

'All right, all right,' she mutters, before stuttering in disbelief as the woman at the entrance tells her it's £22 each. 'Time travel is expensive,' she whispers to Isaac as they step into the West Gate. 'But wow.'

Westminster Abbey feels cavernous: pillars shoot up into Gothic points every few steps, lines running across and down the ribbed vaulting on the other side. Candles flicker along the outer aisles and in the cloisters, and everywhere bears that indefinable smell.

'Churchy,' Thea says, sniffing the air, looking up at the vaulted ceiling.

'Is that your scientific opinion? "Churchy"?'

But the light of a vast stained glass rose window has captivated Thea, tinting everything multicolour. 'It's like the light from a prism,' she murmurs, more to herself than to anyone else.

Isaac lifts his head from the visitor's map he's found and watches her turn in circles as she pieces together the refracted colours of the spectrum.

'The symmetry of this stained glass window pleases me,' Thea says.

'It's interesting – the window looks like a sun, with the yellow at the centre,' he says.

'So it does. And the figures running around the centre make it look like a sunrise,' Thea says, pointing. 'Actually, if it didn't have that book in the middle, I'd swear the window was depicting time travel, refracting light in all the colours of the rainbow.'

Isaac leans his chin on his hand. 'If I remember correctly, stained glass windows were pictorial representations for any of the congregation who couldn't read. "That book" is most likely the Bible – it's in the middle because it's the most important. Makes sense you'd want to replace it with a prism.'

'Sacrilege!' she mocks, then glances at him. 'Hey, you're good at this.' Thea idly counts the petals (eight inner and sixteen outer) forming her spectrum as Isaac deciphers the map. 'It makes me wonder . . .'

'Go on . . .'

'Well.' She clears her throat. 'I wonder if anyone else *has* established time travel before.'

He looks cynical. 'I'm pretty sure you'll be the first. Because otherwise we'd know, wouldn't we?'

'Not if the markers were really well disguised.' She gazes again at the rose window, making her voice light. 'Come on.'

They walk together through the Abbey, pausing for Thea to look up, then down at an intricate mosaic floor – the Cosmati pavement – made up of thousands of pieces of coloured glass. 'I wish Rosy was here to see this,' Thea says.

'I do, too.'

'She'd probably know so many additional details.'

'We'll find her,' he says. 'It's all connected, I'm certain.'

She looks down at the inlaid stone decoration beneath her feet. 'I wonder if the pattern features diamonds? Or prisms?'

Isaac steers her towards the staircase as Thea searches the floor for the symbol of her never-ending doodle motif.

'Which way do we go?' she says, lifting her head. 'Where is she?'

'The Lady Chapel,' Isaac says. 'Upstairs.'

Thea and Isaac stand in a state of bewildered awe. 'Bloody hell,' is all Thea says.

'If you liked the colours downstairs . . .'

The Henry VII Lady Chapel at Westminster Abbey is overwhelming. On each side of the nave, equally spaced as though they're standing to attention in a regimented line, hang large colourful flags – 'Heraldry,' Isaac reads from the guidebook – and the effect is vibrant and overpowering. For the first time today Thea feels a lull in her energy, the aftermath of running on adrenalin and excitement in her post-viral state.

They cross to the tomb of Lady Margaret Beaufort. Surrounded by an iron grille and roughly four feet off the ground, a bronze cast effigy of Lady Margaret lies at peace in the chapel paid for by her son, the king of England.

Thea leans towards her, taking in the countess's head resting on two pillows featuring a Tudor rose, then her wrinkled hands raised in prayer. She wears a widow's dress with a hood and long mantle, and she looks—

'Pious, wasn't she?' Isaac says quietly, peering at the death mask of the old woman, then at the inscription on the black marble tomb chest. 'She looks like a nun.'

'She also,' Thea says, 'looks absolutely nothing like me.'

'Agreed.' Isaac nods, examining the bronze hands for signs of the three distinctive rings she was wearing in the portraits they'd seen at the gallery. They're not there. 'No rings,' he says unnecessarily, because Thea's also craning to see the praying hands. He shakes his head ruefully. 'Oh well. It was worth a shot, if only to rule it out. I'm sorry if I wasted our time.'

'You didn't,' Thea says. 'We had to see if she was a part of all this – we wouldn't be doing this right if we overlooked such a clear aesthetic link. The three rings are important, somehow, I know it.' She reaches for his hand and for a moment Isaac looks confused, before Thea takes his phone from where he's clutching it beneath the visitor's map.

'Oh,' he says, as she unlocks his phone with his passcode without asking for the number.

'What?' she says at his expression. 'We kept no secrets at Christ Church.'

'I don't know your passcode,' he says gently. 'I'd never even begin to guess at it.'

She Googles Lady Margaret Beaufort and swipes through the image results, Isaac watching at her shoulder. She stops when she lands on another painting bearing the three strange rings in the triangle formation, clicking through to read the caption. 'Look – this one is from Brasenose.'

'In Oxford? I've never seen it.' He takes the phone from her, eyeing the shield in the portrait background, which bears a vague similarity to the crest detail behind the Unknown Woman. 'But I've only been to the college once, for Commemoration Week.'

He drops his gaze, clicking the phone shut. They usually try not to talk about Commemoration Week.

They were wrong; they do keep secrets. Even if it's a secret they share.

'I haven't figured out exactly how,' Thea says slowly, 'but the rings are connected to all this. Even if she –' she nods her head at the tomb of Lady Margaret – 'is not.'

Isaac sighs as Thea indicates for them to start walking back towards the staircase to the ground floor.

'What?'

'Well . . .' He looks uncomfortable. 'What you said about Rosy being here . . . She'd probably be able to find some insight into the *Portrait of an Unknown Woman* – she's a specialist in art history.'

'I know,' Thea says softly.

Isaac seems surprised, but says nothing more.

'I didn't know we'd need her background in art history,' she adds. 'But experimenting with time travel? Having a historian around felt like a no-brainer.' Thea lifts her chin as they make their way out from the North Transept, stopping first to pay their respects where Stephen Hawking's ashes lie buried beneath a sunlit arch, then looking up to admire the elaborate screen separating the nave. 'A monument to Isaac Newton,' Thea says with some delight, leaning in to look at the ornate white and grey marble in detail, noticing a figure of Newton lounging against several of his books. 'Look –' she points – '*Divinity*, *Chronology*, *Opticks* and *Philo. Prin. Math.* That last one is his greatest work.'

Isaac's gaze moves between Thea and the words she has read aloud from Isaac Newton's tomb. 'Theology, time, light and mathematical philosophy . . .'

'Wonderful, isn't it?'

He exhales. 'It sounds like the fascinations of someone I know.'

'Are you being sarcastic?' Thea crosses her arms.

'Not at all!' Isaac says. 'You share interests with one of the best scientists in history.' He looks from Thea to the Latin inscription at the base of the choir screen. 'Do you want to know what that says?'

'Yes. My boarding school Latin can only get me so far.'

Isaac squints, and checks a few words against the guidebook. ' "Here is buried Isaac Newton, Knight, who by a strength of mind almost divine, and mathematical principles peculiarly his own, explored the course and figures of the planets, the paths of comets, the tides of the sea, the dissimilarities in rays of light, and, what no other scholar has previously imagined, the properties of the colours thus produced." '

Thea sucks in a breath.

'What a way with words they had,' Isaac says, his hushed voice reverent.

'Do you see it now?' she says, turning to him.

'Don't tell me – Sir Isaac Newton was the world's first time traveller?'

Thea tilts her head. 'No. Well, maybe, actually? He was certainly on the right track.' She wipes her dark fringe out of her eyes. 'More importantly, this tells us Isaac Newton was incredibly – what did you call it, that time you insulted me and we didn't speak again for a year? Oh, yes. *Single-minded*.'

Isaac opens his mouth, but then his phone chirrups, interrupting. He looks down at the screen. 'That's the curator from the gallery – she says we can start to head back.'

'Good,' Thea says. 'Because if the last half hour has told us anything, it's that you're bad at apologies, and it's the Unknown Woman we need to track down.'

'I'm sorry,' Isaac says genuinely, taking one last look at the shrine-like tribute to Isaac Newton's single-mindedness. 'But you do have "a strength of mind almost divine".'

Thea shrugs. 'Perhaps. And if I really did jump back . . .'

'Then the painting will give us the proof. Come on.' Isaac proffers Thea a hand, and they stand for a fraction of a moment too long, holding each other's hands in the colourful light of the Abbey.

'Can we get lunch first?' Thea says, eyeing the place where their hands touched before dropping hers casually to her side. 'I'm bloody starving.'

Thirteen

The lunch rush is over and the greasy spoon almost empty when Thea and Isaac enter. The girl behind the counter looks at them as though they're mad when they ask first about lunch, and then about breakfast. 'It's past lunchtime,' she says.

'I'll have a fried breakfast, please,' Thea repeats politely.

'Give me a fry-up, too,' Isaac says, 'with all the trimmings.'

'I thought you didn't eat bacon –' Thea is puzzled – 'or sausages. And you don't like mushrooms. Not a fan of beans, if I recall.'

Isaac grimaces, then shrugs his shoulders. 'An egg roll would be very nice,' he amends, watching the waitress tut as she scratches through the writing on her notepad with a cheap biro.

'Lapsed, have you?' Thea asks him as they take a seat, moving sticky condiments into the middle of the shiny gingham tablecloth.

'It's easy to eat kosher in New York,' Isaac says, 'but everywhere else, I just . . . try my best.'

'Fair enough.'

'Plus, bacon tastes incredible. I mean, *really* incredible. I'm a bad Jew. Don't tell my mum.' He makes a rueful face and she doesn't laugh, knowing how he hates to lose discipline in any way that could hurt his mother.

She's curious, though. 'When your family moved to the UK, did they change their name?'

'Yes,' Isaac says. 'They removed an S from Mendelssohn, because British people kept spelling it wrong and it was boring to keep correcting them. So we became "Mendelsohn".'

'Really?'

'A token gesture. My great-uncle changed his surname to "Mendel". But it didn't matter – everyone knew they were German Jews, and hated them for it, anyway.'

Thea is shocked. 'I'm sure they didn't.'

'Back then, they did. Some people were extraordinarily kind and generous, but not all. They knew we'd been through something awful, but having neighbours who didn't speak the language, with different customs, was . . . *inconvenient*. We were a burden.'

Thea is contemplative as she watches the rain tap against the glass of the cafe window. 'But you're just as English as I am,' she says. 'Maybe even a bit American.'

'What can I say? I've *gorged* on American culture.'

She puts a hand over her face. 'Do you like it?'

'New York? Yes. I have some good friends.'

'As good as me?' she says.

He doesn't hesitate. 'No.'

She hides her smile as their afternoon breakfast arrives. 'I meant to say – thanks for the pizza.'

'Did you eat it? Good, isn't it? Told you.' He laughs.

'Soon I'll be—'

'As fat as me? I know.'

'No,' she says, confused. 'I was going to say "a pizza connoisseur". You're not fat.' Thea leans back out of the way as the waitress puts their plates on the table.

'I know,' he says, looking at her strangely. 'But last time you said . . . Never mind.'

Isaac's phone vibrates on the table with a FaceTime call from Urvisha.

'I'm not going to tell her what we're doing, yet,' Isaac says quickly. 'Not until we have a proper lead – or proof.'

'Makes sense,' Thea says as he accepts the call.

'Hi, Visha.'

'Ayo says Thea's in London with you,' she says.

Isaac pans round the greasy spoon, zooming in on Thea's fry-up.

'Nice,' Urvisha says. 'Did you have any luck with Rosy's brother?'

'I put an update in the group message – no, unfortunately Edward hasn't heard from her this week.'

'Oh. When are you both coming back? We're trying something here—'

Ayo pops up in the background behind Urvisha, and Thea can see they're in the farmhouse kitchen, the dated splashback tiles just in view. 'Any luck tracking Rosy in history?' Ayo says, hopefully.

'We're working on it, Isaac says.'

'Can we call you later?' Thea says, putting a forkful of bacon in her mouth. 'My food's getting cold.'

'Make sure you do,' Urvisha replies. 'It's important.'

The video call disconnects and Isaac blinks, putting the phone down.

'Do you know what they're working on?' she asks, just as Isaac stuffs the egg roll into his mouth. He gestures at his face apologetically, chewing thoroughly before finally speaking.

'I would imagine they're looking into the science of your prismatic booth. Tell me, when you broke down your theory at the kitchen table, was that the first time they'd heard parts of it?'

She shrugs, cutting another piece of bacon and dipping it in baked bean juice. 'They'd heard variations of the concept before.'

'But it was the first time –' Isaac swallows another chunk of bread – 'they'd heard about the importance of the prism itself. Am I right?'

Thea looks up, pulling a glass prism the size of a pencil sharpener from her pocket and putting it on the table next to the ketchup. She tilts it so it catches the light, miniature spectrums floating across the table, one illuminating Thea's cheek.

'Is that a special one?'

She looks at it appraisingly, cupping it in her hand. 'Not especially. I tried this one before Rosy's leap, with no results.'

'Have you used a different crystal each time?'

'Yes.' She turns it over. 'When I first started, I used basic glass prisms, but they did nothing. Then I tried glass with lead oxide in the mix, which is what makes the difference between plain glass –' she flicks the side of her cheap water glass on the table, which responds with a deadened *ding* – 'and crystal.' She flicks the prism and it rings out with a satisfying *ting* which echoes for much longer.

Isaac wipes his hands with a paper napkin and pushes his plate away, finished. 'Which would you have used for your own jump?'

'I don't know.' She puts the prism back in her pocket. 'There are so many.'

'You don't have a list? How terribly un-Thea.'

She shrugs. 'After using plain glass, then lead oxide crystal like this, I've been trying optic crystal – which is what they use in the

Hubble Telescope. Optic crystal is more expensive; the ophthalmic glass is heated to such a high temperature, it has almost no flaws or bubbles at all.' She puts her knife and fork together, also done. 'Isaac, do you really think I went back in time?'

'Not until we have more evidence.' He stands, waving thanks to the girl behind the counter. 'What can I say? Your desire for hard proof is contagious.'

The National Portrait Gallery is busier when they return, the foyer discernibly louder than when Thea and Isaac were there earlier in the day. They feel a wave of institutional fatigue that often hits during a day's sightseeing, hearing once again the echo chamber of all high-ceilinged grand buildings, which give off a similar resonance, whatever their function – art galleries, abbeys, museums. Bedraggled parents haul uniformed children along as the pair move quickly out the way, past the signs declaring 'Open Late Thursdays and Fridays', and duck into the gift shop.

'Where are we meeting the curator?' Thea asks.

'She's coming to find us – I said we were here,' Isaac says, fingering some Tudor-style Christmas decorations the gallery has on sale, a miniature Elizabeth I figurine and the ever-present Tudor rose. 'Look,' he says, showing Thea, 'an Anne Boleyn made from felt. Alas, she still has her head.'

'Not very festive,' she says. She looks at the piles of art-related merchandise. 'Don't they have anything from the last hundred years?'

Isaac nods at Impressionist printed scarves on the next table but Thea moves instead to a shelf of heavy art books, tilting her head to read the spines.

She stops with delight as she pulls out a book on Barbara

Hepworth. 'Oh my,' she says, flipping open the cover and thumbing through the pages. 'I saw one of these in Yorkshire Sculpture Park as a child. My dad—'

She cuts herself short.

'Go on,' Isaac says softly.

Thea's voice catches. 'My dad took me; I must have been about six. He told me she was the most prominent female artist who'd ever lived. I didn't remember, until now. Seeing this . . .' They stand side by side, turning the pages of the book, looking at artworks combining curved wood and suspension strings, natural ergonomic shapes with geometric lines.

'They're beautiful,' Isaac says.

Thea stops on a full-page print. 'This one,' she says quietly. '*Stringed Figure (Curlew), Version II*,' Isaac reads. They admire the green patinated brass triangle with its folded corners forming wings. But most of all they admire the intersecting strings, the red-brown fishing line held in tension, forming the parabolic profile of the sculpture. 'A curlew is a bird,' Isaac says gently, as Thea runs her fingers across the page, tracing the intricate suspended string pattern with the pad of her finger.

Out of the corner of his eye, Isaac sees curator Helen Claassen walk into the gift shop, but he doesn't interrupt Thea's reverie.

'I didn't remember . . .' she says, a child once more at the Yorkshire Sculpture Park, her hand tucked inside her father's.

'It's part of the Tate collection,' he says softly, 'if one day you'd like to see it again in person. We could go.'

Thea looks up and the kindness she sees in Isaac's eyes stops her from saying another word. Instead she hugs him, and he brings a hand to her back, enveloping her.

'It's okay,' he whispers in her ear, still holding her in position, and with her head against his shoulder she nods.

'Thank you.' Thea notices Helen Claassen walking awkwardly towards them.

'Sorry to interrupt,' Helen says, discomfited. 'I have the documentation you requested.'

'Thank you,' Isaac says, as Thea steps away from him and closes the Hepworth book. 'That's brilliant of you.'

Helen pulls out an A4 sheet. 'This is a facsimile of the sales docket. You can see the gallery stamp and date – see, there, it says 1908 – and here you can read the signature of the seller. An Admiral Joseph Coleman from Edinburgh, Scotland.'

'Coleman?' Isaac says, clamping down his excitement as he lifts the printout to his face, desperately deciphering the signature. 'Like you, Thea.'

Thea peers at the paper. 'I don't have an E in my surname.'

'Names change, mutated by time.' Isaac looks up, clearly animated despite himself. 'Thank you,' he says to Helen Claassen, shaking her hand. 'Would you mind please explaining to Thea the origin of the Tudor rose, while I just . . . grab . . . something?'

While a patronized – and therefore furious – Thea is educated about the combination of the House of York's white rose with the red rose of the House of Lancaster, Isaac surreptitiously carries the Hepworth book over to the till.

'Is it a gift?' the man behind the counter asks, and Isaac nods. 'Want it gift-wrapped?'

'A bag's fine,' Isaac whispers, quickly hiding the book in his rucksack. He walks back to Thea, waving the copy of the 1908 sales docket. 'Come on! Time to prove that you, Thea Colman, are related to one Joseph Coleman, former owner of the *Portrait of an Unknown Woman*.' He can't hide his excitement. 'I think we just found the next step. And I know just where to look.'

Fourteen

They run onto a Tube train at Leicester Square station, laughing breathlessly as the doors start to close, and Thea grabs Isaac's hand and pulls him into the carriage safely. 'Made it,' she says, looking around for a map of the London Underground. 'Where do we get off?'

'We change onto the District line at Hammersmith. It will take twenty-nine minutes to get there,' Isaac says, looking at the app on his phone, knowing she'll appreciate him not rounding up to thirty. The carriage rattles along and they take a seat, the train picking up passengers as they head west out of central London.

'You're sure it will still be open?' Thea asks, looking at her watch.

'It's open until seven – I studied there for part of my dissertation.'

The National Archives in Kew, the official public archive for the UK government, preserves over a thousand years of history in public records. The grounds overlooking the River Thames are beautiful and leafy, a utopia for researchers bound up in the past.

'Do you have any ID on you?' Isaac asks as they wait for a District line train – the least reliable of the Tube lines, but at least they're above ground while they wait. The daylight is fading and the artificial lamps along the platform cause the tracks to glimmer, the wetness from the earlier rain making everything shiny.

Thea looks through her Mary Poppins bag of stuff. 'I brought my passport,' she says, and when Isaac looks puzzled: 'Just in case.'

'*Just in case* I was going to abduct you back to New York with me?'

'Well, you were quite cryptic on the phone. All that "I can't tell you, I have to show you" – remember?'

'Fair enough. Any other identification? We need two pieces of ID to get you a reader's pass.' He grins. 'As my assistant.'

Thea looks annoyed. '*Your* assistant? You should be *my* assistant. Like you said at Westminster Abbey –' she puts on a supercilious look – 'this is my project. You're simply helping me with it.'

Isaac holds his hands up in peace as Thea digs out a wedge of paperwork from the bottom of her bottomless bag, which she'd grabbed as she left the house in Oxford. She roots through it when they're on the District line train at last. 'Council tax bill? Bank statement? TV licence?'

'Any of those,' Isaac says. They reach Kew Gardens station and together cross the road towards the National Archives.

'Pretty round here, isn't it?' Thea says.

'Very green.'

Thea doesn't correct him – that, actually, it's a commotion of falling leaves in rusty amber and burnt sienna, dirty blondes and khaki browns.

'I hope Rosy shows up soon,' she says quietly.

'Me too.'

'All this – it is to find her, isn't it?' Thea's voice is desperate.

'Of course. We're doing our best.'

Entering the archive, they put their bags and coats into lockers in the cloakroom, carrying only the postcard of the

Unknown Woman, the photocopy of the painting's sales docket from 1908, Thea's two forms of ID (her passport and bank statement) and their phones, all bundled inside a clear plastic bag for security.

Thea, somewhat uncomfortably, has her photo taken for her reader's ticket, not deigning to rise to Isaac's teasing as he tells the registrar that Thea is his research assistant, but whacks him on the arm when she's presented with a printed pass that says 'ASSISTANT TO ISAAC MENDELSOHN' in block capital letters on the front. 'You idiot,' she says.

Isaac bites his lip, trying not to laugh. 'Sorry.'

'What are we looking up first? Joseph Coleman's birth certificate? Or death certificate?'

'Neither. They don't keep those here – they're online.' She looks at him, bewildered, as Isaac steers them across the second floor into the reading room. 'We're here for the Royal Navy service records.'

'I see. *Admiral* Joseph Coleman. That's smart.'

'Thank you. I have my moments.' They take a seat at a green-topped desk in the large reading room, a gentle clicking noise tickling the air as people all around type quietly on laptops and grapple with ancient books and records.

At the computer terminal on their bank of desks, Isaac orders up the *Registry of Shipping and Seamen: Agreements and Crew Lists*. 'Some of these are going to be the original log-books,' he says, 'and some we'll have to view on microfiche.'

'Like spies in an old movie,' Thea says.

'Exactly like that. Now, if Admiral Coleman sold the painting in 1908,' Isaac muses, 'I'm going to guess he joined the Royal Navy some time before that . . . shall we guess 1880 to 1900?' Thea nods, not really sure. This is Isaac's world, and she's merely the spectator. 'There are Series II logbooks for the years 1861 to 1938, so we'll probably want to start there.'

Screens around the National Archives show the current status of all orders, and when Thea and Isaac's number is displayed they collect the logbooks from the lockers outside the reading room. They carry the enormous pile back to the wooden desk, and Isaac takes a deep breath.

'Oh,' Thea says, moving closer as he lifts the front cover, the starchy dust odour rising from the pages. 'I love the smell of old books.'

'I do, too,' he agrees, 'but I also love it when crumbly manuscripts are digitized, because then I don't feel quite so much pressure not to break them.'

'I thought you didn't like copies,' Thea says. 'Didn't you say, "A replica can never capture a fraction of the beauty of the real thing"?'

'Huh,' he says, huffing. 'You're right, and I was wrong – the science behind a photocopy *is* a beautiful thing, if it helps books like this live another hundred years or so.'

Thea sits at Isaac's shoulder, leaning forward, but as he turns through pages and pages with no joy, she sits back, then slouches in her chair. She wishes she was allowed to bring a pen in with her – doodling has always helped her think.

'Hmm,' Isaac says after a while, almost admitting defeat. 'This registry only captures about 10 per cent of the agreements and crew lists. So . . .' He moves back to the computer terminal, and brings up all the available reference documents for the Royal Navy. 'Aha!' he says, and Thea sits bolt upright in her chair. 'The *Register of Seamen's Tickets*. They're numerical – but they also record the sailor's name.' He looks at her archly. 'This is where we get to be spies; we have to view the register on microfiche.'

'Goodie.'

Isaac sets up the system and they both lean forward.

'We need to request a date range,' Thea says, and Isaac types *1880–1900*. 'Oh, shit – there are 283 volumes.'

'You didn't use to swear,' Isaac says, starting to scroll.

After a few minutes he says: 'Here we go. Here we fucking go. "Admiral Joseph Coleman of Bedfordshire, England, Royal Navy officer recruitment: 1886. Termination of service: 1910." Twenty-four years in the Royal Navy.'

'And that's definitely our guy?'

'Oh, this is good – Admiral Coleman has several linked documents.'

'Great,' Thea says cautiously, remembering the 283 volumes they've already surfaced.

'This. This is *very* good.' Isaac turns the wheel to bring up the records of baptisms, marriages and burials between 1845 and 1998. 'Joseph Coleman became a father while in the Navy. To little baby Frederick, and bonny wee Ailsa.' Isaac removes his phone from the clear plastic bag and jots the names down in his phone's notes section, taking photos of the documents as he goes. 'Huh,' Isaac says, hovering his finger over the Navy register. 'His record also links to the Merchant Navy register, so he presumably joined as a civilian after being discharged, but . . .'

'Go on.'

'But "Admiral Joseph Colman" in the Merchant Navy –' Isaac makes Thea scoot forward – 'is spelled with no E.'

'Typo?' she says.

'Maybe.'

'Incorrectly linked documents?'

'Not likely.' He reads through Joseph Colman's entry in the Merchant Navy register, scrolling the microfiche against his corresponding seaman's ticket. 'Look – he moved the family up to Scotland.' Isaac points out an address, dated 1902. 'Admiral Joseph Colman in the Merchant Navy lived in Musselburgh, East Lothian.' He looks over his shoulder at Thea. 'Didn't you always say you're half Scottish?'

'My dad's side,' she says, adding by rote, 'I don't have the accent.'

'Here.' Isaac hands her his phone as he clicks into the other linked documents for Admiral Coleman. 'Google the origin of the surname "Colman".'

Thea unlocks his phone with his passcode and opens a mobile browser window. 'It's loading,' she says. 'Do I want the search results from ancestry.co.uk or surnamedb.com?'

'Either,' Isaac says. 'Even Wikipedia will do; we just want the gist.'

'Here we go: "Colman". "This interesting surname" –' Thea smirks, reading aloud from the phone screen – ' "is a Scottish variant of Coleman, which has a number of possible origins, the first being of English origin . . ."' She trails off, looking at Isaac. 'Could it be that simple?'

Isaac glances at the microfiche registers in front of him, at the two names, Coleman and Colman, and the two addresses: one in Bedfordshire, the other in East Lothian. 'It really could be. Dropping a letter because the common name in your new country, where you've just moved your young family, is spelled without an E, sounds like a no-brainer to me.' Isaac signals at himself. 'Look at my family during the war.'

Thea sits back, stunned.

'Have you ever traced your family tree?'

She groans. 'No, I haven't, Isa. Is there no other way to work out whether Joseph—'

'And his kids, Ailsa and Frederick Colman—'

'Is my ancestor?' She looks at him, pleading. 'From here. Or online.'

'I'm thinking,' he says, 'I'm thinking. How can we put together a family tree in a few minutes? Okay . . . yes.' As pens are banned in the reader's room in case any visitor becomes tempted to vandalize an original record, Isaac draws a rudimentary family tree on an app on his phone, using his finger as a pen. 'So we have Admiral Joseph Coleman, spelled two ways – plus his son Frederick Colman, and daughter Ailsa Colman. Let's presume, because of the era, she changed her surname when she got married.

'Now, what's the name of the oldest relative you can remember?' he asks, then blanches as Thea looks like she's been punched, the wallop of her family's absence striking her anew. 'I'm sorry. I wouldn't ask if—'

'My grandmother was called Daphne, and my granddaddy was Peter Colman.'

'Thank you,' he breathes. 'And were they . . . elderly . . . when you were a child, relatively speaking?'

'I don't know, exactly.' She considers his question. 'They'd both died by the time I was ten.'

'I see. So we'll add Peter Colman and his wife Daphne to our tree, further down. If we suppose your grandparents were, what, seventy-something, when you were a child? That could put them as being born in the 1920s. That leaves us two generations, maybe only one, to connect Fred and Ailsa with Peter.' Isaac puts his tongue in his cheek, thinking. 'That could be possible.'

Thea looks at the lines he's drawn with his index finger across the screen, the scrawled names forming her family tree.

She watches as Isaac writes 'THEA' at the bottom, connecting her to Peter and Daphne, leaving a big gap between. 'Alistair,' she says quietly, though he hasn't asked, and Isaac looks at her, alert. 'And my mum was Ruth.'

Without saying a word he draws 'Alistair and Ruth' carefully, tenderly, knowing that the visibility of their names above Thea's could wound her. He speaks very gently. 'Can you open the computer –' he points at the terminal on the desk – 'and click on the section marked "Wills and death duties"? For Frederick Colman,' he adds quickly.

Thea does as he suggests. 'They only have wills up to 1858,' she says, reading through the blurb and clicking a button with instructions. ' "For wills proved in Scotland up to 1925 go to scotlandspeople.gov.uk" . . . That could be the one?'

Isaac nods. 'Open it; let's search Frederick Colman, Musselburgh.'

Slowly, over the next quarter-hour, they connect the dots between the children of Admiral Joseph Coleman, seller of the painting of the Unknown Woman, and Thea. As they discover no will for his son Frederick, and instead an online record of his death certificate showing he died in 1917 during the Great War, they move on to the admiral's daughter Ailsa, discovering she left everything to her own children in her will – who all bore the surname Colman. 'I guess you would,' Thea says, 'rather than let your family name die out.'

Isaac agrees, adding a vertical line down from Ailsa Colman on the makeshift family tree, the branches drawn with his finger given a cursive flair. 'In the instructions about finding wills proved in Scotland,' he says, 'where do we look after 1925?'

She goes back to the help page. 'The National Records of

Scotland.' She hits the button, loading the site. 'Let me guess – I search Ailsa's children's names for their wills?'

'Aye,' Isaac says, attempting a Scottish accent then immediately dropping it with a grimace. 'I wouldn't be surprised if . . .'

'No way.' Thea looks up at him, letting her hand fall from the mouse. 'No fricking way.'

'Back to not swearing, I see,' Isaac says, leaning across her to read it. He hits print, looking round for the reading room printer. 'This is what I hoped to see. "Testament testamentar of Jonathan Colman, deceased 1952." Cancer, how very sad.' The last will and testament of Ailsa's son bears an itemized list of everyday belongings, which Isaac picks up from the printer. ' "To my son, Peter Colman," ' he reads quietly, back at their desk, ' "I leave—" yada, yada, yada.'

Thea's mouth hangs open. 'Peter Colman – my grandfather?'

'I would say so,' Isaac says.

Thea nervously twists the band bearing the brilliant-cut diamond that sits above the joint on her ring finger.

'Ailsa Colman is Jonathan Colman's mother. And Jonathan Colman is your grandfather's father.' Isaac does the maths, the connections making his head swirl. 'Your grandfather's great-grandfather sold the painting to the National Portrait Gallery in 1908.' He prevents himself from doing a hop and a skip, picking up their phones and the clear plastic bag holding Thea's ID. 'This is more than I'd hoped for. Much more.'

Thea gazes at him, still in shock.

'I did ask for hard proof to connect that painting to me,' she says quietly. 'Something even a scientist couldn't deny.'

'You did.'

'I think you might have found it.'

'Where did you get the rings?' he asks. 'Did you inherit them?'

'I've always had them,' she says.

Isaac looks thoughtful as he catches sight of the covering page of Thea's bank statement, gathering the rest of their stuff and helping her to her feet. 'You look exactly like the sitter in the painting. The sitter in the painting is wearing the exact same rings as yours, exactly how you wear them. And you're related to the seller, with a direct line of provenance. Can I make one more leap?'

'Will you get the proof to back it up?'

'It's you in the painting,' Isaac says, 'I know it is.'

Fifteen

They stand outside the National Archives in the fading light, the day saturating into greys and blues as they face each other with rising elation. 'It's you in the painting,' Isaac says again.

'Do you really think so?'

'I used to want you to be wrong about time travel,' he admits, and she tilts her head at the non sequitur.

'I know you did.' Thea shrugs, not moving her gaze from his face.

'This search – I guess this is my way of making amends.'

She speaks quietly. 'I know.'

'I was so sure you were wrong, I even suggested Ayo might want to double-check your physics,' he says, to which she scowls, though it would only be good science to peer-review her work. 'But I believe you really did it. You went back in time.'

'We don't have proof of that.'

'We almost do,' he says as he smiles at her oddly. 'It's you. I knew it was you the minute I saw it.'

'So what comes next?' She moves back and forth on the spot, finding his certainty infectious.

Isaac looks at his watch: 4.45 p.m. 'I have a vague idea, but we've only got about fifteen minutes to try it. Can we jog?'

Thea looks horrified. 'Jog? I don't jog.'

'Imagine you're late for a lecture,' he calls as they take off down the road. 'If you don't make it on time, you have to do the walk of shame through the front of the lecture hall.'

'I do so enjoy disappointing professors,' she says, as a swell of rain drips down onto them from the trees, and they run in the shelter of the endless brick wall that lines Kew. 'It's my new hobby.'

'You *have* changed.' He throws a glance her way, relishing this return to how they used to rib and joke with each other at Oxford.

'And yet I still can't run,' she says, breathless. 'Where are we going?'

'The bank.'

She stops running. 'Which bank?'

'The one we passed near Kew Gardens station. Most banks close at five, so will you please keep up?'

'The *bank*?'

'Thea – please will you trust me on this?'

She picks up her pace to jog alongside him. 'I do.'

'Good.' Isaac laughs as they harrumph along towards Station Approach, their trainers squelching with the dregs of the rainy afternoon. They're both tired, though they won't admit it – the thrill of discovering something new at each step has kept them going. More than that; it's a thrill to rediscover their friendship, and to feel close once more.

Isaac feels the confusion of his feelings keenly.

They may not talk about Commemoration Week, but with his emotions flaring like this it's not far from his mind. They've been close since they first met, but something else tickles at the edges of their friendship for him, and it's nearly always been unreturned. They're too busy for Isaac to think about it much, now – too busy proving what Thea has managed to achieve. How she might change the world. But he senses a flux in her, the potential that his feelings are – for once – possibly returned. If he's not careful, the thought could send him into orbit.

They arrive at the bank in Kew as the security guard bolts the entrance door. 'Please,' says Isaac, 'we'll only be a minute.'

'Sorry, mate. Last counter service is at 4.55 p.m.'

Thea steps forward. 'Oh, please – we'll be very quick. We won't keep you late.'

'Nope,' the guard says, putting Thea and her charm (or lack thereof) firmly in her place. She reaches for Isaac's wrist and waves the watch under the man's nose. 'See? It's only 4.54 p.m.'

Reluctantly the guard lets them through and they rush past.

'Not quite as charming as you were at the gallery,' she quips, 'but just as efficient.'

Isaac tips an imaginary cap at Thea. 'Sometimes it's nothing to do with charm – just plain pedantry.'

'That's lucky. I have that in spades.'

They join the queue at the counter, and Isaac anxiously rubs his temple as an elderly lady counts out her pennies for the poor teller behind the glass.

'Why are we here?' Thea whispers, and with an eye on the clock, Isaac nudges her forward.

'Get your passport and bank statement out,' he says, as they edge towards the front, 'and ask for your full account history.'

Baffled, Thea does as he asks, handing over her bankcard and ID, waving her paperwork.

The teller looks at Thea like she's mad. 'Statements going back *how long*?'

'Since the account was started. Please.'

'Your current account or your savings account?'

Isaac leans forward. 'Savings.'

The teller speaks aloud as she types: 'Theodora Colman, Savings Trust Plus. You want monthly, or yearly?'

'Yearly is fine,' Isaac says quietly, 'or decades, if that's easier.'

Thea tilts her head, confused.

The printer under the counter begins to rumble, and Isaac bites his thumbnail. Thea glances at him, but he notices she doesn't question him – yet – as she graciously accepts the first ream of paper handed to her. 'I hope you have a good reason to murder these trees,' she whispers, as she tucks the statements into her giant bag.

'I think I do,' he replies, taking the next batch from the teller. 'Do you mind if I look?'

'No,' Thea says, 'I don't mind. I'm surprised you'd ask.'

'I'm not looking at the balances, in case you're worried—'

'I'm not.' They flash a quick smile at each other, accepting the final wedge of paperwork before making for the exit past the furious-looking security guard, who had to stay ten minutes late without overtime, as they head out into the autumn evening.

'Can you tell me—?'

'One second.' He turns through the pages, then looks up at her apologetically. 'May I have the ones in your bag? I'm sorry,' he says, 'I promise I'm not being too personal. It's just a hunch . . .'

Out on the pavement, back in the drizzle, they huddle together against the wet. Isaac curves over the paper to protect it from the damp, squinting as he flips back, and back, and back chronologically through the paperwork towards the start of the account, looking for the first entry.

'Isaac,' Thea says. 'Why do you think it's me?'

He looks up. 'Who?'

'The painting. Why do you think the Unknown Woman is me? Honestly?' she says.

'Because she's beautiful,' he says without hesitation. 'Look at every other painting of Lady Margaret Beaufort we've seen today. Her appearance changes, depending on the artist, or the period of the painting – though they all have the same visual fingerprints; she always looks devout, starved, pious, or angry. But this girl . . .' He holds the postcard in the clear plastic bag, sheltering it from the rain. Together they look at the nineteenth-century portrait, the deep reds and warm golds, the neat features and tucked-over hands. Even from only the size of a postcard they can see the tenderness in the portrayal the artist has given her – the painting was not undertaken as a piece of cold, studied work. Isaac smiles. 'This girl is lit from within, like you.'

Thea takes a deep breath, staring down at the papers in Isaac's hands; when she looks up, he's no longer looking at the statements, but at her. 'What are you looking for here, Isa?'

'How did you pay for the barn?'

'The barn?' She frowns.

'How did you have the money to create the glass house? Or a replica laser? Or, in fact, to pay for your entire Oxford tuition fees without a loan? You must know how rare that is.'

'I came into some money when I was a child,' she says uncomfortably. 'When my parents . . .' Her voice trails off.

'And I can see that – here in your statements, when you were twelve, nearly thirteen.' He holds out the piece of paper, but she doesn't take it. 'Most of the money in your account didn't come from that inheritance, Thea. The money was deposited into your account in 1908.'

'What?' She reaches for the sheet of paper, but Isaac rustles through the pile, looking for another.

'See here? This bank account has existed in your name since 1908.'

'That's impossible,' Thea says, 'the bank would have questioned that long ago.'

Isaac shrugs. 'For a savings trust? I'd think not. How many grandparents do you know who put 50p a week in an account for their grandchildren, going on for years . . . It's common.'

'Oh.' Thea looks at the paper again. '1908?'

'The same year the painting was sold to the National Portrait Gallery.'

'But . . .'

'And I have no doubt if we converted the sum on the gallery's sale docket, the shillings and tuppence paid to Admiral Joseph Coleman would match the amount your statement shows, in pounds and pence, credited in 1908. Thea, this is it. This is our proof.'

Thea and Isaac have the beginnings of an answer, but with it a multitude of impossible questions.

Semi-speechless, they get on the train back from west London, ostensibly towards the centre of the city, with no fixed plan of where to head.

'If it's me,' Thea says, as the carriage rocks, 'in the painting, then why don't I remember?'

'I don't know,' he says.

'Why wasn't there a blackout when I jumped?'

'I don't know – maybe you refined the experiment enough.'

'I was working on it before everyone arrived – and after you left. It could have happened at any point,' she concedes. 'But if we've just traced my journey back through time, I would have thought I'd remember it. That seems like part of the fun of time travel.'

'The fun?' He smiles, as they sit shoulder to shoulder on the train, letting the District Line carry them from west to east.

She looks wistful. 'At first, it was the physics,' she says. 'I was excited to try to prove something people had dismissed as impossible. But the reason I've sacrificed my life for it, or so it seems, is because I want to *remember*. I hoped I'd be able to go back,' she says, 'and create new memories.'

Isaac lightly covers her hand where it lies on the armrest between their seats.

'I've forgotten my mother,' Thea says quietly. 'How she sounded, how she spoke.'

He keeps his hand over hers. 'I'm sorry.'

'And why –' her voice changes – 'if that's me, the Unknown Woman, would I let myself end up in a bloody painting? That doesn't seem very smart – I'd probably get kicked out of the Time Travelling Society, if there was one.'

Isaac pats her hand. 'It makes sense you would seek out your relatives. Where else would you be safe? It's true what they say: blood really is thicker than water.'

'Not with you,' she says, but the sudden rattle of the Tube as the train goes into a tunnel masks the words.

'What did you say?' Isaac shouts, gesturing at his ear.

She gazes at his hand, still covering hers, enjoying the warmth. 'You said blood is thicker than water. And I said not when it comes to you. And me. You and me,' she says, and his eyelashes blink twice in surprise.

'Perhaps,' he says, understating it wildly.

Thea's phone rings and they both jump, realizing they're above ground at Baron's Court despite being on the Underground. She moves to answer and Isaac looks away, the moment broken, as the train pulls off again and into another tunnel. 'Damn,' she says, 'I missed it.'

'Who was—?'

'Ayo.'

Isaac wipes the tiredness from his eyes. 'We didn't ring Urvisha back, earlier. She rang during lunch.'

'Oh, yes,' Thea says, but she has no reception now the train is firmly back underground. 'I won't have signal until we get off.'

As the Tube travels further into central London the carriage becomes crowded, the after-work rush hour in full effect. Thea and Isaac are squashed in as commuters stand around them, hanging onto the rails, pushing bags in their faces. The tinny sound from a traveller's headphones bleeds into the carriage, and Isaac nods his head along in time with the irritating buzzing.

'What's your favourite song?' Isaac begins one of his favourite games: baiting Thea's knowledge and taste in popular culture. 'It can be a guilty pleasure,' he says.

'What a stupid expression – if something as benign as the music of a song gives you pleasure, it doesn't require any guilt.'

Isaac rolls his eyes. 'So, your favourite *guilt-free* song?'

She thinks for a moment. 'I don't know. What's yours? No, wait – don't tell me. Something hip that I've probably never heard. You liked it way before it was cool. Maybe some blues? Or some jazz? I bet you like Charlie Mingus. Or some obscure up-and-coming singer-songwriter from Brooklyn . . .' She trails off as she catches sight of his eyes. 'What? You tease me all the time. I'm simply giving as good as I get.' She nudges him.

'It's nice to see,' he says. 'Genuinely.' They sit for a bit longer, aware that Leicester Square is coming up, and without even discussing it they get up, pushing through the passengers, steam climbing the windows from the wet bags and coats.

'Got it.' She nods, satisfied with her choice. 'But it's by U2 – does that mean you're going to tease me all day?'

They swipe out of the station and head into the evening, unconsciously walking back towards the National Portrait

Gallery. It's dark now, the light of the day drained away, and the streetlamps are ringed with the refraction of their own light from the water droplets in the air. 'Not necessarily,' he says. 'You've got about a two-album scope to pick a corker. And they are,' he concedes, 'a fantastic live band. So which is it?'

' "With or Without You".'

Isaac nods. 'That's a nice song. A bit sappy. But nice.'

Thea wrinkles her nose. 'Have you actually listened to the lyrics?'

'Sure.'

' "With or Without You". Think about it. It's Shakespearean – like the witches in *Macbeth*: "Fair is foul, and foul is fair." He can't live with the person he's singing to, and he can't live without them. That's beautiful.'

'Really?' He looks cynical. 'You think Bono wrote something Shakespearean?'

'Of course. The song is about love being a tragedy.'

Isaac is impressed – literary critique is far from Thea's usual wheelhouse. They meander past theatregoers bustling around the box offices opening their doors for the evening shows, past touts offering last-minute tickets, and the glimmer of theatre foyers. 'Chilly, isn't it?' he says.

'Freezing. But it's nice to be outside.'

Without another word, Isaac and Thea walk past the Portrait Gallery and down into Trafalgar Square, the statues and plinths illuminated by spotlights, and the streak of headlights from red buses and black taxis in the perpetual traffic encircling the square.

'The final thing I can't work out,' Thea muses, as they reach the centre of the square, where the four lions keep watch, 'is that, yes, okay, I don't remember anything that happened to me back in time. But why don't I remember anything from right before I jumped, either? Why don't I remember entering the glass house? Or activating it?'

Isaac is looking up at the early evening sky, straining to see the stars over the fug of central London. The drifting rain-clouds block his view, and softly it begins to sleet, the light patter tapping their faces.

'You may have moved through time like water, but you can't expect your memory to do the same. If I could go back—' He cuts himself short.

Thea is also looking up at the sleeting sky, but when he stops talking she looks at him. 'What were you going to say, Isaac? If you could go back . . . ?'

He smiles; it's bittersweet. He has so much to lose and so much to gain by voicing this, by challenging the status quo they've established and maintained for so many years.

But the risk is worth it. Something about Thea is telling him she might react differently, now, from how she would have six years before.

He takes a breath. 'If I could go back,' Isaac says slowly, 'I'd go back to that night. And I'd change everything that happened after.'

Sixteen

They stand under the light of ten thousand hidden stars above Trafalgar Square, the falling sleet dancing around them, lit up by the streetlamps. 'People kiss at university all the time,' Thea says. 'It didn't mean anything.'

'But it did.' Isaac's bittersweet smile changes, becoming more rueful. 'It's only now I can tell you that it did mean something, to me.'

'We simply got carried away.' Thea bites her lip. 'Didn't we?'

∞

The Trinity College Commemoration Ball's theme that year had been *Ad Astra*: 'to the stars'. The tickets were expensive but they'd saved up, knowing the white tie ball was something they should experience at least once in their time at Oxford. It was nearing the end of their second year, and Urvisha, Rosy and Thea got ready together in Rosy's room (the grandest of the three) – Ayo had not yet become a firm friend. Rosy was wearing a white floor-length dress with sparkling, star-shaped earrings dangling down to her shoulders and her blonde hair pulled back.

'You look breathtaking,' Thea had said. 'Isaac is going to lose his mind.'

Rosy had smiled like royalty. 'You look lovely, too.'

Thea had interpreted the theme another way, taking her style inspiration from a different type of star. She wore a form-fitting black column dress with no sleeves, high-necked at the front, with a rounded racer back leaving her shoulder blades bare.

'I get it,' Urvisha had said. *Breakfast at Tiffany's?*'

'A poor homage,' Thea acknowledged. With her long chestnut hair tied up in a simple ponytail, Thea had, for once, taken her omnipresent three rings from her hand and instead looped them through a long gold chain she wore trailing down her back, the diamond sparkling in the light.

Urvisha finished her perfect cat-eye flicks, putting the eyeliner down with a flourish. 'There,' she'd said. 'We all know I'm going to look smoking.' She stood wrapped in a towel next to the others, wearing only a traditional bejewelled tikka in the shape of a crescent moon hanging from her hairline onto her brow. Thea obliged with a wolf whistle. The three women collapsed laughing, then were startled when a knock came at the door.

'Hang on!' Rosy called.

'Oh, crap,' Urvisha said, 'I'd better get dressed.' She eyed the sari hanging on Rosy's bathroom door. 'These things take ages to get into.'

'It will be worth the wait,' Rosy said. 'You're going to look beautiful.'

As soon as the theme had been announced, Urvisha had hunted down a deep blue fabric with embroidered celestial stars, and two long decorative borders of golden stars and moons for the drape. She quickly pulled on her navy blue short-sleeved blouse and petticoat, putting on her shoes first. 'So the pleats are the right length,' Urvisha explained, picking up the long sari silk and starting to wrap it around her waist. Rosy and Thea stood captivated while Urvisha tucked the drape into her waistband, then folded the long length of fabric into pleats the width of her hand. 'I forgot safety pins. Can you hold it while I do the rest?'

She made a face. 'Don't tell my nani.' Thea watched as Urvisha choreographed a mix of drapes, tucks and pleats to get the fabric hanging correctly across her chest and waist. She tweaked and fine-tuned the wide borders, before arranging the drape perfectly over her shoulder. 'There,' she said, admiring her work.

Another knock on the door made them jump and they could hear shouts from the hall. Rosy smoothed down a non-existent stray hair, walking gingerly across the room in her nude heels to open it. 'Sorry about the wait,' she said, as Isaac, dressed in a tail-coat, held out a bunch of white star-shaped roses, smiling broadly. White tie was perhaps the only dress code more brutal to men than to women. While the women wore compulsory floor-length gowns, the men had to wear a cotton pique shirt with a detachable wing collar and double cuffs with cufflinks, a white waistcoat and thin white bowtie, under a black wool tailcoat, fin-ished off with neat black shoes. It was a lot to take in.

Isaac tugged at his bowtie uncomfortably, more used to trainers than shiny shoes, and leaned forward to kiss Rosy on the cheek. 'Hello. You look smashing.'

She pulled back slightly. 'Careful of my makeup,' she said, 'and thank you,' as an afterthought.

Urvisha waved from the bathroom door. 'Hello, Isaac Men-delsohn. You look very smart.'

'As do you, Urvisha Malik,' he said, impressed. 'That is a dress and a half. You look wonderful.'

'Thank you,' Urvisha said genuinely. 'I was a bit worried the student population of Oxford wouldn't be able to handle it. But if you can . . .'

A joke paused on his tongue as Thea stepped out from behind Urvisha, her Audrey Hepburn-style dress flattering and simple, the diamond ring hanging against her back swinging as she moved. 'Fucking wow,' he said. 'Hello, Theodora.'

'Don't swear,' she said, giving him a once-over. 'You look . . . very nice.'

'Thank you,' he said, blushing slightly. 'You look like an icon. Or a dream.'

Rosy tapped a heel silently on the cream carpet. 'I think we need to go, unless we want to be late,' she said, and they picked up pashmina wraps and evening bags on their way out of the door.

'Hey,' Thea whispered as she came up next to Isaac, walking next to each other along the hallway to the entrance.

'If I may say,' Isaac whispered back, 'you look astonishing. I—' But the rest of his sentence was lost as Rosy caught up with them, holding the train of her dress, steadying herself on her heels by holding onto Isaac's arm.

∞

They stand at the edge of one of the fountains in Trafalgar Square, their hoods up against the sleet, watching the centre jettison water more than twenty feet into the air, illuminated against the low light of the evening. 'Why would you want to change that night?' she asks. 'In what way?'

Isaac dips his hand into the pale turquoise water of the fountain, swirling it round. 'We were sober by the time we went home. I don't know why we pretended afterwards that we weren't. We'd had the best time – the best night together. It was all down to you—'

'It was fun,' Thea says simply, watching the patterns Isaac is making in the water, the ripples and the waves. 'But we'd always been friends; it was wrong to think there was something more between us.'

'Friends?' he says, pulling his hand up out of the water. 'You think those were *platonic* feelings between us?'

'Do you think they were romantic?' Thea counters.

'I think,' he replies quietly, over the splashing of the fountain, 'you were so bound up in your guilt about Rosy that you didn't even let yourself entertain what you might really feel.'

Thea is silent. 'She was my friend, too—'

'I know.'

'I would never want to hurt her,' she pleads.

'Thea . . .' Isaac stops; he cannot bring himself to say the rest – *you've made her disappear.*

∞

Rosy had been in a vile mood throughout the ball's formal dinner at Trinity College, a thundercloud marring an otherwise clear blue sky. The group made their way through the champagne reception outside, surrounded by festoon lighting, nodding along to the brass band, before taking their seats at the long tables in the hall dressed like something out of Hogwarts. Starry constellations of lights and candles decorated tables covered with an array of glasses, and surreptitiously the group switched their place settings so they could sit with their friends.

'Hello again,' Isaac said, dropping into the seat between Thea and Urvisha, his white bowtie wilting like an underwatered lily.

'Here,' Thea said. She loosened the fabric, calling on her boarding school days to engineer the perfect hand-tied knot, sticking her tongue out in concentration. While she worked on it, Isaac studiously examined the ceiling of Trinity College's formal hall, not focusing on Thea only inches from his face. 'Thank you,' he said, as she sat back with satisfaction and inspected her handiwork.

'Done,' she said. 'Now you're perfect.'

After dinner they headed outside. The college grounds were filled with marquee tents and fairground rides, all lit up with fairy lights and Edison bulbs as the evening light dimmed towards darkness.

'Here, Rosy,' Isaac had called, waving at Rosalind in her regal white dress. 'Come on the dodgems with me.'

'I've got a headache,' Rosy said, and Urvisha's and Thea's eyes met. 'And besides—' She pointed down at her white dress skimming along the floor, the hem dirtying in the grass.

Isaac reached for her hands. 'Come on,' he said, his tone playful, 'it will be fun.'

'I'm not in the mood.' She snatched her hands back, self-consciously smoothing down her skirt. 'I think I'll go home.'

'Oh Rosy, no,' Thea said. 'We've been looking forward to this all term.'

'I've got some painkillers, if you'd like?' Urvisha opened her bag, but Rosy waved her away.

'Honestly. It feels like I've got a migraine coming on, it's for the best.'

'I'll walk you home,' Isaac said quietly, and she nodded as they moved away from the group.

It was nearly an hour later when, during a big-name band's performance on stage, Isaac rested his hand on Thea's back and she startled at the touch. 'You're back,' she said. 'How's Rosy?'

'We broke up,' was all he said, as he lifted the necklace hanging against the small of her spine. 'These rings are really beautiful – I've never seen you not wear them on your hand, in that odd formation you do.'

'You broke up?'

He shrugged. 'We did. For the second time – or is it the third? But I think that's it, this time. She's not really interested any more,' he said, joining in with the clapping as the headline act finished their set, 'and I fear neither am I.'

Thea touched his hand. 'Isaac, I'm sorry.'

'Please, will you do me a favour? I want to forget about that and have a great time.'

'Who wants to have a great time?' Urvisha shouted from behind them, as the band came back on stage for an encore, playing their most famous single, the crowd surging forwards.

'I do! We all do.' Isaac smiled, Machiavellian. 'So let's have the best night we can – let's forget everything until tomorrow. Deal?'

'Deal,' Urvisha said.

'Deal,' Thea echoed, taking her rings and letting the necklace unfurl down her back as she joined the crowd dancing to the famous song, in the dark marquee filled with warm, sweating bodies.

∞

Thea walks from the fountain to the steps outside the National Gallery. Despite the wet, she sits down and stretches out across a few steps, leaning back to look at the sky.

Isaac follows, feeling the ground before he, too, sits down.

'Look there.' Thea points through the falling sleet to the distant lights above. 'The North Star.'

'Are you sure?' Isaac squints. 'I think that's Venus.'

'Isn't it amazing that the light we're seeing is millions of years old? Anyone can be a time traveller, simply by looking at the stars.'

He breathes in and out before speaking, putting the exercises from his mindfulness app into practice. 'I wish I could time travel,' he says at last. 'Not just back to the ball – but so we could re-do this past year, as well. I'm sorry we haven't spoken.'

She's quiet. 'Me too.'

'I spent a year wanting you to be wrong about time travel. Wanting you to give it all up so I could have my friend back. I'm sorry.'

She looks at him, nonplussed. 'Your friend never went anywhere, Isa. But mine has. I'd do anything to bring Rosy back.' She focuses on Venus, or the North Star, bright in the London sky. 'I didn't mean for this to happen – any of it. I wish I could remember what I did. If only I could undo it—'

'You'll find her,' he says. '*We*'ll find her.'

∞

They'd had their last drink at two in the morning, after the band had finished their set, and they'd sat out in deckchairs. Isaac's tailcoat was around Thea's shoulders. Urvisha was riding the dodgems and dangerously careening around the course, crashing into everyone she disliked. Thrilled, she'd fist-pumped at Isaac and Thea, making them both laugh.

'Hi, Thea.' Ayo Adebamowo from her Physics class stood next to the deckchairs in a striking red dress, and Thea sat up at her greeting.

'Hi, Ayo – you look lovely. Have you met Isaac?'

Ayo reached out and shook his hand. 'Nice to meet you, Isaac. This is my husband, Lao.'

They both stood to shake Lao's hand. 'I've heard so much about you,' Thea said, as he said precisely the same thing, making them both smile. 'Though I'm not usually dressed quite so formally.' Thea indicated her Hepburn dress.

'Me neither,' Lao said, casting a rueful glance at his tightly fitted tails. 'It's a rental.'

'Mine too,' Isaac said easily. 'Awful things, aren't they? I feel like an over-dressed penguin. I've lost half the bits and pieces of the suit already.'

They chatted for a few minutes, before Ayo touched her husband on the arm. 'We'd better get back – we said we'd be home by one.' She grimaced: 'We're already late.'

Thea bade them farewell. 'Easy to lose track of the outside world, here.'

'It's nice to meet such a lovely couple,' Lao said, and Thea blushed.

'We're not . . .'

But they'd already gone, clutching hands, a halcyon image of a young married couple that, amid the hedonism of the night, stood out to both Thea and Isaac as some sort of aspirational bright light.

Breakfast was served at five o'clock – a retro food truck appeared in the quad, serving gourmet bacon and sausage sandwiches. Isaac dutifully queued up beside Thea, taking his roll and handing it to her as she finished hers. 'Thanks,' she said, licking brown sauce from the corners of her mouth.

'Well, we made it,' Isaac said grandly, gesturing around Trinity's Garden Quad, as the sand-coloured buildings of the college brightened in the first light of dawn like a damp beach warmed by the sun. Thea watched the unseen sunrise illuminate the party, until at last she could see the details that had been stolen by the dark: the chimneystacks, the stone mullion work on the college's oldest building – and the fallen students, too drunk or tired to continue till morning, asleep at the edges of the gardens. 'What do you want to do next?' he asked, handing Thea his pocket square in place of a napkin. 'Shall we go home and watch a film?'

She looked at him in confusion. 'It's morning.'

'No,' Isaac said, leading the way out of Trinity, joining the crowds in white tie on the streets heading back to their own colleges. 'It's still night. It's a really, really long night, the Commem Ball. Biggest night of the year. It isn't over yet – it doesn't stop until we go to sleep.'

∞

The National Gallery behind them sounds an intercom, announcing its closing time in five minutes. 'The thing is, Thea,' Isaac says, 'it wasn't just a kiss – and you're wrong when you say it didn't mean anything. There was something there between us.'

'I don't know,' she says, as hordes of tourists leave the gallery, pouring past them. A spray of water splashes up with every step. 'I can't think about that night too much.'

Isaac waits for the stream of people to become a trickle, until finally the last person passes and, once again, it's only the two of them. 'And what about now? I don't think I'm imagining it, am I?'

'Now?'

'Us.' Isaac looks at her, huddled on the steps in her yellow raincoat. 'We never talked about it back then, and I'm scared to risk our friendship now . . .'

She closes her eyes against the last of the tumbling sleet. 'What are you trying to say?'

'Something's different. Since I came back from New York . . . and this bizarre adventure we're on today . . . there's a *click*. But I'm scared – no, I'm terrified – to tell you how I feel.'

'And how do you feel, Isa?' Uncertain, she needs him to spell everything out. They can't get this wrong.

'There's something between us, Thea. I know it.'

At that moment – exactly the wrong moment – Thea's phone rings again, and with an exasperated sigh he indicates she should answer it. 'Go on,' Isaac says. 'Take the call. They've tried three times already. And at least we have something concrete to tell them.'

'That's true,' she says, reaching for it. 'Hi, Ayo.'

'Thea? You need to come back – we've had a breakthrough.'

'Is it Rosy?' Thea asks.

'You need to come home.'

'It's not my home,' Thea says automatically.

'What's up?' Isaac says, questioning.

Thea hears Urvisha snatch the phone from Ayo. 'Are you guys on the train yet?'

'Not quite yet,' Thea says. 'We have something to tell you—'

'When are you leaving?' Urvisha interrupts, and Thea and Isaac glance at each other.

'What is it?' Isaac asks loudly. 'Is Rosy there?'

'Just get back to this ghost-forsaken farm, will you?' Urvisha says. 'Like, right now. Everything is turning batshit crazy.'

Seventeen

Euston station is full of weary commuters stalking heads down to their trains. As Thea is jostled for the eleventh time, she gives up on trying to read the departures board and waits for the announcement instead. 'Are you sure you want to come back with me?' she says to Isaac, who has stocked up on 'train goodies' – bags of sweets and chocolate he's fruitlessly trying to stuff into his already full bag. 'Give them here,' she says. 'You'll never get them in your rucksack.'

'Did you know "rucksack" is German for "backpack"?'

'I did not.' Thea takes the confectionery from him, putting it all in her own bag. Whereas usually she'd find some other piece of trivia to answer him with, playing a ping-pong game of Did You Know, instead she's thinking about the lengthy journey north. 'You definitely want to come back to Dunsop Bridge; you wouldn't rather stay here in London?'

'And miss Ayo and Urvisha's big reveal? Not a chance,' he says. 'I want to know what they know. And I want to see the look on their faces when we tell them about you.'

'They probably know,' Thea says softly. 'If they've been looking in detail at the equipment and my notes, they might have spotted that the experiment has been carried out multiple times.' They'd already begged Ayo to tell them what her breakthrough was, but she'd retorted that she couldn't tell them, she could only show them – which had had Isaac rolling his eyes, until Thea pointed out he'd said precisely the same.

'Is it Rosy – is she back?' Thea had asked desperately, again and again, praying it was true.

'We have a lead,' Urvisha had said, and that was all they could get out of them over the phone.

Thea and Isaac board the train to Preston, finding the last two seats together in a busy carriage with people chatting noisily into their phones, the windows fogged with condensation from all the warm bodies. As they settle in they feel the exhaustion hit: they've been so busy running around looking for clues, this is the first time they can sit without having to rush somewhere.

'Tired?' Isaac asks, offering her a sweet, stating the obvious. Though not the *obvious* obvious – they've hardly spoken since Thea's phone rang, interrupting the mood.

'Knackered.' She leans gently against his shoulder, watching as London falls away, its graffiti and trackside houses threatening to tumble onto the rails. They find an easy silence, like they always have, watching the landscape change into darkened fields dissected by the odd motorway, flashing with headlights. 'We're going to get back quite late,' she says, her voice sleepy.

'I'll wake you when it's time to change.'

She nestles into him, so Isaac lifts his arm around her, creating a nook. 'Cosy,' she says as she drifts away into sleep, his cheek resting against her hair, and he follows not long behind.

He wakes to an empty train and the loud, repeated announcement that it's the end of the line. 'Thea,' he says, 'wake up.' She groans and he nudges her again. 'We're at Preston – we need to make the connection. Unless you want to spend the night finding some dodgy hotel—' He blushes as he realizes how that sounds.

'Sounds pretty good to me,' she says, her eyes still closed, then flying open as she hears the inference in her words. 'Oh, come on,' she says, suddenly wide awake. 'What are you waiting for? We're going to be late.'

'Typical,' Isaac mutters as they run across the platform. Their second train is much less comfortable, a regional line run by a small company, with crisp packets shoved between the seats. The lights are garishly bright and Thea groans again, putting her hood over her face.

'On second thoughts, maybe a hotel was a good idea.'

'We'll be back soon.'

'There's another train after this,' she corrects him, 'and don't even think about falling asleep this time or we'll end up in the depths of the Yorkshire Dales.'

'How shall we stay awake?' he says, cringing as everything he says becomes suddenly ripe with double entendre.

'Did you know,' she starts, eyes closed, 'that the milk of a hippo is bright pink?'

He smiles. 'I did not. Did you know that if you shaved the hair of a leopard, its skin beneath would still be spotty?'

'I like that one.' She covers a yawn with her hand. 'Did you know the polka dot has nothing to do with polka? Purely marketing, because the polka dance craze was so popular they added "polka" onto everything.'

Isaac frowns. 'What does that have to do with animals?'

'Spots – dots.'

Isaac rolls his eyes. 'So lateral. Fine, then; did you know the French navy's famous Breton shirts have a pattern ratio of two to one, base colour to stripe?'

She sits up. 'Now that *is* interesting.'

Isaac smiles, looking out of the window. 'Give the girl a ratio and she's fully awake.'

'What do you think they want to talk to us about?' Thea says, getting out the postcard of the Unknown Woman from Isaac's bag.

'Could be anything,' he says, as she rummages a bit deeper in his backpack.

'Oh, Isaac – no wonder your bag is so full.' She brings out the Barbara Hepworth coffee-table book he bought in the Portrait Gallery shop and wraps her arms around it, taking care not to damage the corners of the dust jacket. 'You didn't need to buy this book, it's expensive.'

'It meant something to you,' he says simply, 'so of course I did.'

'Thank you,' she says, her arms still clasped around the book, gazing out of the window at the night whizzing past outside. 'I got you something, too.' She reaches down into her own bag, bringing out a pin badge.

' "I Tweeted A Curator",' he reads, taking it from her. He starts to laugh. 'Thank you! What a wonderful souvenir.' He pins the round badge bearing the gallery logo and the Twitter bird proudly onto his navy coat lapel.

They get off the train as they arrive in Clitheroe, long after midnight, and Thea yawns widely as they walk to the station car park. 'I think I should drive,' Isaac says, and Thea makes a face.

'Safer with me driving a bit tired than you driving on the wrong side of the road,' she says, getting in on the driver's side. 'We'll put the windows down; you can talk loudly and keep me awake.'

Isaac huddles down in his seat, trying to remain warm despite the October night air blasting in through the fully open windows. They play another game of Did You Know before moving onto the classic I, Spy, but as they drive into the village, past Puddleducks tearoom, Thea swerves across the road and pulls the car up next to the bridge.

'Woah!' Isaac says, then: 'Sorry, I thought you'd fallen asleep at the wheel and were going to kill us in the ditch.'

She looks cynical. 'No.' Her face uncreases as she turns off the engine. 'I wanted to tell you, before we get back to whatever it is Ayo and Urvisha want to discuss with us, that I've had an amazing day with you.'

'Me too,' he says.

'I didn't know what to expect when I arrived in London this morning. And I want to say thank you.' She shifts in her seat. 'I know you can't stay in the UK indefinitely, and soon you'll have to go back to New York . . .'

He doesn't say anything, not wanting to bring the outside world in quite yet.

'. . . But having you here through this insane situation has made a huge difference. You've been such a support. Thank you, Isa.'

'I wanted to help prove you were right,' he says quietly.

'What do you mean?'

'I saw how much it hurt you to consider you might be wrong. So, I thought if I could help prove you were right . . .'

'About Rosy?'

'About time travel.' He smiles. 'I will do anything it takes to help prove you are right, Thea. I promise.'

She takes her hand from the gear stick and rests it on his, aware the gesture is small, but that to step any further would be to move irreversibly away from friendship, and she can't be certain, in this moment, that they're ready. All she knows is he has her back, no matter what – and she's not quite sure she's ever had that before.

'Come on,' Isaac says. 'Let's face whatever it is – together. If they've found out you jumped then we can show them our own evidence, and if they've found Rosy . . .'

'Then so much the better,' she says quietly. She drops his hand, gently, switching the engine back on and pulling the car back onto the road; without speaking, they turn at the trees, up the track towards the farm.

Thea pulls up at the turning circle outside the farmhouse and they look at each other in alarm. Every light is on, the farm lit up like a distress beacon. The front door is unlocked – when Thea puts the key in it swings open, and she meets Isaac's eyes. 'Go on,' he urges. 'Everything will be fine.'

They drop their bags in the hall and Thea calls out, 'Ayo? Visha? Are you guys here?'

They hear noises from the kitchen so they head that way, but as they open the kitchen door the heat hits them squarely in the face. 'Oof,' Thea says, 'it's boiling in here.'

Ayo looks up from where she's sitting at the kitchen table breastfeeding her child. 'I turned the Aga on full,' she says. 'It's really warmed up the place.'

'You're telling me,' Isaac says, coming through the door, swiftly averting his eyes. Ayo throws a blanket over the baby against her breast and carries on.

'Visha!' she calls. 'Thea and Isaac are back.'

'So what's happened? What's the news?' Thea says without sitting down.

'Would you like some tea?' Ayo says.

'I'll make it.' Isaac walks to the kettle. 'You all – clearly – need to talk. I'll listen.'

Ayo shifts her little boy onto the other breast and continues his feed. Thea's textbooks from Oxford sit in a crate on the corner of the table next to Ayo, her notebooks splayed across the surface. 'Urvisha, come on,' Ayo shouts, and they hear thumping from upstairs as the ceiling beams shake, then a *thud – thud – thud* as Urvisha drags something heavy down the stairs.

'What the—?' Isaac moves to the door, looking into the hallway.

'Hello, Mr Chivalrous,' Urvisha says drily. 'No, don't worry, you don't have to help with this heavy case – I can quite manage.'

Isaac beams. 'I wouldn't want to presume you couldn't.'

Urvisha pulls an enormous suitcase across the room, scratching the ancient farmhouse flooring. 'You're back. About time.'

'What's the breakthrough?' Thea says. 'And what's in the case?'

'You look tired,' Ayo says. 'It can probably wait if you want to get some sleep.'

'NO, IT FUCKING CAN'T,' Thea says, and everybody turns to stare at her. 'We've travelled five hours from London to talk about exactly this – so, please. Tell us.'

Ayo's baby starts to cry, and she pats him gently on the back, lifting the blanket and saying 'Beebo!' in a mangled game of peekaboo to distract him from his tears. A gurgle emanates from beneath the blanket, and after a minute he settles.

'What about *your* breakthrough?' Urvisha says, walking over to the sink but stopping to finger Isaac's pin badge on his coat lapel. 'Looks like you had a busy day . . . sightseeing?'

'You can't even begin to imagine,' Isaac says.

Thea indicates for Urvisha to sit down at the table. 'Please – tell us what you know.'

Isaac blinks at Thea's choice of words, noticing Ayo twig the phrasing too, but she doesn't question it.

'Come on, then,' Ayo says, gesturing for them all to sit. 'Urvisha and I have been running some numbers. We've been going back through the science, taking a closer look at the glass house and the laser.'

Thea nods. 'Go on . . .'

'We also reviewed the theory,' Ayo says tentatively, holding Thea's gaze.

Thea nods again, not enjoying the idea of her work being checked. 'And?'

'We found something really quite interesting.' Ayo gets up slowly, her left hand cradling the baby's head, and she puts him down in a portable cot next to her on the bench, shushing him as he snuffles and grumbles. 'Go to sleep, little one, that's right,' she croons.

The old-fashioned copper kettle whistles loudly on the hob, making them all jump; the baby stirs but doesn't cry. Isaac stands to make the tea. He pours out four mugs of chamomile, thinking they could all do with some calming, their nerves are so fraught.

'Ayo,' Thea says, her hand shaking slightly as Isaac hands her the mug, 'what did you find?'

'We solved it,' Urvisha says bluntly, parking her suitcase next to the table and throwing herself down onto a backwards chair, straddling it and using its back as an armrest.

'Seriously?' Isaac says. 'You can't sit like that.'

'I'm being edgy,' she says, scowling at him.

'Well, you're setting us all on edge, so why don't you turn around and sit like a normal person?'

'You solved it?' Thea echoes, ignoring Isaac and Urvisha.

'We solved it.' Ayo's face is kind. 'Your physics was brilliant – extraordinary. But when we examined the laser and the logbook, all your research notebooks and reference texts—'

'You read my notebooks?'

'—We realized it is quite possible for somebody to jump and come back.'

Isaac and Thea avoid meeting eyes as Isaac takes a sip of calming chamomile, then changes his mind and reaches for Thea's hand. They're both about to speak, when—

'Guess what?' Urvisha says, tapping incessantly on the table, making them wince. 'We were wrong.'

Thea sits forward, Isaac's hand still on hers; it's time to confess. 'You weren't wrong—'

'It's not a time machine, Thea,' Ayo says gently. 'That second compartment you built? That was a clue. And your theory of spacetime . . . Just because it's happening in space, it doesn't mean it's happening in time.'

'It *is* – it *does*. We have the proof,' Thea says, reaching for the Portrait Gallery postcard.

'It's not a time machine,' Urvisha repeats. 'We're certain.'

'Then what is it?' Isaac asks quietly, rubbing the tiredness from his eyes.

Urvisha's eyes take on a gleam. 'It's a portal.'

Eighteen

'A portal?' Thea says.

'What type of portal?' Isaac asks, grimacing slightly as he recognizes he's back in the land of scientific explanations requiring simplification for his benefit. 'Or should I say, a portal to *what*?'

'Not what. Not when.' Urvisha's the cat that got the cream. 'But where.'

Thea sits back in a daze, a frown upon her face. She leaves the Portrait Gallery postcard in her bag, waiting for further explanation.

'We misunderstood the time crystals. And the theory of relativity,' Urvisha says, grinning.

'All the paradoxes of time travel,' Ayo says to Thea, 'all of the reasons *it's never been done before*. Changing the past so that it affects the present. Killing your grandfather so you cannot be born. Would any of those be an issue if, say, instead of jumping to the past, you jumped to a parallel timeline, instead?'

'A parallel timeline,' Thea repeats.

'No paradoxes. No conflicts. Wouldn't that be the simpler explanation?'

'Occam's razor,' Isaac says. 'The simplest explanation is usually the right one.'

Ayo nods. 'Precisely.'

Thea snaps to attention. 'But – going back in time . . .'

'We thought about that, too,' Urvisha says. 'If you can jump to another timeline, then theoretically you could jump to a different marker on that timeline, such as a different year. *Seemingly* moving back in time.'

'But the key part is that, whether you've gone back in time or not, you've jumped onto a parallel timeline,' Ayo finishes. 'In a different universe.'

Isaac stays very quiet as he tries to digest what the team is describing. He watches as Thea takes out a notebook, bending the spine as she starts writing notes – ever the diligent scientist.

'So the portal you're describing,' Isaac says at last, 'it's the glass house?'

Ayo checks her baby is sleeping soundly on the bench next to her. 'Yes,' she says simply.

'The glass house is the trap. It's a conductor. And it's also a shield,' Thea says without looking up.

'And it's also a *portal*,' Urvisha says, emphasizing the last word.

Thea doodles her endless pattern of interlocking diamonds and prisms in her notebook for a moment, her brow wrinkled in concentration. 'What you're saying,' she says, 'is that it's not time crystal theory – nor special relativity. It's not even about wormholes. What we're dealing with here is the many-worlds interpretation.'

Isaac groans. 'Of course there's another theory. Quick, get the salt and pepper pots out – I am going to need some demonstrations to understand *anything* after the day we've just had.'

'You're not going to keep up,' Urvisha says rudely. 'You can't learn this stuff through a quick demonstration with Thea's crusty salt shaker.'

'Try me,' he says, folding his arms.

'Fine.' Urvisha squares her jaw, both physically and mentally. 'Schrödinger's cat.'

'I know that one!' he says. 'It's about a cat being alive and dead at the same time.'

Urvisha wrinkles her nose. 'An entanglement paradox – a thought experiment illustrating the problem of quantum mechanics applied to everyday objects, such as a cat. According to quantum superposition, the cat may be simultaneously both alive and dead.'

'I hear the word *quantum* and I'm lost.' Isaac throws up his hands. 'I tune out.'

Thea pats him on the shoulder. 'Don't worry. What you need to know is that one of the first multiverse references was made by Schrödinger. In a lecture, he joked that his Nobel equations seemed to describe different histories that weren't *alternative* histories, but were really happening *simultaneously*.' She looks up at Ayo and Urvisha. 'Isn't that right?'

Urvisha folds her arms. 'Sure. Of course you know everything. But what you didn't look at in detail, when you were putting your theories together for time travel, was quantum mechanics.'

Isaac yawns. 'I don't think I can take quantum mechanics tonight. You said it's possible to jump and come back?'

'Yes,' Urvisha says, picking up her cooling mug of chamomile. 'It's perfectly possible, now we know what we're dealing with.'

'So we'll be able to retrieve Rosy?' Isaac doesn't mention the *Portrait of an Unknown Woman*. He can't muddy the waters, there's too much going on. But he thumbs the pages of Thea's bank statements and Admiral Coleman's sales docket, quickly flicking open his phone to make sure the document photos he took are saved safely.

'Hang on, Isaac. I want to know what I missed,' Thea says,

though her voice is so quiet the three others sit forward, straining to hear. 'I want to know how I was wrong.'

Urvisha takes a sip of the tea. 'Quantum decoherence.'

Isaac stands, picking up the paperwork. 'I don't know what you're all talking about,' he declares. 'You said it wasn't a time machine, but now you're talking about quantum this and quantum that and I can't follow.' He looks at them expectantly. '*Keep it simple, stupid.*'

Thea flashes a taut smile at her friend, sensing his frustration. 'All right. I'll take quantum-*everything* out of it and explain MWI – the many-worlds interpretation – like they would have done in our Philosophy class, rather than Physics. Okay?'

'Okay,' he says solemnly.

Thea takes her notebook and draws a flat line across a blank page. 'Here's our reality. It's always been viewed as a single unfolding history. Yes?' At the very beginning of the line, she writes 'Big Bang'. At the far end, she scrawls 'Right Now'. And somewhere quite near that, for Isaac's benefit, she adds a dark circle and writes 'Nazis – Very Bad'.

'Now, instead of this single unfolding history, imagine reality as a many-branched tree, where every possible outcome can be realized.' She draws branches sprouting off from the line, running parallel in all lengths and sizes. 'Every possible alternate history and future is real, each representing an actual universe. So in one universe, Hitler lived. In another, he was killed by a time traveller. And in another, he was never born at all. Do you see?'

Isaac nods.

Thea fractures each line into smaller branches, so that every one has multiple lines growing out of it at every point. 'Each tiny, infinitesimal decision made by you or me, every choice faced by every single electron, causes a new branch to grow: a new timeline . . . an infinite number of timelines. A multiverse of parallel timelines, parallel universes.'

'I see,' Isaac breathes, looking at the tree she's drawn, at how the branches radiate out, away from the central timeline, until there are many.

'In one world, Schrödinger's cat is dead, and in a parallel universe, the same cat is alive.'

He looks up from Thea's notebook. 'So in a parallel world, I'm a millionaire?'

'Sure.' Thea nods. 'Isaac Mendelsohn is walking down the street in downtown Manhattan. In this world, he's late and hurries along without looking down. In another parallel world, he stops and finds a lottery ticket, becoming a multi-millionaire.'

Isaac is quiet. 'So in the many-worlds interpretation, there's a parallel world out there where Rosy isn't missing.' His eyes graze Urvisha's huge suitcase, and it breaks his concentration. 'Going somewhere? It's the middle of the night.'

'I'm glad you asked,' Urvisha says, standing, a fidget of excitement in her stance. 'Now you're caught up, we're going to run the experiment again.'

Thea and Isaac look at her, uncomprehending.

'Let's find out where the portal goes. That way we can find Rosy at the other end.'

Ayo looks at her sleeping child, concerned. 'Now?'

'It was your idea,' Urvisha says, pulling the suitcase over to the door, taking her coat down from the peg, then turning when none of them moves. 'You said we could run it again when Thea and Isaac returned—'

'I meant in the morning, but if you really can't wait . . .' Ayo says, getting to her feet, carrying her son in his portable crib. 'But only if the baby monitor signal reaches to the barn.'

Isaac's curious. 'Visha – what's in the case?'

Her expression is flat. 'Everything I might need in another world. I'm going to go and get Rosy.'

'We can't—' Thea begins, looking at her notes and doodles. 'We need more time.'

'Everything's set up and ready to go,' Urvisha says, opening the kitchen door so a freezing gust of wind wraps around the room, chilling them all.

Isaac and Thea sit, stunned, at the kitchen table.

'Coming?'

They stand robotically, looking at one another from each side of the kitchen table. Thea moves to get her warmest coat as Isaac slides out the *Portrait of an Unknown Woman* postcard from its place tucked inside the sheath of papers, and puts it snugly into his back pocket. 'I feel like my head is going to explode,' Isaac says to Thea under his breath.

'It's a lot to take in, even for me,' she says thoughtfully, as he helps her into the down-filled parka.

'Come on!' Urvisha strides out into the night.

'This is ridiculous,' Thea says, but she's lost the upper hand.

The group step out into the courtyard. The sudden darkness after the illuminated farmhouse makes them pause, and they let their eyes adjust before making their way to the kitchen garden with its untended vegetables growing wild and tall, past the paving stones – *one, two, three* – past the cylindrical dovecote, towards the outbuildings. The wheels of Urvisha's suitcase grate against the quiet night, as she leads the way to the double-height black-timbered barn.

'This is all happening so fast,' Thea says to Isaac, as they hang back. 'Do we even know if the glass house – the portal – can transport luggage along with a person?'

'If your glass house truly *is* a portal, I think we've got bigger problems than its baggage allowance.'

∞

The door to the barn is ajar, a crack of light seeping out. Urvisha hauls it open and Thea gazes at her experiment setup, familiar but somehow different. The photographic lamps aren't on, and the glass house looms large in the dark, glistening and ominous.

'The lamps weren't important,' Urvisha says, noticing her stare, but Thea's in a daze, her mind working overtime. 'It's all about the laser.'

'Are you all right?' Isaac whispers to Thea, watching as Urvisha makes her way over to the laser.

Thea turns on the three photographic lamps, looking out of the barn towards the dark line of trees behind the farm's fences. 'The many-worlds interpretation,' Thea mumbles, to herself rather than to the others. 'Every tiny, infinitesimal decision made by you or me, every choice faced by every single electron, causes a new branch to grow. So the question is . . .' She trails off as Urvisha heaves the case over to the prismatic glass house.

'What's the logic there, Visha?'

Urvisha rough-handles her luggage, leaving it just outside the door. 'I'm hoping if I leave a suitcase with everything I need *here*, then in a parallel world there will be a suitcase with everything I need *there*.'

Isaac wrinkles his forehead. 'The worlds are like a mirror?'

But nobody answers him.

Ayo sets up the baby monitor, Thea's camera and Urvisha's laptop on the workbench, making small adjustments to ensure the perfect angle is captured between the laser and the booth.

'Thea – you were saying something about a question?' Isaac asks.

Thea stares at the outline of the trees, their individual branches masked by the darkness and the distance. Concerned, Isaac peers out of the barn to spy what she's looking at, but to no avail.

'The thing about the many-worlds interpretation is that the worlds run in parallel until they split,' she says at last. 'Here, one decision is made, and there, the opposite decision is made.' Thea rubs her neck, reasoning to herself. 'The timeline splits at the exact point of decision. One goes left, one goes right.'

'So it *is* like a mirror,' Isaac says.

'I need time to think this through,' Thea says, almost like she's talking to herself rather than Isaac. 'There's something about that split that's bothering me.' She puts her notebook on the workbench, drawing two parallel timelines like train tracks, diverting one left and one right in a Y-shape. 'Two worlds running in parallel until I leapt. They split, and now they're different. So—'

'What do you mean, *you* leapt?' Urvisha stares at Thea from where she stands by the glass house, and Isaac shifts uncomfortably.

'It's theoretical,' Thea says. 'If there is an infinite number of timelines, a multiverse of parallel worlds that you can jump into, then which decision – which choice, which *precise moment* – split our two worlds?'

Urvisha shrugs. 'We know that. It was Rosy's jump.' She returns to the laser setup and control panel, not seeing Thea's face and the uncertainty all over it.

Isaac mouths a question, and Thea shakes her head.

'Ayo?' Urvisha says. 'Can you help set the laser?' Ayo walks across to the box and, checking against Thea's notes, enters the same strength and brightness settings used for Rosy's experiment, double- and triple-checking that they are correct.

'Time for go or no go.' Urvisha confirms the power to the barn is stable, then checks the recording devices are live. 'Go.'

'Why are we rushing this?' Thea asks.

'It does seem a bit soon,' Isaac says.

'Rosy's been gone for days,' Urvisha retorts. 'It's time one of us goes to retrieve her.'

'Go,' Ayo says, verifying all the doorways to the barn are clear, then standing next to the laser, ready to fire.

Both Ayo and Urvisha look at Isaac and Thea. 'Well?' Urvisha says expectantly. 'You want Rosy back, don't you?'

They can't argue with that. 'Where do you want me?' Isaac sighs, pulling the heavy door closed and walking deeper into the barn.

'You're tech-savvy – you take over the computer, monitoring the National Grid. The program should run itself, so don't worry. You only need to keep it running. I'll get in the glass house.' Urvisha walks to the prismatic glass, clambering past her oversized suitcase. 'Thea?' she says impatiently.

'Yes,' she says, at last.

'Make sure you use the same prism in the door that you used for Rosy.'

'Okay,' Thea says, still deep in thought. She carries her notebook with her, reading her notes. 'How do we know where you're going?'

'Everything's the same, isn't it?' Urvisha says. 'I'm going to bring back our friend.'

Thea chews her lip.

'Keep all the recording devices running,' Urvisha prompts. 'Go.' She raises her fist into the air from inside the glass box.

'Isaac, all set?'

He nods hesitantly.

'Then we are cleared for launch. On three?'

'It *is* a mirror, of sorts,' Thea says, tracing the parallel train tracks with her two fingers, splaying her hand where they split into separate paths. 'But I don't think the timelines split where you guys think it did. Before Rosy jumped, when I— Well.'

'Three,' Urvisha says, irritably.

But Thea's train of thought can't be derailed. 'If we were running in parallel with an identical world, then feasibly, at the precise same moment we jumped from our world to theirs . . .'

'Two.'

'Somebody would have to jump back the other way.'

She emerges from her reverie with an adrenalin spike of shock. Urvisha firmly says: 'One.'

Something's different. Since I came back from New York . . . and this bizarre adventure we're on today . . .

You have *changed.*

It's only now I can tell you that it did mean something, to me.

This is all wrong.

That's why Thea doesn't remember jumping from here: because she didn't.

'Wait!' Thea calls out, but it's too late: Ayo fires the laser, and once again the light is blinding. Their vision of the barn is violently drained of colour. Thea runs towards the laser, jabbing at the button to stop it. Nothing happens – Ayo must have tweaked the design. Thea shields her eyes, waving to Ayo.

'Stop!' she shouts, but she can't be heard.

As the light in the barn turns white, bleached in the moment, Thea follows the wire from the laser's control panel to the fuse box, making the decision before she's blinded and can no longer see. She yanks at the cord, flips all of the circuit breakers, then finally wrenches the fuse box's master switch off.

There's a scream, and the barn is plunged into darkness. They stumble to reach for their head torches, which are lying discarded on the benches, and two beams illuminate the cavernous barn in streaks.

'Is it a power cut?' Isaac says, looking at the extinguished photographic lamps.

'Urvisha!' Ayo shouts. 'Oh Lord, no – help!'

A figure lies slumped inside the glass house, the weight pressing against the door until it swings open, and Urvisha tumbles out onto the floor.

Nineteen

Thea is so horrified she can't speak, transfixed by the truth she has gleaned. In the aftermath of her literally pulling the plug, Ayo and Isaac run to where Urvisha lies unconscious on the floor. For a fraction of a moment, Thea suffers her epiphany alone.

The word *epiphany* can be used too lightly, she finds herself thinking. But the moment you suddenly feel you understand, or become conscious of something very important to you – that's a true epiphany.

It can also mean a manifestation of a divine or supernatural being, which Thea doesn't want to think about right now.

Isaac rolls Urvisha into the recovery position while Ayo tries to wake her: 'Urvisha! Visha! Can you hear me? Wake up, please!'

Isaac feels for a pulse, fumbling in the dark of the barn. He begins mouth-to-mouth, pumping on Urvisha's chest as Ayo holds her hand, moaning softly.

Thea breaks free of her shock and moves to the fuse box, flicking the master switch back on so the lights blink back into life.

Ayo looks up in surprise – they'd presumed it was another ill-fated power cut – but Isaac doesn't falter as he beats a steady rhythm with his palms on Urvisha's chest – *one, two, three* – then pinches her nose and breathes into her mouth for a further count of three.

Thea drops down onto the cold floor next to Ayo and Isaac, taking Urvisha's other hand.

A wail goes up and Thea, Isaac and Ayo look at each other in confusion, until Ayo grabs the baby monitor from the work-bench. 'I forgot.'

'Go to the house and call an ambulance,' Isaac says, still pumping.

'We shouldn't have rushed this. I can't believe someone else has got hurt.' Ayo gathers herself and jogs to the barn door, turning back to take in the horrific scene before fleeing towards the farmhouse.

'Help me,' Isaac says, and Thea realizes he means her.

'What can I do?' Thea says, snatching a look at him. He'd seen what nobody else could: *You* have *changed*.

Urvisha suddenly coughs and splutters, coming around.

'Oh, thank God,' Isaac says. 'Visha? Can you hear me?' Isaac doesn't let go, though Urvisha opens her eyes and looks at him wildly. 'Are you all right?'

'What happened?'

'The experiment failed.' They help Urvisha sit up. 'Careful – you weren't breathing two minutes ago.'

'That was, without doubt,' Urvisha declares weakly, with 20 per cent of her usual verve, 'the worst wake-up kiss I've ever had.' She blinks a couple of times, then smiles at Isaac. 'Thank you.'

'You're welcome, Sleeping Beauty,' Isaac says softly.

'Bleurgh. And what the hell did you do?' Urvisha asks Thea. 'Huh?'

'While Isaac saved my life, what were you doing?'

'If you're making jokes,' Isaac says, with about 10 per cent of his usual wryness, 'then it's safe to say you're back to your old self.'

'Help me up,' Urvisha says, standing slowly.

'Rest a minute – Ayo's calling an ambulance.'

'What? No!' Urvisha is horrified. 'They'll ask all sorts of

questions. I'm fine – I'd just like to sit down. Somewhere other than a freezing barn floor.'

'You need to see a doctor,' Isaac says.

'I can go tomorrow,' she insists. 'Isaac – go and stop Ayo, will you? Cancel the ambulance.'

'You are *so* stubborn,' he says, as he jogs ahead of Thea and Urvisha. Thea flicks off the barn lights as they shuffle out into the courtyard, Urvisha's arm around her neck as they move slowly back towards the kitchen garden.

'How are you feeling?' Thea asks gently.

'Nothing more bruised than my ego,' Urvisha replies as they hobble into the house.

Thea needs to talk to Isaac about her epiphany, but the priority is Urvisha.

They make her comfortable in one of the spare rooms, and Thea runs to get another duvet while Ayo fusses around making a hot drink, baby Bolu held against her in a makeshift sling.

'Is that,' Urvisha asks, looking at the white fabric Ayo's used, 'one of Thea's Miss Havisham dustsheets?'

'It's all I could find.' Ayo sits down next to Urvisha on the bed, cradling her son, but taking the other woman's hand in hers. 'Are you sure you're not hurt?'

'This is one hell of a comedown,' Urvisha says, rubbing her temple with her other hand.

'Idiots,' Ayo says. 'We can't let this happen again. First Rosy –' she pauses – 'and now you. No more rushing.'

'I just wanted to find our friend.'

'Isaac?' Thea calls from the top of the stairs. 'Can you come up and help me for a sec?'

In the farmhouse's master bedroom, moonlight pours in through the draughty metal-framed window. He stands in the doorway as she lifts the duvet from the bed. 'What an insane evening.'

'What an insane day.' The *Portrait of an Unknown Woman* feels almost a distant memory, in light of what she's subsequently learnt. 'In the barn,' she starts, 'I was thinking about the many-worlds interpretation, and what that might mean for me. What it might tell us about my jump.'

'Right,' he says, still by the door, a little nonplussed.

She puts down the duvet and pulls out her notebook, opening it to the page where she'd drawn the jump.

'It's important.'

He walks further into the bedroom and traces her Y-shaped diagram with his hand, the moment when one timeline breaks left, and the other, right. 'You were saying something about two worlds in parallel until a single decision causes the split.'

'Exactly. One goes left, the other goes right.'

'Okay,' he says. 'And so . . . ?'

She looks around at the room that had belonged to her parents, now hers by default. She picks up the duvet again, feeling the comfort of it against her skin. She has to tell him, as much as she doesn't want to.

'You were right, in a way, when you said the parallel world was like a mirror. I'm trying to work out when the timelines broke apart. And down in the barn, everybody kept talking about Rosy's jump. But you and I – we know something they don't.'

He nods, putting his hand gently on her arm.

'This is about my jump, Isaac. It's why I don't remember, and why I've been a bit . . . *different*, recently. Before the timelines split, until that *very* moment, the parallel worlds were identical. So if somebody from here jumped *there*, then somebody from there jumped *here*.'

He looks at her blankly.

'That must be why I don't remember jumping,' Thea says, her heart breaking. It hurts to tell him this, but he needs to know. 'Because I didn't. If the portal leads to a parallel world, then everything that happened here *before the landing* also happened in another world. Exactly the same. So at the same moment I jumped from this world . . .'

'. . . Someone jumped back the other way.' Isaac bites his lip. 'Do you see?'

'Don't be ridiculous,' he scoffs. 'That's crazy.'

'Look at the science . . . we have all the proof we need.'

Isaac falters. 'Really?' If Thea believes there's enough proof, there probably is. 'No way.'

'You said yourself I've been different,' she says, and as it did for Thea, this hits home for him.

'Oh, hell.'

'*Now* do you see?'

'It can't be. Do you think . . . ? I can't believe it.'

'Everything that happened *before the landing*,' she repeats, her voice a murmur, 'also happened in another world.'

He looks at her hard. 'What are you saying, exactly? Spell it out for me.'

'I didn't jump *from* here. I jumped *to* here.'

Isaac drops his hand from where it's still resting on her arm. 'You're not you, you're the other you?'

'Yes.'

'Oh, God. You're the Thea from the other place. You've ended up in the wrong world.'

Thea sits down on the bed, the feather-filled duvet spilling out of her arms. 'I don't – I can't—'

'Breathe,' he says, clearly concerned.

She takes a breath, and regroups. 'The physics is sound.'

'I'm sure,' Isaac says. 'You're rarely wrong.'

It's nearly two in the morning, and Thea feels broken; this revelation is the latest in a long day of revelations.

'You're from the parallel world,' Isaac repeats, his voice less disbelieving this time. The repetition is making it more solid. Whereas before they had the outline, now the truth is starting to be filled in.

'I believe so, yes.'

'But how can that – how can that be?' Isaac looks at her, really searches her face. 'How can you be in a world where you don't belong? Because the way I feel about you . . .'

She looks at him sombrely. 'I don't know.'

'What about all the markers we found in history? The *Portrait of an Unknown Woman*, sold by Admiral Coleman, the money in your bank? Didn't you go back in time?'

She lifts her hands, bewildered. 'I honestly don't know.'

'Perhaps the truth really is one of the simple answers we were trying to discount today. A strong family gene,' Isaac says, 'or the app revealing your museum doppelganger.' He pauses almost imperceptibly at the word *doppelganger*, sucking in the new resonance it carries for them.

'Maybe my journey to another universe bent time as a dimension,' she says. 'Jumping to another world – we don't know what happens to the past when you glance against the strands of time. Remember, if it's happening in space, it's happening in time . . .'

Isaac waves his hands, as if he couldn't even begin to understand what she is saying.

'There will be a better explanation . . . I just can't quite grasp it yet.' She sags back on the bed, feeling the after-effects of the exhaustion of the day, and now this. In the other room they hear the murmur of Ayo and Urvisha talking, the snuffling of Ayo's child. 'I can't believe I was wrong about the glass house. I was wrong about the whole thing.'

'You weren't. Look at what you've built,' he says.

'I was wrong. But you're right about something.' He straightens his shoulders and smiles. 'I don't belong here. This isn't my world.'

With those words everything crashes down around them.

'This is a headfuck,' Isaac says, taking the duvet from her and putting it onto the mattress behind them. 'The Thea I knew at university is in your world, and you're in ours.'

'An impossible situation,' she says, turning to face him on the bed. Behind him she can see the curtains she remembers from her childhood, a William Morris pattern she never had the heart to change. 'Everything is messed up because she's there, and I'm here.'

'You're here,' he repeats. 'And she's there.'

'This is impossible.'

'Totally,' Isaac says. His face looks as though it might crack. 'Especially because of how I feel about you.'

'And how's that?' she says, her voice faltering, but at last wanting to hear it.

'Thea, you know – you must know.'

She puts her hand to his cheek. 'Is this what you were going to tell me tonight in Trafalgar Square?'

'Was that only tonight? I was going to say—' He breaks off. 'I was going to say that I've spent the last year wanting you to be wrong about time travel, so I wouldn't lose you.'

She bites her lip.

'And I was angry that you'd leave me if you succeeded.'

'Why?'

He inhales. 'Why? Because I love you, Thea – I always have.'

'Oh,' Thea breathes, putting her head in her arms, and Isaac rests his hand against her back as they sit on the edge of the bed in a bedroom that, in a different world, belonged to her parents. 'And that's why this is impossible; because I feel the same,' she says, sitting up. 'I'm in love with you, Isaac.'

She leans into him, brushing his unruly hair away from his face before she puts her lips lightly on his.

The intimacy takes him by surprise and after a moment he pulls back slightly, resting his forehead against hers, their eyes fixed upon each other.

He exhales.

'This is fucked up, don't you see?' Thea's voice is sorrowful. 'I'm in the wrong place. I belong there, and the other Thea –' she stands, not even wanting to think about what she's saying – 'she belongs here.'

'And me?' Isaac says. 'Where do I belong?'

'With me.' But even as she says it, she feels the scientific untruth of the words. Because this is his world, and not hers. The idea that life would be this cruel wounds her. Just as she's found a place where she truly belongs, it turns out she's in the wrong place entirely.

∞

Isaac's not sure whether his heart has turned arrhythmic inside his chest or whether all of his internal organs have been startled into failure.

She loves him back.

It's heartbreaking for him to realize he's always been in love with Thea. But just when she appears to return his feelings, for the first time in their long friendship, it's a Thea from a different world.

None of this makes sense.

Though, really, everything is starting to make sense: the changes he's seen in her across the past . . . how long?

Does he love *this* Thea because she returns his feelings? Or does he love the Thea with their shared history, who never mistook their platonic friendship for unrequited love? Is it possible that he loves them both?

She touches his hand and he's startled anew by the confession she just made. *She's in love with me.*

'Thea wouldn't have known it was a portal, when she jumped,' Thea says, and he closes his eyes, unable to truly reconcile the thought of two Theas – one in love with him, one his old friend. 'I'm worried she's in another world and doesn't even realize.'

'But you're in parallel, aren't you?' he says. 'So if you've just realized, then surely she's just realized, too?'

'No.' Thea rubs the baby hair on her temple, which has always been her tell that she's thinking hard, in whatever world he's known her. She points again at the Y-shaped drawing in her notebook. 'We split apart at the landing. We're no longer in parallel. Everything that's happened here since I arrived is different from what is happening there, where I came from.'

He feels the hopelessness rise up inside him. Everything that's happened since she arrived . . . is everything.

'I pulled the plug on Urvisha's jump,' she says, out of the blue. He looks at her without speaking, listening. 'I couldn't let someone else jump when I didn't believe it would actually take Visha to Rosy.'

'That's understandable,' he says.

'I figured out what had happened, and I knew I'd have to put it right.'

'Okay,' he says, nodding.

'Isa.' Thea takes a deep breath. 'It's up to me to get them back.'

He pauses. 'Them?'

'Rosy. Thea. I have to return them to their rightful place,' Thea says.

Isaac looks down at their entwined hands. 'You want to go back.'

'No. But I must.'

He deflates. Just when he thought that he and Thea could possibly be together . . .

'Why?' he asks. 'Can't you stay here, and the . . . other . . . Thea, there? The worlds are the same, aren't they? Nobody would ever know.'

She visibly balks at the suggestion. 'I wish we could. But everyone seems to be displaced, and I'm the only one who knows what's going on.'

'You want to be right again,' he says sadly.

'I *am* right,' she corrects, but her voice is soft. 'This isn't about me. It's about the other Thea . . . and Rosy.'

He stands, offering her his hands, not even wanting to think about what he's going to say next. 'I'll help.'

Thea's shocked. 'You will?'

'Of course I will. I promised, didn't I? "Anything it takes".'

'I mean it. I don't *want* to go back,' Thea says, standing to face him in the bedroom. 'I want to be with you, here. But the others . . . I have to.'

He closes his eyes. 'So I'll help you.'

It's brutal, holding to a promise despite your heart screaming at you to break it. Isaac cannot even begin to comprehend why she feels the need to do this, nor why he's offering to help. But perhaps that's what real love is: sacrifice.

Thea lets go of his hand and the gulf between them becomes real. 'I need to get to the glass house.'

Isaac opens his eyes. 'Now?'

∞

Ayo and Urvisha have both fallen asleep with Ayo's little tot in his travel cot beside them, when Thea and Isaac tiptoe down the stairs.

'They aren't going to let me jump back,' Thea says quietly as they reach the ground floor. 'And they shouldn't find out. I need to go while they're still asleep.'

Isaac tries to hold back from complaining, but she watches as he can't stop himself. 'Would it not be better— We could get some sleep, and think about this in the morning?'

The idea of spending one night together is tempting. But if they wait too long, she'll chicken out entirely. It's like ripping off a plaster: better quick and fast.

Isaac moves to turn all of the lights down, but Thea stops him. 'No,' she whispers. 'It might wake them.'

She asks Isaac to head out to the barn with her, and they repeat the routine of stepping into wellies and warm coats. Thea winds an old knitted scarf around her, then pulls another from her coat pocket, rising up on the balls of her feet to wrap the long woollen scarf around Isaac's neck. He puts his hand on the small of her back, pulling her to him, and silently, so as not to wake the others, they hold on to each other in the doorway to the cold northern night.

She hugs him a fraction longer than she should.

Thea opens the door carefully, not making a sound, so her friends won't hear. It feels like a lifetime since that night in

Oxford when she crept out with the intention of breaking into the Beecroft by herself. What would have happened if she had done it alone?

They lift their wellies carefully so the rubber boots don't make a telltale scuffing noise against the courtyard pavestones, then pass through the kitchen garden with its vegetables so wild it's like a garden at the end of the world, then past the crazy paving slabs – *one, two, three,* – and out towards the barn.

It's a clear night and, unlike in London, they can see all of the stars.

'Do you remember,' Isaac says, 'what you did that was different from the others?'

'The other experiments?' Thea says, gazing up at the moon as they get to the shadowy outlines of the black wood outbuildings.

'It must have been different. Rosy's jumps were either very short, or she didn't swap places. So for you to end up here, and the other Thea to end up there . . .' He can't finish his sentence, and she takes his hand in the dark.

They make their way through the outbuildings to the barn, the door still open from when they'd rushed out carrying Urvisha, only a few hours earlier. The glass house isn't illuminated by the stage-like lighting of the three photographic lamps, and the prismatic texture of the glass is grey and dull.

Thea glances over it, then at the laser, then back again. 'That doesn't look quite right,' she says slowly, and Isaac walks over to examine the laser, though what he hopes to deduce is anyone's guess.

'Did Urvisha change something?' he asks.

'No, I don't think she did.'

'Do you think you did something different before?'

She flicks on the power for the three photographic lamps so the entire barn brightens and, illuminated, the glass house once again radiates its familiar ethereal glow. Thea fingers the pocket in the glass house door where she normally inserts the prism. 'I've been putting the prism in the path of the laser beam, here, so it acts like a lens.' She takes out the prism already tucked in the door; a fairly standard one of cut glass, which she lifts so it throws refracted rainbows wherever it catches the light. 'But maybe it doesn't need to be there.'

Isaac watches the spectrums falling onto the floor and across the other surfaces in the room, laughing as one lights up Thea's face. She moves the prism between her forefinger and thumb so it catches the light even more, and Isaac is momentarily blinded by the brightness of the light bouncing off the prism and the diamond ring on her hand.

'Ouch.'

'Sorry,' she says. Then she does it again, the diamond flashing in his eyes.

'Hey! That hurts!'

'I'm wondering . . .' She moves the prism to her other hand, stretching her palm flat and regarding the three rings she's wearing in the triangle formation. Like in the *Portrait of an Unknown Woman*, the stone on her ring finger sits highest, up between the two joints. *So it doesn't look like an engagement ring.* She twists her hand, throwing the reflected light from it once more.

Thea starts dragging the laser towards the glass house. 'I'm going to rest the laser against the prismatic glass – I think that's what it needs.' Her eye once again catches the hole in the glass door, and she looks around the barn for something to raise the laser up to a similar height. She sees a rickety old wooden ladder resting against the wall and drags it over, placing the laser box on the rung level with the small pocket in the door, so when it's fired, the beam can shine almost directly through into the glass house.

'There,' she says, stepping back to take in her work. She can easily turn the laser on from the glass house – it's so close it's practically inside.

Isaac moves Urvisha's suitcase away from the glass house. 'What's the small antechamber for, at the rear?'

'Thea?' The voice comes from somewhere near the kitchen garden, or the three paving stones. 'Isaac?'

'It's Ayo,' he says, moving to the door.

Thea runs through the checks, the laser's control panel casting an otherworldly green glow on her face. She turns on one of the battery-powered head torches, leaving it lying on the control panel. Without anyone else to record the video, monitor the National Grid and check for the all-clear, there's little else to do.

She takes a breath.

'Are you sure—?' Isaac breaks off.

'Go on,' she says. 'Ask.'

'Are you sure this will work? That you'll jump to wherever Thea is – and Rosy, too?'

'I'm sure,' she says, smiling. She raises the back of her hand, waggling her fingers, the gleam from the ring matching the proverbial light bulb above her head. 'I used my own diamond when I jumped to this world. That's why it worked.'

Isaac stares at her hand, pulling the postcard of the Unknown Woman from his back pocket, where it has been stashed with Thea's notebook. He holds it out to her and a smile blooms across her face, once again sure that it's her.

'A plain glass prism with lead oxide crystal was never going to work properly. But this – I was *connected* to it.'

He beams at her visible happiness at solving at least part of the riddle.

'I wanted whatever was inside the glass house to be carried away on the light wave,' Thea says, gazing at the diamond. 'But it never fully worked when I was trapping the light inside pieces of glass. But to carry a person away, all the way to a parallel world, using a family heirloom – a personal link . . . that's how you jump all the way.'

'So now we know.' Isaac sighs with relief. 'We use the ring.'

'Are you guys out here?'

They hear Ayo somewhere near the dovecote, her voice getting louder.

Thea reaches for the plug and turns off the photographic lamps, plunging them into blackness.

'Thea?' he says gingerly, seeking her outline in the dark barn. 'I'm coming with you.'

'You can't—'

'I can.' His tone is insistent, and the fact she doesn't interrupt him again means he has her ear. 'I can go with you, then return with the . . . *other* . . . Thea.'

'But why?'

'Isn't it obvious? We just found each other. I don't want to be without you – not yet.' He finds her hand in the dark.

She mulls it over, her eyes adjusting to the gloom. From outside they hear footsteps crunching on the gravel, and Isaac moves closer towards Thea's silhouette.

'I'm coming,' he says.

'Hello?' Ayo's voice says; she must be near the first outbuilding.

'All right.' Thea pulls him into the glass house with her, and though he can't see much in the eerie light given off by the prismatic glass, he can feel the warmth of her body against his own.

'On three?'

'Not this time.' She stands face to face with Isaac in the enclosed space, the small glass seat pressing into the backs of her knees. She tilts her head up. 'I say we just go.'

As she fires the laser into the glass house and their world turns white, she kisses Isaac long and hard, and the light carries them away.

III

A Prism Full of Light Years

Twenty

Joined as one as they cease to exist, Thea and Isaac feel the gravitational force acting upon them as they are pressed together with an intensity unlike anything they've ever experienced. They lean into the kiss, the pull between them powerful, as their history and their future merge with their present within the tiny glass house.

Through his closed eyes, Isaac can sense a blinding whiteness outside the glass house, plus something even brighter inside it. As Thea moves her hand to his face, he knows at once it's her family heirloom: the diamond on her finger glows vividly, the light colourless. He lifts her hand, interlocking his fingers with hers, and without even opening his eyes he can see the halo outline of her ring clearly through his eyelids. She pulls back, looking at their interlaced hands, as a great ripping sound fills the air.

'The blackout, maybe,' she whispers, her mouth next to his ear, then she kisses the lobe and that part of his neck. They touch as though it is the first time, discovering each other anew. This isn't like before – a sleep-soaked hangover of comfort sex, familiarity driving them together, the tinge of guilt keeping them apart. This Thea is in love with Isaac and he is in love with her.

The light drops, and Isaac's eyes spring open in alarm. Thea's diamond ring emits a light like a beacon, engulfing the interior of the glass house, lighting her jaw against the dark, so he runs his thumb across it, cupping her face.

Their stomachs plunge as though they're rising a million storeys in a glass elevator. The colour outside turns yellow, then orange, then red as they climb, catching the grooves of prismatic glass in lines the shades of the sun. The glass refracts the light inside the glass house, drifting spectrums of colour across them both. 'Did you know,' he says, 'there are only really six colours of the rainbow? Indigo isn't—'

'Not *now*, Isaac,' she whispers, turning so they can both face outwards. Thea sighs, luxuriating in the warmth of the light, her gaze flicking to the warm pressure of Isaac's hand on her waist, then up to his cheekbones as the light dips. 'Beautiful, isn't it?'

The red dusk turns a deep blue before their features are completely lost in shadow. After a few moments of darkness, patches of light appear, dotted haphazardly on the inky black outside.

'Oh my—' Isaac says, and though he doesn't finish the sentence, the sentiment is enough.

'We're among the stars.'

They press their faces to the glass. Condensation from their breath pools on the surface and Thea leans against the wall, her face cooled by its smoothness. The glass house has turned almost translucent in the vacuum of space, showing the sprawl of stars around them.

They see each other clearly in the light of the nearest star and laugh a little, awkwardly. Isaac lifts her chin gently with his forefinger, and as the three stars of Orion's Belt glitter outside he leans towards her and says, 'You're beautiful.'

She laughs.

'You are.'

She glows from the compliment and the prismatic glass shimmers as they head into a haze of fuggy stardust.

As they exit the nebula and it darkens once more, the odd twinkling star causing ripples of light, Thea cranes to see the purplish radiance of the Milky Way, then lets out a cry when she catches sight of something.

'Do you see it?' she says, her hand up to the glass, pointing as best she can.

Isaac leans against the surface next to her, moving to look where she is staring.

'See? There!' Her voice is urgent and he twists as much as possible, straining to see.

'The ecliptic,' he breathes, the curved line plainly visible to them in the glass house. They can see the arc of the planets: there's Mercury and Venus, just like when Thea and Isaac saw them for the first time, together – but also Jupiter, Mars, the Moon . . . and Earth.

'Oh my God,' Thea says, near tears. 'I never thought I'd see a conjunction that includes Earth in my lifetime.'

They gaze at the blue planet from the glass house, picking out the oceans and continents from their unique viewpoint, noting the way our pale blue dot fits into the sweeping curve of the ecliptic among its neighbouring planets.

'We're the only people seeing this alignment,' Isaac whispers, 'in the entire universe.'

She smiles. 'This is our conjunction. It's ours.'

Isaac holds his hand against Thea's waist. He cannot bear to let her go. 'It's as though we're standing on the edge of the universe,' he says, repeating something she said a long time ago. 'As though, for once, we could wave and the other planets might see.'

She looks at him, almost seeing through Isaac in that moment, finally aware of the truth: he's been in love with her since they met. Isaac has always been in love with her.

She reaches up and kisses him, softly. It's a feather-like kiss, full of love and loss. 'You see the world like I do,' is all she says.

'We're so lucky,' he says quietly, though the truth is they're desperately unlucky. Because how could it happen that Isaac would love Thea in his universe, but she would only return his love in a world where she couldn't stay?

They leave behind the Milky Way and the ecliptic dissolves out of sight, the glass house once again becoming opaque as the light outside bends away. Another great ripping sound fills the air, the noise so loud they both cover their ears, when suddenly their world – Isaac's world – is gone in an instant as the rear compartment snaps free. They tumble backwards into the smaller antechamber, collapsing on the floor of the glass house.

'What the—?' Isaac says.

'Oh God,' Thea says.

'So that's what—' he says, but she lifts a finger to his mouth, her eyes on the spectacular view outside. They freefall in the microgravity of Thea's world, the glass house sinking down with the inevitability of Newton's apple.

'Sshhh,' she says, and he understands, holding her tightly as they descend through the stratosphere towards daylight, a sprawl of stratus tinted with fire greeting them as they fall back to Earth.

'Red sky in the morning,' Thea says quietly as they land, and together they watch the sun rise.

∞

If they were expecting a parallel world to appear different to the naked eye, they are disappointed. As daylight creeps across

Thea's world, Isaac reaches for the portal door, pushing it open carefully to see the world beyond.

'Where are we?' he says, as they both sit up, the spell broken.

Thea kneels to lean out of the door. 'We're still in the barn.'

'The barn?' he says. 'In my world?' He uses the possessive lightly, only for clarity.

'I'm not sure.' Thea steps out, looking round. The same cold stone floor, workbenches and photographic lights are arranged at familiar points, the laser pointing towards the glass house. She wanders round, touching the equipment gently, looking at her setup.

'Have we gone back in time?' Isaac asks, as he steps out, too, glancing round with interest but also suspicion.

'No – we've moved sideways,' she says, gazing back at the glass house. 'It should be the same time, on the same day. Just a different place.'

'Does it feel . . . like home?'

'I suppose so,' she says. 'As much as the other world did.'

'Looks like the diamond worked, then.' Isaac is suddenly more alert. 'Hey, do you think Rosy was wearing a diamond when she jumped? She always wore fancy jewellery. Could that be why she went?'

Thea shakes her head slowly. 'I'm not sure. She used to wear a sapphire . . .'

'It's possible, then.'

'The crystalline structure doesn't lend itself that well to trapping light.' Thea gazes around. 'We'll have to see what we can find out.'

'Shall we head outside?' Isaac says, sensing her reluctance to leave the sanctity of the glass house and her equipment.

She finally takes the plunge, pushing the heavy barn door

open to reveal the early morning, the flat, hazy clouds at low altitude burning off their redness as the sun fully rises.

'Shepherd's warning,' Isaac says, and Thea claps her hands together. 'What did I say?' he asks, bewildered.

'That's what that means!' Thea almost bounces on the spot, a piece of the spacetime puzzle clicking into place for her. 'Red sky at night – shepherd's delight. But red sky in the morning – why would that be a warning?'

'I have no idea what you're talking about.'

She waves towards the glass house. 'The glass house – it diverts the blue and violet end of the spectrum, more than the red and orange. The red wavelength continues on a direct course and is reflected off the clouds, so the sky turns red –' she beams – 'and the blue light is scattered by the portal.'

Isaac looks at her, eyebrows raised.

She rolls her eyes. 'A red sky is an after-effect of a time leap. A red sky means somebody has jumped.'

'Ah. Shepherd's "warning".'

She grins again. 'Come on. Let's go and explore my world.'

The outbuilding courtyard is disappointingly familiar. They walk past the dried-out firewood and dovecote, making their way across the three slabs of crazy paving – *one, two, three* – until they're at the kitchen garden, just as overgrown as the garden back in Isaac's universe. The morning air is fresh, and the flowering vegetables are covered in spider webs that glisten in the light with dew.

'Thea,' Isaac says, stopping in the middle of the overrun courgettes. 'Do we need to be worried about meeting . . . the other you?'

She tilts her head, then moves to avoid a spider weaving an intricate web. 'I honestly don't know,' she says.

'Because in all the science fiction I've seen, meeting yourself is never a good idea.'

She hides a smile. 'This isn't a movie, but if you're worried about violating the laws of physics . . .'

He shrugs. 'I don't know about the laws of physics, just the books and the films and the games and the—'

'I get it.' She smiles openly. 'Let's be careful, then. Statistically speaking, depending when the timelines split, there's a much smaller chance of . . . the other you . . . being here in Dunsop Bridge, than me.'

He looks at her soberly.

'So you go first. See if . . . the other me . . . is in the house. And I'll wait here. Avoiding some sort of self-paradox.'

He makes a face, wondering if she's mocking him.

'Don't let me meet my grandfather,' she murmurs, 'or step on any butterflies.'

Isaac walks hesitantly from the overgrown garden to the kitchen door, crossing his fingers the other Isaac isn't, in fact, here in this parallel Dunsop Bridge. He tries the handle, but the door is locked. He turns it again to no avail, then knocks on the glass, the sound loud in the early morning. 'Thea?' he calls. 'Are you in?' He waits, then tries again. 'Theodora?' It's early, but at Oxford she always woke up at six to start her studies before class. He scratches his head, trying to remember if he's ever seen Thea stash a key somewhere, even for her rented house in Oxford . . . He reaches up on top of the doorframe, running his hand along the splintered wood until he finds it. 'Bingo.' Quietly he inserts the key in the lock, turning the handle until the door opens into the kitchen of Thea's farmhouse.

He coughs. Not to warn he's in the house, but because he has a tickle in his throat. He covers his mouth with his hand

and notices the dust he's disturbed, the airborne motes around him. Dustsheets cover the kitchen table and hang suspended from the light fixture, giving a spooky effect. 'Thea?' he says again, more weakly.

'Huh.' He walks out into the hallway. A covered chandelier hangs from the ceiling; the only sign of life is Thea's crate of textbooks at the bottom of the stairs. She's here, then. He picks up the book on top, thumbing through it, then flicks over the cover of the next one down to see what else is in the pile. So far, so familiar. But why is the farmhouse untouched, like nobody's been staying here?

'Thea?' he says, and coughs again. The onset of a headache throbs at the back of his head. He jogs up the stairs, taking them two at a time, putting his head round the door to where he last saw Ayo and Urvisha sleeping like inverted commas in the spare room. The bed is covered in white sheets, the dust on top long settled. All of the other rooms are untouched, so he heads, a little confused, to the master bedroom.

He pushes open the cranky wooden door. There are no dustsheets – it is exactly as it was when Thea told him she loved him, in another world entirely.

He sniffs, his nose streaming, then walks back out of the room, running down the stairs and out of the kitchen door.

'Thea?' he calls towards the garden. 'It's safe – there's no one here.'

She steps out from the shrubbery and he catches his breath as chestnut strands of her hair catch the morning light, her green eyes shining in the cold. 'Come and see this,' she says, beckoning him over.

He walks back into the wilderness of the kitchen garden, and Thea leads him to a medium-sized pond. She moves aside some weeds to reveal an old water feature, the huge basin of murky water topped with slimy green pond scum. She feels along the outside of the feature for something, and Isaac rubs his temples, confused and feeling worse by the minute, until the stinking water begins to drain out. 'Do you notice anything?' she says, intently watching the water. 'Keep looking.'

Isaac's sinuses are burning as he sniffs again, the cold making his nose run. 'What are we looking at?' he says finally.

'The direction the water's draining. Does that strike you as weird, at all?'

He blinks, watching the water run away down the drain. 'Tell me.'

'Objects not attached to the surface of the Earth – like water, cyclones and hurricanes, even winds – will rotate clockwise in the northern hemisphere, and anti-clockwise in the southern hemisphere. It's a consequence of the Earth's rotation,' she says. 'In your world, in the northern hemisphere, the vortex of this pond's drain in Dunsop Bridge, England, will flow clockwise. But here, the water is moving anti-clockwise. Like a mirror image.'

'Can you tell me what that means, so we can get on with why we're here, please?'

She looks at him, frowning. 'Are you all right?' she says, reaching for his hand. 'You're burning up.' She moves her hand perfunctorily across first his wrist, then up to his forehead. 'Christ, Isaac – are you okay?'

'I feel a bit weird,' he admits, the illness sliding into place and clamping visor-like over his eyes. 'I must be coming down with something.'

'Let's get you into bed,' Thea says, and for once, he can't even make a coy joke.

Twenty-one

Isaac is sick. As the fever grips him, climbing to 40°C, he calls for his mother, which Thea finds touching but also curious. She wonders if she has ever done that; she supposes everyone calls for their mother at times of distress, whether they've been comforted by them or not. Her memories of her own mother are hazy, though she holds on to the few she has tightly, terrified that the tighter she grips, the more likely they are to shatter and recede from view altogether.

Isaac wakes as if from a dream, reaching out for Thea's arm where she sits on the bed next to him. 'Hello,' she says, but he speaks at the same time.

'Which hand do you write with?'

She shakes her head. 'You've had a terrible fever,' Thea says, 'I think it's the flu.'

'Are you right- or left-handed?' he insists, looking at her hand as though he could imagine it holding a pen.

'I'm ambidextrous.'

He lies back. 'That's probably why you didn't notice,' he says. 'The water – what did you call it?'

'A vortex.'

Isaac nods. 'This world is a mirror of . . . my world. My water goes clockwise, your water goes anti-clockwise.'

'Two worlds in *reflection* symmetry,' she muses. 'Wow. Two possibilities there, I suppose: the reflection only began after my and Thea's jump – one world goes left, the other goes right.

Or there could be hundreds – thousands – maybe millions of mirrored worlds. Every possible universe piled up on top of each other.' She smiles. 'How are you feeling?'

'Crap.'

'You've had a terrible fever. I probably gave you the flu when you came to Dunsop Bridge – I was pretty ill then, myself.'

He squints. 'Have you seen anyone?'

'No – the house is deserted.' She looks around in the afternoon light at the bedroom that once belonged to her parents. It's hard to believe the same tragedy could play out on more than one timeline, in more than one universe. 'There's nothing to eat, I'm afraid,' she says. 'Are you up for heading into the village to get something?'

He sits up, rubbing the sleep from his eyes. 'I suppose so.' He moves from the bed, his skin aching, finding the rest of his clothes and taking large doses of paracetamol and ibuprofen with a glass of water Thea has put on the bedside table.

They wrap up and head down the lane of trees, the fallen leaves crackling underfoot. 'Same time of year,' Thea notes. They admire the open fields beyond the farm's borders as they head into the village, following the low stone wall. Isaac runs his hand along the shingle in an echo of another time, remembering to lift it in the exact place where previously it was cut by a jagged loose stone.

The chequered Georgian windows of Puddleducks look warm and inviting, so they cross the road towards the tearoom. Isaac pushes open the door for Thea, but as she makes to walk in, he quickly slams the door shut, holding it closed.

'What the hell?' she says.

'We can't go in there,' he whispers urgently: '*Thea's* in there.'

She peers through Puddleducks's steamed window, trying

KATIE KHAN

to see in. 'Oh.' She hesitates, trying to decide what to do. 'You go in,' she says at last, 'and I'll go for a wander. Maybe we could meet past the bridge, down by the river?'

'Sounds like a plan,' he says, his voice betraying his nervousness. 'Shall I get you something to eat?'

'Anything will do,' she says, waving her hand in thanks.

∞

He pauses for one moment alone before he pushes the door to the tearoom open again, letting the noise of chattering locals and the clash of plates seep out. The bell on the door jangles as he walks in, and a few people look up. Thea Colman is sitting at a table near the middle, facing him, and he urges himself to walk across to her – noticing at the last moment that she's sitting opposite someone else.

'Hi, Thea,' he says, as he pulls up level with her table, then almost falls to the floor with shock. 'Rosy!' he exclaims. Then: 'How are you? You look well,' as he desperately tries to recover, attempting to appear nonchalant.

'Isaac?' Thea says curiously. 'You look dreadful. What are you doing back from New York?'

He looks at her. 'I'm in New York?'

'Aren't you? We spoke yesterday,' she says. 'You were raving about the pizza.'

'Of course I was,' he says, his mind working like mad. In this world, he hasn't yet travelled back for his visa. At least that makes it easier here – one Isaac on each side of the Atlantic. 'I thought I'd surprise you,' he says weakly. 'Surprise.'

'Sit down,' this Thea says, motioning at the seat next to

234

Rosy. Cold-weather coats hang over the backs of their chairs and Isaac notices they're both wearing walking boots.

'We're taking a hike up to— Isaac, are you poorly?' Rosy says, looking at him with concern.

'I've had the flu. Nasty bugs flying round at this time of year.'

Thea stares at him hard. 'Let's get the bill,' she says, pushing her chair back with a loud grating noise, making Isaac and Rosy jump.

'Already?'

'I need to get something to eat—' Isaac protests.

'Grab a sandwich to go,' Thea says, moving to the till to pay for hers and Rosy's. 'Let's take a walk and catch up. Rosy, do you mind heading back to the house? I need to talk to Isaac,' she says, 'alone.'

Rosy's lips form an O of surprise. 'Of course,' she says easily. 'I'll see you back there.' She reaches across to hug Isaac, then remembers his flu and pats him formally on the shoulder instead. 'Lovely to see you. Maybe we can catch up later?'

'That would be nice,' Isaac says genuinely. After all the worry and concern for Rosy's wellbeing in his world, seeing her smiling in Puddleducks here has thrown him, not only for a loop, but for an elliptical orbit.

He orders two sandwiches, stuffing one into his pocket. 'Saving it for later,' he says at Thea's inquisitive gaze. She stalks out of the tearoom and Isaac hurries behind, looking forlornly at the display of scones and cakes as he steps back out into the open air without having eaten a thing. He unwraps the wilting sandwich, taking a bite as he catches up with her on the main road through the village. 'Where are we going?'

She strides in the opposite direction to where the other

Thea is sheltering by the bridge over the river. 'The Hanging Stones.'

The Whitendale Hanging Stones are a few miles from Dunsop Bridge, through the dramatic Dunsop valley. Adorned with purplish ferns and dark green conifers, the hills undulate in a series of knolls, and Thea and Isaac climb the valley, panting slightly at the incline. They cross a weir where the water runs flat on one side, the other in whitewater rivulets.

Isaac stops, ostensibly to read a weathered information board about the local area, but really to catch his breath. 'How far is this walk?' he says, still feeling the palpable effects of the flu.

'Only a couple of hours.'

Fuck.

'How was your journey?' Thea says casually beside him, reading the sign too.

'Turbulent,' he says.

'Travel far, did you?'

He casts a glance at her. 'New York to London?'

She skips across some stepping stones rising out of the water, then waits on the other side for him to do the same. 'Oh, I think you travelled a bit further than from New York.'

He considers the implication. 'How do you know?' he says finally, as they walk through the boggy land past Whitendale Farm, a remote, low-level network of buildings nestled in the valley.

'Did you know,' Thea says, 'that news of the end of the First World War took six weeks to reach Whitendale and the neighbouring farms?'

'I can believe it.' Isaac is cold and unwell, confused by her frosty behaviour and how she seems to know where he has come from, so he doesn't answer in the usual jaunty manner for their game.

She arches an eyebrow, but slows her pace to allow the struggling Isaac to keep up. 'I got the flu, too,' she says softly, over the wind blowing across the fell. 'After I jumped.' He looks at her, saying nothing. 'You're in a new world, Isaac; you don't have the antibodies here. Everything you built up as a kid was for the germs in our own universe.'

'Oh,' he says. She knows everything – of course she does, she always has. He also takes a moment to realize that might be why the other Thea – *his* Thea, he reasons – was recovering from the flu in London. 'So you remember?' he says.

'I know that I jumped.'

Isaac is shocked, and he takes a few moments to collect his thoughts as they hopscotch along a muddy path, avoiding dips and puddles filled with brown water, until they get to a traditional kissing gate. They filter through in single file: Thea first, Isaac second.

This isn't a walk; it's a hike. Ramblers would spend an entire day tackling this route, and weeks beforehand planning it. Isaac meekly follows Thea, who clearly knows the paths backwards, as the minutes turn into hours. His skin has a sheen, his temperature still not back to normal.

They stand where the moors meet the sky, the green and purple hills rolling angrily beneath the grey clouds. Isaac feels almost vertiginous.

'It's like we're on top of the world, isn't it?'

'Yes.' He snatches a look at her, his old friend standing to his right, behind her some deeply sinister rock formations.

Thea sees where he's looking. 'Wolfhole Crag. Well done, we're nearly there.' She leads them south, and finally Isaac sees them: huge boulders like melted faces on the side of the fell, as though Mount Rushmore has come to Lancashire, a clumsy homage by a sculptor with an indelicate hand.

The Whitendale Hanging Stones hug the knolls of the fell like they might tumble down the hill at any moment. Thea and Isaac make the final push up towards the rocks, choosing to stand on the flat top of the smoothest one.

'The official centre of the country,' Thea says, pulling her North Face jacket around her. 'If you include the four hundred and one outlying islands.' The wind batters clumps of ferns and heather around them, the vegetation bristling in the breeze.

'You find it creepy up here, don't you?'

Thea shakes her head. 'No, I like it.'

Isaac pinches the bridge of his nose, partly to relieve his painful sinuses, partly to make sense of what he's hearing. He's sure Thea had told him the Hanging Stones were 'creepy' and 'meditative' . . . He'd compared standing stones to gravestones, and she to the Holocaust Memorial. Hadn't they?

'Can you tell me what happened when you jumped?' he says. 'And how come you can remember, but—'

'But what?' she says lightly.

He decides not to tell her there is another Thea, not to tell her the chaos she has caused by switching to a parallel timeline. 'Oh, nothing,' he says. 'So you remember what you did to get here?'

She sits down, dangling her legs over the top of the Hanging Stone in a manner Isaac finds horribly precarious. 'A lot of it has to do with you,' she says. 'When I first got back to Dunsop Bridge, you said something about my memories at the farm being "only ghosts". I thought a lot about confronting those ghosts – I was working out in the barn when I realized the key to travelling back in time was a personal connection to the past. And here I am.'

He considers what she's saying. 'You jumped then?'

'Yes. Right after I left Oxford, my first day at Dunsop Bridge.'

Holy wow. Every single exchange he's shared with Thea since he arrived from New York has been with the other Thea. The revelation takes his breath away. 'That's earlier than we thought.'

'We?'

'Ayo, Urvisha and me. We've been working as a team – trying to piece together the timeline.'

Thea swings her legs, watching the laces of her walking boots catch the wind. 'And Rosy?' she says.

There's no way around this one. 'Rosy is missing,' he says.

'What?'

'She jumped, too.'

She puts her hand up to the side of her head, holding the long brown strands escaping in the wind. 'No, no, no – please don't tell me that.'

'I'm afraid it's true.'

'When did she jump? How? What method did you guys use?' Thea stands, her ponytail whipping around her, the fabric of her coat flapping as she faces Isaac. 'Have you looked for her? Tried her family, the Bodleian – anything?'

Isaac reaches out a hand and puts it on her arm, trying to soothe her distress. 'We've tried all of that. Everything. We've looked everywhere. Including her brother in London. That's how I found . . . I followed some clues through time, for you.'

She looks at him blankly. 'If Rosy has disappeared, we need to find her. If this is a many-worlds scenario, as I suspect it might be, then we can't let anyone get trapped between alternate universes. That could be catastrophic.'

'For who – the world?'

Thea flinches. 'For the individual, most of all. I jumped here. Then Rosy jumped – where exactly, we don't know. And now you've jumped here, too; we need to be careful we don't draw tangled strings between parallel worlds that are impossible to unpick.'

'Like knitting,' Isaac says, but he's actually thinking about the Barbara Hepworth sculpture Thea had loved in the book at the gallery: *Stringed Figure (Curlew), Version II*, its cotton strands criss-crossing like a geometric pattern.

Thea tips her head in the direction of home. 'Come on – let's go back and try to solve this, however best we can.'

Isaac stumbles as they follow the fence along the severe ravines of Whin Fell. The descent is steep and they struggle to keep their footing as they reach the remains of a stone shingle wall, climbing over a wobbly stile with great care, matter-of-factly holding out a hand for each other to traverse it safely. 'Thea,' he says, 'you knew it was a portal, then?'

She steps down from the stile. 'No. I came to the conclusion when I woke up on the floor of the barn, having arrived seemingly back in the same place, yet with significant differences.'

'Do you know why you'd remember everything about your jump, but . . . others . . . may not?'

Thea pauses on the path. 'That's an interesting question. I suppose it depends who instigates the jump; in this case, it was me,' she says, jabbing him as they pass the weir with the rotting information board and the dry-stone wall that lines the road back into the village. 'But it might also have something to do with which prism was used. I'd have to think about it.'

Isaac hurries to catch up after checking beneath the bridge for any sign of the other Thea, peering at the empty towpath next to the river.

'I have to ask, Isaac,' she says, as they cross the bridge and head past Puddleducks and the Post Office. 'How on earth did you follow me here?'

Twenty-two

Thea had waited under the bridge for Isaac for quarter of an hour, then half an hour – hands shoved deep in her pockets – then three-quarters of an hour, stamping her feet to keep warm. After a freezing hour she said 'Sod this' aloud, and began the walk back to the farmhouse, taking care to ensure she didn't meet the other Thea, walking around in her life as if she owned it.

Perhaps she did.

Perhaps they were two halves of a whole.

Isaac was right: this was such a headfuck.

Perhaps it was like having a twin.

Maybe that's unfair to twins. She'd always imagined what it might be like to have a sibling; someone to play with, fight with, and – if she was truly honest – share her grief with. To feel like someone else in the world understands the hell you're going through, losing both your parents. Not the mention the compounded hell of losing them so young, before you even know a fraction of your own personality. Going to boarding school had given her someone to share a bunk bed with, dormmates and roommates. But until Thea met Isaac at university, she hadn't known the best friendships could feel like falling in love.

Reading C. S. Lewis as a child had introduced her, in her teen years, to two quotes he'd written about friendship in *The Four Loves*. She'd felt a certain kinship, at first, to his idea that 'Friendship is unnecessary, like philosophy, like art . . . It has no survival value; rather it is one of those things which gives value to survival.' But as she studied for a joint honours degree in Philosophy, and came to appreciate first the subject's worth, then friendship's, she switched allegiance to a different quote. 'Friendship,' C. S. Lewis had written in the same book, 'is born at the moment one man says to another, "What! You too? I thought that no one but myself . . ."'

Thea walks back towards the house, opening the front door carefully, catching it before the locks clatter shut to announce she's home. The dustsheet that was covering the miniature chandelier in the hallway when she and Isaac headed into the village is now draped over the bannisters, and she stares at it for a moment. A noise comes from the rear of the house, a sort of *woof!* like the sound of a gas boiler being lit, and she pads towards the kitchen, peering round the door.

Thea's heart shatters and she emits a short gasp as she sees this world's Rosy, fresh from Puddleducks where she'd just left the other Thea with Isaac, wearing a lacrosse team jumper and furry boots, hair looped up in an inimitable posh girl's bun, standing next to the Aga looking satisfied.

She steps back, feeling for the warmth on the top plate, then sees Thea by the door watching her.

'You're back!' Rosy says. 'That was quick.' Then: 'And you've already changed, clever thing. How was the walk? Where's Isaac?'

Without answering any of Rosy's questions, Thea moves across the kitchen and throws her arms around the tall blonde girl, holding her tight in a bear hug. 'I thought I'd lost you,' she whispers.

'Silly Billy,' Rosy says fondly, stroking Thea's hair, which is damp from the cold outside. 'We just had lunch together and I came back here, like you told me.' She points towards the Aga. 'I've got this thing lit, so the house should soon warm up.'

Thea stares at Rosalind, at the regal arch of her brow, her smooth high forehead and the petite bow of her lip.

'Thea?' Rosy says. 'You're, umm, putting me rather on edge. Have I got some leftover jam or clotted cream on my face?'

'No,' Thea says, stepping back. 'I'm . . . happy to see you. Thrilled you're here.'

Rosy pats her arm, moving away to tidy some mugs and other detritus in the sink. 'Well, I'm pleased to be here. I can help make it more homely, before the others arrive.'

'The others?'

'Ayo and Urvisha are going to head up after they finish their tutorials on Friday. For the weekend,' Rosy explains.

For one purely selfish moment, Thea wants to have Rosy to herself. She doesn't want to think about the others – she only wants to talk to Rosy. She's about to suggest they take a walk somewhere, when—

'Hello, boy!' Rosy's lurcher rambles sleepily into the farm-house kitchen, butting up against Rosy and then sticking his head in Thea's crotch, wagging his tail. 'Did you have a nice sleep?'

'Oh,' Thea says in surprise.

'I couldn't leave Cyril at home after I went back to visit my father; I want to spend a bit more time with the old boy.' She ruffles the lurcher's ears, tugging at him and giving him a good fuss.

Everything is different here, Thea rationalizes, since she and the other Thea both jumped and swapped places. She reminds herself she hasn't gone back in time just because Rosy's here – the clocks have continued marching on, time remaining one of the only constants. It's the same day in both worlds, in the same month, the same year . . . It's simply a case of two worlds no longer in parallel. Like the Y-shaped drawing in her notebook, the timelines have split.

Thea reaches down to pet Rosy's dog, her mind whirling. 'Hi, Cyril.' The lurcher sniffs her, curiously – and irrationally she wonders if a dog can sense a person is from another universe. After all, they've supposedly been known to detect cancer in humans simply by smell.

'Shall we take him out for a quick walkies?' Rosy says, interrupting Thea's reverie.

'Oh, yes please.'

And, like the millions of times they've left the house this autumn, whether they were in this world or the other, they bundle back into their coats and warm boots, and Rosy pulls a well-worn lead from her waxed jacket's pocket, heading towards the wood bordering the edge of Thea's farm.

∞

Isaac and Thea walk back towards the house, keen to warm up inside, arguing all the way through the woods. 'How did you get here, Isaac?' Thea says. 'Tell me.'

'It's a long story.'

'I've got time,' she says, gesturing at the road winding in front of them through the trees bordering her farm.

'How did *you* get here?' he deflects instead. 'What prism did you use?'

She frowns at him. 'I used the diamond in my ring. But why do I get the feeling you knew that already?'

'Can you explain it to me?' he says. 'How it works?'

'I can try,' she says, diverting them towards the barn. Then she grins, breaking the tension between them that's been evident since he appeared in this world. 'If you think you can keep up with the science.'

'Always my own personal brand of Kryptonite.'

Like every other time someone has opened the heavy, double-height barn door, it creaks, and Thea hauls it round using all of her strength. If she's surprised to see the experiment setup looking a little dishevelled after the latest landing, she doesn't show it, and instead walks over to the workbench running along the longest side of the black wooden barn, switching on a lamp and pulling the head over to light the surface. 'I'm going to pose some rhetorical questions,' Thea says, so Isaac grins – it's typical of her to announce that she will not require any answers, to avoid the awkwardness of him trying.

'What is the historical significance of the diamond?' she says. 'Why is it the most popular family heirloom, passed down across generations? What is the enduring appeal of this particular stone for an engagement ring?' Thea shrugs, the emphasis of her rhetorical questions fading between them, as she slides her ring from where it sits by the knuckle of her ring finger.

'When it comes to diamonds,' she continues, rummaging in a cardboard box under the workbench, bringing up a magnifying loupe and looking through it at the stone in her hand, 'there are four Cs: cut, colour, clarity and carat. The third and fourth don't matter in this instance. The most important is number one.' She hands him the loupe. 'Do you know about diamond cuts?'

Isaac shakes his head, peering at the diamond, which he brings up to his eye.

'When a diamond is cut with the proper proportions, light is returned out of the "table" – see here.' She runs her finger over the flat top of the diamond. 'That's the table. But if it's cut too shallow, light leaks from the bottom; too deep, and it escapes out of the sides.' She turns the diamond sideways, displaying its perfect depth, its beautiful proportions. 'This is a good example of a well-cut diamond. Do you see?'

Isaac hesitantly touches his finger to the table of the diamond. 'It's stunning,' he says, putting down the loupe. 'What about colour? You said the third and fourth of the four Cs were the least important – so colour is important?'

Thea bends the neck of the lamp so the bright light shines across the desk. 'A diamond's "colour" actually refers to its lack of colour. It's the absence of colour that's prized: the highest – and therefore most expensive – grades are those where the colour is barely visible under magnification, let alone to the naked eye. This,' she says, turning the diamond over so it catches the light from the lamp, throwing sparkles out from the top of the round, brilliant-cut stone, 'is considered grade D: absolutely colourless.'

'I'm guessing that's extremely rare?'

Thea nods, clicking off the lamp.

Isaac looks around, alarmed. 'I hope that thing is insured.'

Thea doesn't acknowledge the joke. 'That's why the best diamonds are the most expensive . . . there's real skill involved in cutting the stone. The best ones provide the most clean and clear route for the light to travel through the diamond. The path of least resistance.'

Isaac nods, listening hard.

'But this stone has a tiny inclusion, which to any diamond dealer would make it less valuable than a flawless stone. It's not visible to the naked eye, so we'll have to look through the loupe. For our purposes, it's the flaw that makes it interesting: it's a crystal inclusion.'

'Crystal,' Isaac repeats.

'It's a mineral crystal contained within the diamond, and in this case, it's a tiny diamond within the diamond.' She looks up at him. 'It was always interesting to me – I liked the idea of a crystal flaw hiding inside, capturing emotions, holding a feeling within its facets; catching even the most difficult sentiment – such as grief. I would look at the ring on my finger and think, if my grief is only contained in that tiny diamond-within-a-diamond, then I'm protected from it, and it can't hurt me . . . Well. Imagine how much of a family's history such an heirloom could hold inside the stone . . .' She trails off.

'I understand,' Isaac says softly.

'There's a scientific element to time travel and the glass portal,' she says, 'but I also think there's something personal – some sort of alchemy between the person and the prism – that we'll never even begin to comprehend.'

She starts as Isaac puts a postcard down on the bench, its corners worn. A woman, wearing an embroidered hood or headdress over her dark brown hair sits, hands together, an unusual triangle of three rings adorning her fingers. In the background a reddish symbol hovers behind the woman's head, reflecting the warm ambers and maroons of her dress. 'What is it?' Thea says, reaching to pick it up.

Isaac taps the postcard lightly with his index finger. 'Thea, I'd like to introduce you to the *Portrait of an Unknown Woman*.'

∞

As Cyril the lurcher canters through the wood, his long, skinny legs graceful despite his age, Rosy and Thea lag behind, feeling their way across the uneven ground as twilight descends through the trees. The afternoon light is dropping fast, the first sign that winter's on its way.

'We haven't had much of a chance to talk,' Rosy starts. 'Properly, I mean.'

Thea chooses a good stick from the ground and throws it for Cyril, and despite his age he hurtles after it with the elegance of a racing dog chasing down his prey. 'I feel like we haven't spoken in ages,' Thea says truthfully.

'I would have come sooner,' Rosy says. 'I hated to think of you all alone here with only your memories. But I had to go home, first – to speak to my father.'

The Thea from a parallel world recalls Urvisha's description of her visit to see Lord de Glanville, a man adrift from his children, unsure of their whereabouts or happiness. 'How did that go?' she says cautiously, unsure what Rosy may have already said to a different Thea.

Rosy rewards Cyril for bringing back the stick, then throws it with the power of her lacrosse arm. 'I told him I won't be joining Edward at Sotheby's. Not now, and not in the future.'

Thea widens her eyes. 'Oh, wow. Good for you.'

'I started to feel like, maybe – and this is no disrespect to my brother – that maybe I was meant for something more, something better.'

'Ad majora natus sum,' Thea murmurs and Rosy, with her extensive classical education, smiles.

'Thank you, yes. "Meant for greater things", that's a more elegant way of putting it. There is so much I want to see, so much I want to do . . . and I'm not sure valuing the paintings of my father's friends, until I meet a suitable husband, is the best way for me to spend my days.' Rosy smiles so Thea does, too, because if there's one thing Thea has learned from her ability to put her foot in her mouth in all social situations is that it's best to let the person speaking lead the emotion. If they laugh, you can laugh. But if they're sad and you laugh – well, then you're an arsehole.

'How are you finding it – being home, I mean?' Rosy says.

Thea shrugs. 'I've always tried to spend the minimum amount of time here. During school holidays I frequently stayed in the dorms; while at Oxford – well, you know better than anyone, I'd stay with friends and their families.'

Rosy smiles at the memory, shaking off her kindness as though taking in a stray at Christmas was the same as leaving leftover turkey out for the foxes. 'You're always welcome. So long as you bring a Yule log.'

'Thank you. Truly.'

They walk through the trees, patches of shadow starting to overtake the patches of daylight. The texture of the trunks is slowly steeping with colour like a mug of tea being brewed, and Thea and Rosy stop for a moment next to a tree with carvings in the bark.

Rosy leans in to read the initials etched in the wood. 'A. C. and . . . What letter is that?' She reaches to trace the markings with her finger, the initials set in the middle of a round sun, surrounded by beams that radiate outward.

'R,' Thea says quietly. 'For Ruth – my mother.'

Rosy runs her finger over Ruth's R meditatively. 'I'm sure they loved each other very much.'

'Probably,' Thea says. 'But when both your parents die unexpectedly when you're twelve, your memories take on a shimmer. You can't rely on them as you'd hope.' She traces her father's initials in the bark. 'I don't really remember how they talked to each other; whether my father would help my mother in the kitchen, standing behind her to warm them both by the Aga after a long day out on the farm. I don't know whether that's an image I'm remembering, or whether it's the haze of an image I've created.'

Rosy nods, full of empathy, letting Thea speak about this because it's so rare.

'I don't know if my mum loved my dad, or was exasperated because he made her up sticks to live on a farm. I like to think she did.'

'But at twelve,' Rosy says gently, 'you must remember how they were with you.'

Thea smiles, wistful. 'I didn't pay enough attention, Rosy. I didn't bank enough memories – I didn't know I'd need them so soon. On the day of the crash . . . I'd gone out to the Hanging Stones without telling anyone where I was going. I was angry because I'd told my parents I didn't like boarding at my new school, but they didn't listen – they said everything would get better with time.' Thea looks at the dark outlines of the trees around them, the branches forming shapes like the silhouettes of scarecrows. 'It's dangerous to go out on the fell in bad weather. There was a fog over the moorlands, but I marched on, regardless.'

Rosy puts her arm around Thea, moving away from the initials so they can talk and walk together.

'My dad was working the harvest so my mum took a bicycle down to Whitendale Farm, to try and catch up with me that way. When my dad heard I'd gone missing in the fog, he took the car. But there was so much mist by then, it was impossible for him to see . . .'

'Oh, Thea, no,' Rosy moans, realizing what's coming.

'My father hit my mother's bike. She went into the dry-stone wall. The screech of brakes – followed by the crunch – could be heard across the fell, I'm told. I must have been crossing the weir at the time, gushing water covering the horror.'

'But your dad . . .'

'He couldn't forgive himself – when it was me he should have been punishing. It was my fault, I was so stubborn. He hanged himself near here soon after.'

Rosy doesn't dare breathe, doesn't dare to ask where. She understands now why she feels so much sadness in the landscape; the brutality of the rolling hills can be beautiful, but there is also a tangible menace emanating from the moors. Confronted with what she now knows, she can understand exactly why someone would study Physics and Philosophy, asking the biggest questions of our known universe. In one fell swoop, Rosy can see why somebody who'd lived Thea's experience and every subsequent trauma might dedicate her life to working out how to rewind time.

'I'm so sorry,' is all she can say.

Thea shrugs. 'There are two ways to move on from something like this: you push it down and suppress it, or you use it in everything you strive to do with your life.'

'It's strange,' Rosy says, as they step over a fallen branch. 'Honestly? I always would have thought you were the first type of person. But perhaps I was wrong.'

They reach the far side of the wood, away from the farm. The remaining visible light is masked by the trees. 'We should think about heading back,' Thea says, her arm around Rosy's waist as the two women return to the house – where Isaac and Thea sit at the kitchen table, having a cup of tea.

Twenty-three

Rosy and Thea walk up the drive towards the front entrance of the farm. Cyril trots in front, the light now entirely gone from the sky. But as they arrive at the gravelled courtyard, a streak of headlights coming up the drive behind nearly blinds them. The car pulls into the courtyard, reversing awkwardly over the turning circle, and Rosy and Thea look at each other in confusion.

'Where in holy hell are we?' Urvisha says, getting out of the passenger side.

Thea pinches the pressure point behind the bridge of her nose. 'What are you doing here?'

'You're early,' Rosy says. 'Days early.'

'Surprise!' Ayo rolls down the window and makes a face at her own driving. 'I'm a bit out of practice.' She gets out of the car, leaving it parked awkwardly. She remembers at the last moment to turn and lock the rental, looking proud to have been so conscientious.

'Interesting parking,' Thea says as Ayo walks inside with her, looking round at the dusty farmhouse.

'This is quite a place you've got here – very shabby chic.'

'I like it!' Rosy says.

'Very Miss Havisham,' Thea says at the same time, appreciating that although two parallel worlds may split and go their own separate ways, some things will never change.

Isaac comes into the hallway from the kitchen, meeting the

group by the door. 'What are you doing here?' Urvisha says, then looks at him closely. 'Are you sick?' She breezes past him. 'Don't give it to me, I don't want it.'

'Nice to see you, too,' Isaac murmurs, then looks to where Thea is standing by the front door, smiling at her friends. 'Why don't you put your luggage upstairs?' he says loudly to Urvisha and Ayo.

'Good idea,' Rosy says, taking up the mantle of playing host. 'Let me show you to your rooms.' She leads the two new arrivals upstairs, past the white dustsheets lying across the bannisters, and Isaac hurries out of the front door.

'Have we gone back in time?' he says to Thea quickly. 'They've all turned up, just like in the other world.'

'We haven't time travelled,' she says. 'It's a coincidence – similar personalities making similar decisions. Friends will be friends, whatever universe they're in.'

'We should get out of here,' he says, 'before they see there's two of you. You're wearing a coat – that's good, they might presume Thea in the kitchen has taken it off. Where should we—'

'How are you feeling?' she says, resting the back of her hand on his forehead, and he startles at the compassion, feeling again the kick between them, their shared warmth and affection.

'Like I'm building up a childhood's worth of antibodies in a day,' he says, and her eyes widen.

'Of course, that makes sense.' She looks wistful. 'Did the other Thea tell you that?'

He takes her hand from his forehead and holds it in his. 'Yes – but you'd have figured it out, too. She's had longer to mull things over, because she remembers the jump.' He pulls her out into the darkness of the courtyard, leading her to one of the farm's old cars. 'We have to get out of here – before it gets too messy.'

'Sure,' she says, though she's tired and wants to sit for a moment among friends. 'Where shall we go?'

'Start driving,' Isaac says, 'and we'll find our destination on the road.' She opens his door and takes the key from the glove compartment. 'Risky,' Isaac says.

She waves at the remoteness of the landscape around them. 'Who's going to steal an old banger from here?' She starts the engine and as it turns over it chugs, before they pull away, down the drive towards the village.

There are hardly any streetlamps as they wind past the Lancashire villages, along roads edged by the omnipresent dry-stone walls, the trees and ferns watched over by electricity pylons looming large in the dark.

'Where am I heading?' Thea says.

Isaac opens the glove box in front of him and pulls out an ancient A–Z. 'London,' he says, throwing a glance at her reaction.

'At this time of night? It's already dark.'

He opens the A–Z. 'There's something I'd like us to look at.'

'Let me guess,' she says, diverting left as she sees a sign for a motorway. 'You can't tell me . . . you can only show me?'

'Something like that,' he says good-naturedly, 'but I promise it's not such a dramatic revelation this time.'

They drive in silence for a while, finding the quiet companionable as they watch the landscape roll by.

'I waited by the bridge for you for an hour, you know.'

'I'm sorry. Thea – she made me join her for a four-mile hike.'

Thea's alert to the significance of the distance. 'She took you out to the Hanging Stones?'

'Yes.' Isaac winces as they pull onto the motorway, the bright lights harsh after the darkness of the countryside. 'We talked a little about what she could remember after the jump, since she landed here.'

'She knew you were . . . from her old world?'

'Yes. She said perhaps she can remember everything because she instigated the jump.'

'Well. How was it?' Thea says, hoping her question isn't quite as transparent as it feels.

He rests his hand on where hers sits on the gearstick. 'It was just like the old days,' he says, 'and when I say "old days", I mean the very platonic old days when we were just friends.'

'Oh,' Thea says. 'I'm sorry.'

'I'm not.'

She looks down at his hand on hers, relieved. 'Did you walk by Whitendale Farm? Did she tell you what happened there?'

'She didn't mention anything in particular. Why?'

'I just wondered.' She brakes as a car pulls into their lane in front, and in the pause as she takes her hand back, she looks at Isaac, his profile lit by the streetlamps outside. 'This is all getting terribly complicated,' she says.

'I know.'

Isaac knows he needed to get them away from Dunsop Bridge, but really what he's doing is buying time as he thinks about his and the other Thea's last conversation. He'd shown her the path he'd mapped through time; from the sitter in the *Portrait of an Unknown Woman*, wearing the three rings that both parallel Theas wear on their hands, to the sales docket of Admiral Joseph Coleman – later Colman – and his great-grandson, Thea's grandfather. But he hadn't been greeted with the smile of delight he'd expected. Instead, Thea had frozen as he'd shown her the photos on his phone of the supporting documents, including her own bank statements with the payment for the painting in 1908.

'Don't you see?' she'd said. 'This is bad – very bad.' She'd paced around the kitchen, pulling the white sheet from the table and throwing it irritably to one side, a sparkle of dust motes flying up. 'The painting, the seller, the sitter . . . We're getting entangled in time.'

'Entangled?' Isaac had said.

'I know you probably think this is charming,' she said, sliding the postcard towards him. 'It bears all your hallmarks. But we're messing with timelines outside our control. This is a history which wasn't meant to be changed.'

'So what do we do?' Isaac had asked.

Thea had pulled out a notebook, starting to map their chronology. 'We have to detangle our timeline, leaving as little out of kilter as possible. Which will start with us both going back. We'll have to go home, you and me.'

Isaac stares out of the window as they move from motorway to motorway, progressing down the country towards London. They stop at a neon-bright service station, every poor bastard there sporting a greenish tinge as though they were all travelling after some hellish bender.

'We're going to arrive in London at crazy o'clock,' Thea says, sipping her thick milkshake as they sit overlooking the road, the rhythm of the passing cars slow at this time of night: a flash of headlights every five to ten seconds, the bending of the engine noise in a red shift.

'That's good,' Isaac says. 'We can watch the sunrise.' His phone rings, but it cuts off before he can mute the call, so he puts the phone back in his pocket.

They enter London from the north, past empty retail parks and a huge shopping centre surrounded by uninhabited car parks. There's little traffic as Isaac directs them using the ancient A–Z; there's no rush as they discover new ring roads and one-way systems not marked on the well-thumbed pages. They laugh, following wherever the road takes them, finding themselves further east than either of them has ever been. 'Take that road,' Isaac says, pointing across her so she doesn't miss it. 'We need to head west into central London.'

They move on a relatively straight route from the east of London towards the river, passing Tube stations closed for the night and corporate-looking hotels. 'I spent some time with Rosy today,' Thea says quietly. 'It was so good to see her.'

Isaac is gentle. 'Of course, she's your Rosy from this world,' he says. 'But she's not the Rosy we lost – the Rosy from my world is still missing.'

'I know,' Thea says, forlorn. 'I feel guilty every day.'

'Thea,' he starts, 'did someone swap places with Rosalind, like how you swapped places with the other Thea?'

It's a good question, and she thinks about the answer. 'I don't think so, no,' she says. 'During Rosy's experiment, we used an optic prism. I don't think it was powerful enough, and it had no personal connection to Rosy. You and I – we only got here by using my family heirloom.'

This chimes with what the other Thea had told him about diamonds, so he's quiet.

'Do you think she's trapped somewhere, then?' he asks. 'If it was enough to make her disappear, but . . .'

'. . . Not powerful enough to make her reappear.' Thea nearly crashes the car, so she pulls over. 'Shit. I'd always presumed she was trapped somewhere in the past, you know? Like London in the 1980s or something. Not trapped . . . between worlds.'

They look at each other in horror.

'Oh my God,' Thea says. 'She could be in the glass house somewhere . . .'

'Calm down,' Isaac soothes, 'I'm sure she's not. Don't imagine the worst-case scenario—'

But it's too late: both of them can't stop imagining Rosalind stuck somewhere, unable to return.

'We have to help her,' Thea says fervently.

'Of course. That's why we're here.'

They pull out on to Victoria Embankment and, with no forewarning, they're suddenly next to the River Thames. Thea swings the car into a parking space near a glorious bridge and puts the handbrake on, turning off the engine. 'Here,' she says. 'This looks like a good place to watch the dawn.'

They're parked opposite a pier, festoon lighting strung along the riverbank, the white structures of the bridge alight like sails of a ship. Preoccupied, they lean their seats as far back as they'll go and Thea digs some old woollen blankets out from the boot of the car. She spreads the blankets across them, her legs tucked up by the handbrake, resting lightly against him. As they reach the coldest part of the night before dawn, she leans into him, her head on Isaac's shoulder, and absently he strokes her hair as they move in and out of sleep.

'Isaac.' Thea shakes him awake gently, but he moans and rolls to the far side of the car seat, away from her. 'Isaac, wake up.' She leans over him, trying to get his attention, but after his bout of flu sleep has him in its grip.

'Gerroff,' he says, pulling the blanket over his face. 'Five more minutes.'

Thea shakes the stiffness out of her limbs, and climbs on top of him in the passenger seat. The windows are wet with the breath of condensation, but light is breaking across the sky so she pulls his ear. He moans again, and she laughs, sticking a finger in his open mouth.

'You are really annoying,' he grumbles, opening one eye.

She pokes him in his open eye.

'Ow!'

'Wake up –' she laughs quietly – 'you're missing the sunrise.'

He lowers the blanket, looking at the windscreen but also at Thea, sitting on his lap being playful. He can't bear for this to be over. 'Come on, then.' He opens the car door and they brace themselves for the cold, feeling the creeping chill as Thea climbs out of the door first, then pulls him after her.

She takes his hand as they jog to the pier, the festoon lighting still ablaze, and after a second's pause she hurdles the railings and indicates for him to do the same. They run down the pier, the wood creaking beneath their feet, and since no boats are moored they sit on the edge of the dock, watching the sky.

As dawn finally emerges across the eastern sky they settle, her head on his shoulder, hand in hand. The light is totally and utterly yellow, the sky around the sunrise turning white.

'It's strange seeing London so empty,' he says, and she agrees. There's a silence while he tries to form his next sentence in the right way. 'What do you think would happen if I didn't go back? If I stayed here, with you?'

She widens her eyes, watching the blooming skyline. 'I was thinking about this when I was with Rosy earlier,' she says, the timbre of her voice even. 'She's the Rosy from my world, who's been spending time with the other Thea, while I've been with you. And now she's here, and you're here, and I'm here, too . . .' She looks down at the water beneath their feet, the tide beneath the surface of the Thames surprisingly strong. 'I'm worried about the ripples we're creating. They're getting bigger and bigger,' she says.

He nods slowly, watching the same section of water beneath their feet ebb and flow. This was the answer he'd feared.

'Actually, maybe water makes a good metaphor for time. Not only do the waves spread, rippling out far and wide, but also, if you put something into water that doesn't belong there, precisely the same volume of water is pushed out of the way.'

' "Something that doesn't belong there" – like a person?'

'That's my fear,' Thea says. 'Me being in your world, or you being in mine, means we are pushing spacetime – or something else, something we haven't grasped yet – out of our way. And where is that going? What are the repercussions of us both being out of time?'

'I don't know.' He considers the idea.

'It's wrong,' she says. 'So I don't think you can stay.'

The festoon lights click off above their heads, clearly programmed to do so during daylight hours, and they jump in surprise.

'Why are we here?' she asks. 'In London?'

'Let's get breakfast, then I'll show you.'

The Tate Modern opens to visitors at ten o'clock and, after stashing the car in an all-day car park for an extortionate fee, a sleepy and rumpled Thea and Isaac head across the Millennium Bridge to the monolith of the gallery.

'More art,' Thea says, apprehensively. 'Don't tell me you've found me in another painting?'

'Ha very ha,' he says. They walk into the Turbine Hall, the sloping, descending floor of the cavernous entrance space covered with a plush, brightly coloured striped carpet. Visitors lie across the floor at various angles, their eyes on the ceiling. Isaac and Thea glance at each other in confusion, before looking up.

'Oh, my,' Thea says, as she spots the giant metal pendulum above their heads. The mirrored sphere swings steadily back and forth across the Turbine Hall, reflecting the faces from the striped carpet, unceasing in its movement.

'It's a commission by an artists' collective called Superflex,' Isaac reads. 'Did you ever come here when it was a giant setting sun?' But Thea is mesmerized by the swinging pendulum, and doesn't answer. 'Theodora?'

She watches the motion with a slight frown, tracing the arc with her finger.

'Earth to Thea.'

She repeats the movement, her hand hovering at a particular moment in its swing. She's startled as a fragment of a thought comes to her, then realizes her phone is ringing with a video call. 'Urvisha is FaceTiming me,' she says, showing Isaac.

But as she slides to answer the call, she can hear her own voice saying, 'Hello,' and Urvisha asking her what she wants for breakfast.

'What—'

She shows Isaac what's happening, and he hurriedly disconnects the call, putting his thumb over the camera. 'What happened?' she asks.

'Thea answered.'

'How is that possible?' she says.

'Haven't you ever had it where your phone and your laptop both ring with the same call because they share a number?' he says. 'Multiple devices synced to the same telephone number, the same email address, the same account in the cloud.'

'But my number is mine,' Thea begins, then realizes that in a parallel world, parallel Theas would have parallel phone numbers. 'God,' she says, disgusted. 'Is nothing my own any more?'

He holds her phone, trying hard not to blink when she tells him her four-digit pin so he can unlock it and unsync it from the other Thea's phone. 'One nine zero eight,' he repeats. 'Did you change that recently?'

A blush creeps across her cheeks. 'I wanted to remember our day in London.'

He snorts, secretly touched.

They don't talk much as they walk through the brightly lit rooms upstairs, bypassing the most famous pieces in the collections as they head straight for the reason Isaac has brought them here.

'Oh,' Thea breathes, taking in the sculpture in front of her. 'It's the curlew.'

Barbara Hepworth's *Stringed Figure (Curlew), Version II* stands in front of her, regal in its prominence. The green brass picks up the ambient light from the huge white gallery room and shows off the patina.

'In real life you can see it's an abstract bird,' Isaac says, pointing to the folded corners of the triangle that form the wings. But Thea is staring with terrifying intensity at the intersecting strings of reddish-brown cotton.

'Forget water – this is how I imagine time,' Thea says, her voice a whisper. 'Multiple strands of tight cotton strings, held in suspension – crossing each other but never meeting.' She looks up at Isaac, the happiest he's ever seen her. 'Timelines. Spools of string, connected but all separate.'

He marvels at how she uses metaphors, from the ripples in the water by the Thames to the twanging of strings as spacetime.

Perhaps it's part of a genius mind; the ability to visualize a meta-physical concept as a physical entity.

Thea leans in so that Isaac has to stop her from touching the strings in case one of the guards sees her. 'Isaac, do you believe an artist could imagine time like this if she hadn't seen it?'

'Isn't that what artists do?' he says.

'Look at it. Doesn't it strike you as weird that this is so exactly what we're experiencing? I mean, this strand could be my leap to your world –' she follows a taut string with her finger – 'and this could be yours, crossing mine the other way, converging. And here is Thea, in a tandem opposite me . . .' She trails off, entranced. 'If only the strings were suspended within a round shape, you could ostensibly say it was the Earth—'

'Hepworth made a sculpture exactly like that,' Isaac says quietly. 'There's a picture in the book. Round, like a world made from split wood. It's called *Pelagos*.'

'What does that mean?' Thea asks.

Isaac smiles: finally the Linguistics part of his degree has some worth. 'It means "sea",' he says, surprised. 'That's so odd – you're talking about strands of time and the ripple effects in water. And so is one of the best sculptors who ever lived, who died long before you were born.' He takes her hand. 'Do you think . . . ?'

'Oh my God,' Thea breathes, admiring Hepworth's sculptures, tracing the tensile strings with her fingers, a physical representation of the entanglement she and her friends are causing. 'This is telling – no, *showing* – us something.'

'What?'

'It's saying . . . ' Thea follows three strands to where they converge in an intricate cross-pattern, light shining through the strings. 'Our timelines are about to get seriously fucked up.'

Isaac can't even laugh at her swearing, because she's right.

Twenty-four

They take the same route back up to Lancashire, drawing lines on an invisible map of the country, tracing every road they've travelled on this quest. Isaac is at the wheel while Thea naps beneath his jacket. Some of her best thoughts come in the state between dreaming and waking, but it's hard to clasp them without falling into deep sleep and forgetting everything you've conjured.

As they drive north, Thea is thinking about seeing her friends again: Ayo, Urvisha and Rosy, all waiting at the house. Her house.

She can't imagine what it's like for the alternative Ayo and Urvisha back in the other world, who've lost their Rosy – she can't imagine what it would be like not to have seen her, not to have felt the sweet respite from guilt, spending time together yesterday in the wood. She must fix this, for everyone's sake.

Rosy is a prisoner of time and Thea holds the key to her release.

'Isaac?' she says sleepily, and he turns down the ancient car radio, which is playing some obscure indie rock. 'You said Thea remembered everything?'

'I did – she does,' he says, his eyes on the road.

'Did she wake up on the floor of the barn, too, after our jump?' she says, and he flicks a look at her because she sounds mournful.

'Yes. Before the others even went to Dunsop Bridge. You were there on your own.'

Thea bites her lip, envisaging the timeline. 'Oh yes. I was looking at the grandfather clock pendulum, and you messaged me something about ghosts. Then I went out to the barn . . .'

'Sounds right.'

'It was before Rosy jumped,' she said.

Isaac nods.

'I lost her. The other Thea was here.' She's quiet for a moment, before she speaks again. 'If only I could go back and change it so that Rosy never jumped,' she says. She rests her face in her hands for a minute, before the rocking motion makes her feel travelsick, so instead she watches the horizon.

∞

Isaac is unnerved by her comment, remembering a conversation he'd had with the other Thea, and what she had said – somewhat more brutally – when they'd discussed quantum entanglement. 'I wish there was a way to go back to the point when the timeline split,' she'd said, 'and undo every deviation that has happened since.'

But Isaac doesn't want to undo everything that's happened since. And he hopes this Thea doesn't want that, either.

The spanner in the works is Lady Rosalind de Glanville, missing somewhere in time. He wishes he could be okay with leaving her out there, potentially lost somewhere in the deep vacuum of space.

'Do we really have to go back?' she says, and he nearly swerves off the road.

'To – Dunsop Bridge?'

'Yes. Where did you think I meant?'

'Never mind,' he says, returning his focus to the motorway.

'Hey – red car.'

'What?' Isaac says, reaching to turn off the radio.

She gives him a sleepy smile that makes him melt. 'Yellow car,' she says, and he scans the nearby vehicles for the offending colour. 'Damn,' he says. 'If I'd have known—'

'Red car. Come on, Mendelsohn, you're losing three-nil.'

'This is a stupid game for two people,' Isaac grumbles, crossing his fingers he can prove his reactions aren't entirely dulled. 'Aha! Red car,' he says, and they debate the position of burgundy on the colour wheel – if it's a valid red – past the Midlands, into Lancashire and all the way to Dunsop Valley beyond.

They arrive mid-afternoon to find an unexpectedly sunny day up north. After the rains of London and the chilly night they'd spent in the car, turning stiff from the cold and sore from sleeping in the seats, it's a delight to see the rolling moors lit with all the different shades of autumn. 'Where shall I head?' Isaac says as they reach the turning for the farm, and Thea squints towards the house, looking for signs of life.

'I don't know. We need to sit and draw the timeline, I think, and work out what to do – maybe we could use your jazzy drawing app.'

'Only if you repeal the use of the word *jazzy*,' he says, parking the car outside the farm. 'We're probably best going back out to the barn,' he says apologetically. 'Keep a low profile.'

'Okay,' she replies easily.

She gets out, stretching her legs before walking round the side of the farmhouse to the kitchen garden, nipping quickly behind the wildly overgrown plants in case she's spotted. They make their way across the three paving stones, past the dovecote, then turn towards the barn—

'So you see,' the other Thea is saying, 'I built a replica of the Beecroft laser, right here in the barn.'

'Fuck,' Isaac says, backtracking.

Ayo, Urvisha, Rosy and Thea stand by the open door of the barn, letting the afternoon sunshine light up the dark wooden interior as they examine the setup.

Thea stands rooted still, as though she wants them to turn and see her. But Isaac nudges her, then tugs at her arm, and after a beat she reverses back a few steps and shelters by the dovecote, a tall, cylindrical brick building from the eighteenth century. Thea quietly kicks at the low, rotting door with her toe until it gives, and they hurry in.

The inside of the round building is filled with small stone nest holes at every height around the walls, with a central wooden pivoted post supporting a revolving ladder.

'Wow,' Isaac says, looking up and turning round.

'My father used to keep pigeons.' She eyes the pigeonholes as though they might still be inhabited, not rotten and long empty. She hops onto the ladder with such familiarity that he almost reaches out to stop her, in case the wood splinters, but he realizes he's being irrational as he watches her climb the ladder with ease, up to the oak arms at the top where she peers into the nearest nest box. 'There might actually be some squabs living in here,' she calls, and he makes a surprised face.

'Squabs?'

'Young birds.'

Isaac stares up at Thea, his back to the door. 'Do they produce eggs? Eggs would be nice for breakfast,' he says.

'You're always thinking about your stomach,' a voice says from behind him, and he whirls round to see Thea standing in the door.

But she's up the ladder.

Two Theas.

'Hi. What are you doing h . . .' she says, but her voice trails off as she sees Thea at the very top by the conical ceiling, climbing the ladder in the exact way her father used to when she was little. 'Who . . . what . . . the hell?'

'Oh, fuck.' He looks from Thea to Thea in dismay.

Thea looks down from the ladder at her doppelganger standing in the low doorway. 'Hi,' she says, her voice echoing gently inside the brick holes.

'This is . . . Oh. I'm officially lost for words.' The Thea in the doorway pulls the rotten wooden door shut behind her. The light inside immediately drops, the small bird holes creating shafts of sunlight across the dovecote.

'First time in your life, I'd expect.'

Both Theas scowl at Isaac, and he mouths 'Sorry.'

'So this was the secret you were keeping – why I couldn't quite make your story add up?' Thea says from by the door.

'Yes.'

She scratches her head. 'I suppose it stands to reason that, in two parallel worlds, two versions of the same person would make the jump.'

Thea climbs a little way down the ladder, clearly not yet willing to come all the way back to the ground.

'This is – weird.' She looks down at Isaac and he looks up at her, a pleading expression in his eyes. *Please don't make this weird.*

She's wearing a white top, the same one she slept in last night – looking down at a version of herself wearing a navy top.

Light and dark, Isaac thinks, *yin and yang. She'll be bad cop, you be good cop.*

'It's really nice to meet you,' the bad cop says from by the door, and the good cop on the ladder wears a look that says: *damn*.

'You, too.'

'Statistically speaking,' Thea continues, walking a little further into the dovecote from the door, 'we might be the only people in our parallel worlds ever to meet ourselves.'

'True,' Thea says lightly, still standing on the rungs of the ladder. 'And it only took a prism full of light years to do so.'

Isaac hides a smile. He thought it would be hard to tell the Theas apart, but it's easy: one is his friend who sometimes talks like Spock; the other, the love of his life, who is becoming increasingly poetic.

'I'm worried Rosy didn't meet her – what do we call it? *Doppelganger* seems so predictable,' Thea says from the ladder.

'Counterpart,' the Spock-like Thea suggests, then frowns. 'I agree, I don't think she made it this far. The methodology doesn't sound quite right—'

'It wasn't,' Thea says, coming down a few more rungs. 'I was there, and we didn't use the correct prism. It was a plain optic crystal.' Colour floods into her cheeks at her own perceived failure. 'I hadn't made the connection then, like you had.'

The other Thea shrugs, nonchalant. 'It was just luck I tried the diamond that day – and it probably was for you, too. We'd have got there with the theory eventually.'

'Thank you. I agree,' she says, and Isaac rolls his eyes – two Theas, puzzle-solving together? The dovecote is claustrophobic, and he wishes, as they both clearly do from the way they're eyeing each other, that they had a larger space for this unexpected meeting.

'Are the others—?' he starts.

'They're heading back to the house.' Thea walks from the door to a nest box, tipping out the contents from the pigeon-hole, her navy top almost disappearing in the gloom at the bottom of the dovecote.

The other Thea hops from the lower rungs of the ladder until she's also standing on the stone floor, covered with stray pieces of straw. 'Each of these holes used to house a bird,' she says dreamily. 'Can you imagine?'

'Yes,' Thea says simply.

'Imagine when they were all in flight, spooked perhaps, div-ing for the holes to the outside world. The squawking, the flapping of wings – their paths crossing in the air . . .'

Both Theas stand staring upwards, imagining an intersec-tion of birdwings before they both look at each other. 'The timelines have got so muddled,' one says, and frankly it could be either of them.

'I know.'

'The ripples of us both being here – and Isaac . . .'

'We don't know what the fallout will be.'

The Thea wearing white leans against the oak ladder, look-ing down at the loose straw covering the stone floor. 'We jumped before Rosy; I fear she's fallen between our split time-lines, lost somewhere.'

'I know.' Thea examines a fossilized eggshell fragment, turning it round on her thumb. 'I was saying to Isaac that I wish there was a way to go back to the split, and undo every deviation that has happened since.'

Isaac sucks in a breath; the thought of undoing everything he feels is too much to bear. But he sees the Thea in white jolt at the idea, and he recognizes the frown, how she rubs the baby hair at her temple, deep in thought. Somewhere a spark has been lit in her mind. It's not yet a light bulb moment; more like the tiny flicker of a match being scratched.

'If only it really *was* a time machine,' the other, more pragmatic Thea goes on. 'Not a portal.'

'You want to go back to the split,' the Thea in white repeats, 'back to that *particular* moment in time?'

'If it was possible, it would bring Rosy back. Wouldn't it? Because she never would have jumped.'

Thea exhales. 'Perhaps the original theory could help us out, here. If you travelled faster than the speed of light then, theoretically . . .'

'. . . You could arrive somewhere before you left.' Isaac nods, chiming in. 'I know this one.'

They both look at him as though remembering for the first time he's still there. The Thea wearing navy taps her foot. 'But it wasn't time travel. We were wrong.'

'The theory still stands, though, doesn't it?' Other Thea says, still leaning on the ladder, her white top illuminated by the shafts of light coming in through the pigeonholes.

'I suppose so.'

She moves away from the ladder, thinking hard. 'We both got here by slowing the speed of light in a prism. And the trapped light inside that prism oscillates, like a pendulum.'

'I see . . .'

'*Like a pendulum*,' the Thea in white repeats. She runs her hand along the rounded wall of the dovecote, thinking hard. 'The trapped light in the prism is bouncing back and forth, interacting with more matter because it's been slowed, oscillating between two states like a pendulum.'

Isaac and the Thea wearing navy both stare at her.

'It's oscillating between two states,' she says again, more emphatically. 'This is pure time crystal theory! Urvisha and Ayo discarded the concept of spacetime, because it didn't suit their hypothesis at the time. But it's worth remembering that everything happening inside the prism with the speed of light is happening in space, so it's also happening in time.'

Triumphant, she looks at their confused faces – well, one confused, one less so. 'Imagine it in four dimensions,' she says. 'The movement inside the prism – the pendulum swing – isn't only between left and right, up and down. That's what it is in *space*. But in *time* – the pendulum is swinging between the past and the present.'

'Oh,' the Thea in navy says, breathing in.

'This is four-dimensional spacetime. So if we fire the laser as the light wave is trapped at the slowest part of the pendulum arc, when the pendulum is swinging towards the past . . .'

The other Thea considers. 'Then when it carries us away, it would take us towards the past.'

'Yes! You *could* travel back in time.' She appeals to Isaac, who is watching them bounce physics between them in the confined dovecote. 'Now we know what we're dealing with, we can manipulate it in our favour.'

He squints, trying to recall everything he's learned in the last few days; all the theories, all the science. He's determined to keep up with the Theas but it's no good.

'Hold on. What are you saying?' Isaac says. 'That it *is* actually a time machine?'

'It's both. It's a portal, because a jump takes you onto a different timeline. And it's a time machine, because you can also jump to *a moment in the past* on the other timeline.'

'Specifically,' the Thea in navy says quickly, 'we could jump to the moment before both Thea and I jumped.'

Isaac looks between them. 'And what would that mean?' he says, fearing he doesn't want to know the answer.

The Thea in white finally speaks. 'If you and Thea return to your world at a time before Rosy ever made the jump, she'll be there when you go back. You'll arrive before you left – and before she left, too.'

The other Thea nearly bounces with excitement at the potential solution. 'It would put Rosy right back where she belongs . . . Rosy would never disappear.'

Isaac speaks quietly. 'What about me?'

'Nothing can be left out of place on the timeline, or it might not work,' Thea says, and the kindness in her tone tells him which Thea she is.

'What if we return there, and another version of us jumps here?' he says.

'I don't think it works like that,' she answers, before the other Thea can speak. 'Remember the mirror.'

Isaac gives her a look. This is not the time for further extended scientific explanations.

'Two worlds in reflection symmetry,' she reminds him. 'When the timeline splits, one world goes left, the other goes right.'

'She's right.' Thea steps back from where she's been listening by the door, so he can see her navy top in the light of the pigeon-holes. 'Our two worlds are paired because of what we've done. The other worlds aren't out of kilter – not yet, at least.'

'Especially if we jump back to before this began, and return it all to the way we found it.' The Thea in white moves towards him. 'We're detangling the timelines. It's what we have to do.'

'Oh,' he says, his last bastion of hope smashed. 'So . . . I definitely have to go back, too?'

She looks at Isaac with imploring eyes. 'Remember the *Curlew*? And the displaced water?' she says.

'And the *Unknown Woman*?' the other Thea interjects. 'We're not just changing our time, we're changing all of time.'

'We need to detangle the strings,' Thea says. 'Everything will go back to the way it was if I stay here, and you both jump back to before all this ever happened.'

The other Thea smiles broadly, determined. 'It's the only way to save Rosy.'

Twenty-five

Isaac whispers 'No!' and both Theas look at him: one, uncomprehending, the other with her heart breaking. The latter looks away first, closing her eyes as though her eyelids could shield her from the tide of emotion, from the truth of their situation.

'We can't do this,' Isaac says to both of them. 'There must be another way.'

'There isn't,' Thea says, though she's gentle. 'It's my fault, Isaac – Rosy is gone because I was careless. Because of that, our friend is missing.'

The original Thea stands by the dovecote door, an understanding dawning as she looks from Isaac to Thea, and back to Isaac. 'Guys – you haven't, have you?'

'There has to be something else we can try,' he says. 'Something that won't . . . *undo* . . . everything.'

'Oh, crikey,' the other Thea says with a grimace. 'This is very messy indeed.'

'Can we have a minute?' Thea asks. 'To sort this out.'

She nods. 'I'll be in the barn.'

If Thea dares look at Isaac's anguished face, she'll shatter. So she simply nods, her manner brusque. 'Right. Thank you,' she adds, as the other Thea exits the dovecote, pulling the door behind her to give them some privacy.

'Let's get out of here,' Thea says, claustrophobic in the small cylindrical building.

'Really?' he says, looking hopeful.

'Oh – I didn't mean . . . Let's take a walk.' She takes his hand to soften the blow, stepping from the building out into the fading afternoon light. She remembers at the last moment to look around for the others and to avoid being seen. It's hard to believe this is her world; she's been behaving like an intruder, tiptoeing around the farmhouse and away from her friends. But she belongs here. Her farm, her barn, her dovecote . . . but not her Isaac.

'I could stay here with you,' he says, as though reading her mind.

A wave of fresh exhaustion hits her. They walk across the kitchen garden towards the woods that border the farmland. She knows they'll have to go to the glass house, momentarily; she knows there's no real time left to make him see this is the only thing that can be done.

'This isn't your world, Isa,' she says quietly, as the sky takes on the baby blues and pinks of candyfloss, as though the day knows it has one last moment in which to dazzle, and exerts itself in a display of colour before the inevitable fade to night.

'It doesn't matter – I'm sure I could stay here and be with you. Nobody will even notice that I'm gone.'

'It would be wrong.' She blinks. 'We have to reset the time-lines back to the way they were,' Thea says, inhaling hard when he reaches for her hand as they walk between the trees. 'If you stay in this universe, when you belong in the other, you could get lost between worlds, too.'

He looks distraught. 'You don't know that.'

'No, I don't. Not for sure. But I'm not willing to risk it. We need to put everyone back where they're meant to be.'

He pauses. 'You are so goddamned *stubborn*,' he says. 'Tell me, do you want to be right, or do you want to be happy?'

She's silent.

'I don't think you could live with yourself if it meant having to live with being *wrong*.'

'That's not it,' she says, though he's closer to the bone than she might expect. 'It's my fault, Isaac: I made Rosy disappear. I can't live with the guilt of that.'

'It's not your fault—'

'Don't you see?' Her voice breaks. 'It's always been my fault. I have *never* done right by Rosy when it comes to you.'

He pauses. 'I'm responsible for that, too.'

'And that's why we can't. We can't risk doing anything that would mean the timeline doesn't go back to the way it was.' Thea picks up a fallen branch with a spray of dying leaves, and she begins to tear them off, yellowing leaf by yellowing leaf. 'With every jump, with every displaced person, the strings of time entangle, weaving a web where people could get hurt . . . the effects unknown.' She throws the leaves up into the air and, mesmerized, Isaac watches them float to the ground, landing in chaos.

'You could come with me,' he suggests. 'It doesn't have to be the other Thea. If there was one of you in each world—'

'That wouldn't work; we'd still be out of time,' she says gently, letting go of the branch so it falls to the ground with a crunch. 'Don't you think the fact we both got sick when we landed in each other's world is a hint? We're not meant to be there – we don't belong.'

He blanches. Knowing someone is right, even if you don't want to hear it, is an uncomfortable feeling; staying quiet, even more so. 'Well, fuck. This is awful.'

'I know.'

'Do you? Or do you not give a shit because you've got another Isaac here, who's probably in love with you, too?'

Her eyes widen in surprise. 'Is that what you think – that I could move what I feel for you onto him, like you're the same? Because you should know more than *anyone* how specific it is to be in love with an individual, and not someone else because they look or sound like them.'

He's silent.

'Jesus.' She kicks the branch and it disintegrates, woodlice crawling out and scuttling away across the forest floor.

'I'm sorry. It's— I feel like I only just found you.'

'I know,' she says. 'I feel the same.'

His face is desperate. 'Please, Thea. You're saying I can't live here with you. But I'm not sure I can live *without* you. I could stay—'

'You can't,' she says, the catch in her voice betraying her emotion.

He puts his hand pleadingly on her but she shakes him off, instead putting her arms around his waist in a tight hug. Surprised, he holds her, then after a moment finds her mouth with his and kisses her as the light fractures behind the trees. It's a desperate kiss, the weight of their situation pressing down upon them both.

She pulls back, reaching to touch the bow of his lip with her index finger, committing the shape and feel to memory. 'You essentially just quoted "With or Without You",' Thea says as they hold each other again, seeking the warmth of one another. 'I told you it was Shakespearean equivocation,' she whispers, trying anything to lighten the mood, and he smiles into her hair, the moment bittersweet.

'It will be my favourite song, when I get back.'

She lets go of the hug but not of him. 'If I thought there was any other way—'

'I understand.' He pulls her under his arm and she tucks herself around his waist, one hand resting on his chest, and they walk this way through the wood together, entwined for perhaps the last time. 'The problem with you being a genius,' he says, 'is if there was even a chance of there being *any* other option, I know you'd have explored it.'

'Think about the sculpture we saw. How many times did the deep red fishing lines cross one another?' She looks up at him expectantly, and he nods. 'Just once,' she answers. 'More than once, and the strings would be tangled, knotted. Some might even snap. So although I want you to stay here with me – or me to come back with you . . . we can't.'

He leans his chin against her hair and she rests her hand against the back of his neck. He can feel the coolness of her three rings against his skin, and the warmth of her taunting him in every place they touch, from their knees to their faces. He tilts her head, kissing her again before he no longer can. And she in turn pulls him closer, tighter, realizing when she'd started the experiment she had wanted memories she could transport back across spacetime, without considering that the grief might not come from those memories, but from finding the great love of her life in an impossible parallel world.

The thought of grief sobers her. She takes his hand. 'Promise me something. When you get back, you can't let this – us – consume you.'

'But it's so unfair,' he says. 'You'll flit into my mind every time I speak to the other Thea. When I see Rosy or the others, I'll remember. Every time I walk around a London gallery, or rent a Boris bike, or go for a fried breakfast in the afternoon, I'll think of you.'

She smiles in agony, gesturing past the trees back towards the farmhouse, diverting his attention away from the sorrow she knows is emblazoned across her face. 'I doubt I'll ever be able to go back to the barn without thinking of our journey here together.' She tightens her grip on his hand. 'You chased away the ghosts for me, Isa. Because of you, I feel more connected to my past than ever.'

'I can't believe I'll never see you again.' They look at one another in anguish, marking the silence as their last minutes together tick by.

'Do you remember,' she says slowly, regarding the fading pastel colours of the sky, 'the ecliptic? That feeling – as though we were on the edge of the universe.'

'As if we could wave, and the other planets would see.'

She smiles. 'I'll wave.'

'I'll wave back,' he swears. 'Every single conjunction, I'll be there.'

'No,' Thea says quickly, 'not all. There's a conjunction almost every week, if you look hard enough; we'd be grieving each other all the time. I want you to move on with your life.'

'How could I?' he says. 'How can I possibly do that?'

'Please, Isaac,' she begs, holding onto him. 'Only the rarest alignments. A once-in-a-decade conjunction.'

'When we can see five planets at once,' he says, understanding, 'lined up with our viewpoint on Earth.'

'Earths,' she amends gently, and the distinction almost breaks him. 'Believe me, I'll be looking at the same arc, looking for you.'

He nods, holding himself together. 'Our alignment.'

With his thumb he gently wipes away a lone tear rolling down her cheek. She blinks and another tear catches in her eyelashes like rain on a spider's web. Without saying a word, both understanding their fate, they walk together past the house, past the overgrown kitchen garden like something from the end of the world, across the paving slabs – *one, two, three* – past the dovecote, and round the corner to the outbuildings.

∞

The other Thea is waiting for them. The glass house is alight, illuminated by the photographic lamps like something out of the Blitz, the beams strong. The control panel for the laser is aglow, ready and programmed. She stands by the prismatic glass making a couple of final adjustments. 'Are you ready?' she asks them both, and when neither answers she lifts her shoulders apologetically. 'We have to go back, Isaac. I'm sorry.'

The Thea at Isaac's side stares at the glass house, imagining the ray of white that will soon fire from the laser, covering the man she loves in light until he disappears from her world. 'How do we stop anyone following in our footsteps?' she asks, and Isaac moans at the question.

'As far as we know,' Thea says from by the glass house, 'in our time, the experiment has only ever worked using this ring.' She raises her hand so the diamond glitters, and Thea raises hers in response; two identical diamonds dancing in the light.

'We dismantle the laser,' Thea next to him says, 'and we—'

'—destroy the rings.'

Isaac is visibly shocked. 'That's a family heirloom. We traced it all the way back to the painting. For all you know, those *are* the rings of Lady Margaret Beaufort.'

Thea puts her hand on his shoulder. 'It has to be done.' She looks across to her doppelganger; so similar and yet, somehow, so different. 'Rosalind got lost when we used any old prism.'

'There's more.' The Thea by the glass house examines the

small hole in the door. 'You destroy the chamber here, and I'll break the glass house when I get back to my world.'

Isaac puts his hands to his eyes. 'All that work – it's your crowning achievement. All that . . . magic . . . Do you really have to go full Frodo?'

Thea slides the ring from her finger and sets it down on the bench beside him. 'Yes. We have to destroy the rings.'

'And everything else.' The Thea wearing navy opens the door and steps into the glass house, urging Isaac to do the same. 'It's time to go home,' she says.

'I'll help with the laser,' Thea offers, leaving Isaac's side to get into position, sweeping her hand along the workbench as she moves across the room. The laser is raised once more, at the same height as the tiny hole in the glass house. 'Do you want to give me your ring? I can fire the light into it, and send you . . . home.'

Home.

'Can't you use your ring?' Thea frowns inside the glass house.

'I think my ring works due to its connection to me, and your ring works through its connection to you.' She considers. 'They're linked, I think – they're what sent us to the same place, each time. To send you home we should use yours – I can destroy it after you've gone. After all, they may look the same –' she smiles, the confession so open she feels naked – 'but they might be entirely different on the inside.'

The other Thea holds the glass house door, weighing her options. 'Yes, all right.' She, too, slides her ring from her finger and, after a pause, hands it to Thea, who moves with it to the laser.

'Isaac?'

Before he steps into the glass house he cups her face for the last time, running his thumb against her jaw and down the edge of her neck. She leans in, pressing against him to mask the drop of something light into his pocket, before they break apart. 'I love you,' he says quietly.

'I love you, too.'

'I'll see you at the ecliptic,' he says, before they close the door. 'Don't forget to wave.'

'I'll be there.' She clenches Thea's ring in her hand as she stands between the laser and the glass house. 'Shepherd's warning.'

'What do you—'

As she fires the laser, unable to say an extended goodbye lest her heart collapses from the grief, Isaac raises his hand on the inside of the glass.

'Thea, no— Wait!'

'Goodbye,' she whispers, resting her hand briefly on the outside of the glass, her palm over his. They both shut their eyes as the light in the barn turns painfully white, and their vision of each other is bleached in the moment, violently drained of colour.

Twenty-six

Oxford, June 2012

The end of the Trinity College Commemoration Ball in the early hours of the morning was a curious sight: the streets of Oxford were suddenly strewn with students in white tie. Women in full-length gowns – some barefoot carrying their heels – were accompanied by men in tailcoats eating kebabs, as they made their way along golden streets, the honeyed stone of the city providing the perfect backdrop to their ana-chronistic hedonism.

Isaac and Thea broke away from the crowd, making their way more soberly back to Christ Church. Isaac's undone bow-tie hung loose around his neck, his top button popped. 'What do you want to watch?' he said as they walked to his accom-modation. 'Do you want food? I have biscuits.'

'A nice cup of tea,' Thea said sleepily, 'and a lie-down. I need to get out of this dress.' She indicated her Hepburn-esque black dress, uncomfortable after twelve hours of wear, and Isaac lightly touched the necklace hanging down her back as she walked up the stairs in front of him.

He opened the door to his cramped room, remembering at the last minute he'd told the bedmaker not to bother cleaning that week, nor had he washed up his dirty mugs. 'Sorry,' he said.

She shrugged. 'I'm used to it. Can I borrow a t-shirt? I really can't breathe in this dress.'

'Of course.' He moved like lightning to his chest of drawers, throwing her a t-shirt from a Cuppers tournament he'd taken part in during the first year.

She flopped down on his bed, unzipping the dress at the back. 'Can you help? I can't reach,' she said, and he sat on the bed next to her, lowering the zip while looking to the sky in prayer.

Isaac rarely used Yiddish phrases because they reminded him of his grandmother, but as he averted his gaze while undressing Thea, *'Oy, vey'* was the only expression that came to mind. *Woe is me. Help me through this.*

Thea looked up, trying to see what he was staring at on the ceiling, then made a face at his odd behaviour. He turned away as she stepped out of her dress and into the t-shirt.

'Err, Isaac?'

'Yes?'

Thea arched an eyebrow. 'It's really short. The t-shirt, I mean.'

'Oh.' He pulled another from the drawer, an oversized American football top purchased during his time in the States, and threw it towards her, where it landed just short of her on the floor. She bent to retrieve it and he bit down on his own knuckle.

She watched Isaac make tea for her, pulling the bowtie from his collar and throwing it aside. He didn't have to ask how she took her tea: they'd spent a lot of time together this way, comfortable and relaxed, while other students went on nights out. The best thing that can happen to a homebody is meeting another.

He unbuttoned his white pique shirt as Thea watched from the bed, eyeing him speculatively as he handed her the mug, feeling the tingle of attraction in the lower part of her belly. Hell, this was complicated.

She scooted over as he sat down, setting up his laptop for them to watch a film. 'Any preference?' he asked, and she shook her head, still shaken by the kick of feeling she appeared to have for her closest friend.

She tried to rationalize it away: an acknowledgement that someone was handsome, or beautiful, wasn't necessarily attraction. But when he grinned at her as the title credits came up, she again felt the pull between them and couldn't dismiss how much she wanted to bite the lip that was smiling broadly at her on his bed.

'*Stargate*?' she said, wrinkling her nose.

'Trust me, you'll love it,' he said, wiggling down so they were lying next to each other, Thea near the screen and Isaac behind her. He handed her the better pillow and she bunched it under her head, watching the opening credits.

'What's it about?' she said.

'James Spader discovers a portal that transports him to another world.'

'Sounds far-fetched.'

But as they lay there, watching the film, it became hard to concentrate on James Spader's world-hopping as Isaac became aware of Thea's bare legs lying against his front, and she aware of his bare torso behind her back. Eventually she turned, so they were face to face, and she looked at him plainly.

He raised an eyebrow. 'Is there—?'

But she cut him off, kissing him before he could speak, before they could question what on earth they were thinking.

They rolled over, so first she was on top, then he was, the splash of tea and the crash of the mug hitting Isaac's floor the only distraction as an entire night of attraction was unleashed between them.

'That dress,' he whispered.

She ran her hands across his chest, feeling every part of him. 'You should smarten up more often – it suits you.'

They scrambled out of their remaining clothes.

While the light of the day strengthened outside, finding their rhythm and moving together in different ways, Isaac and Thea reached their climax – as a bell rang out across the college.

'Is that—?'

They sat up, looking towards Isaac's stone window, peering out to see Tom Tower at the entrance to Christ Church. 'Some drunken fool's climbed up to Great Tom,' Isaac said.

'They're going to be in so much trouble,' Thea said, pulling the bed sheet around her and leaning forward to see, too. 'Look – the bell's swinging.'

Isaac looked back at her, laughing, and they bit out a tangled kiss. But it was over so quickly – too quickly – and they were becoming hyper-aware of their situation, of what they'd just done.

They lay back down together, but the spell was broken by the prank of the swinging bell: Isaac got up to go to the bathroom, and Thea reached down to clean up the spilled cup lying on the floor.

Isaac's phone lay next to the mug, splashes of Earl Grey on the screen. She picked it up to wipe the phone clean with the corner of her borrowed t-shirt. The screen lit up at her touch, a message preview clearly displayed. Sitting up, Thea read it with dismay.

I'll always love you, Isa. You were right, we should get back—

The rest of the message was truncated by the preview, and

without opening his phone there was no way to read the rest of Rosy's message.

But she'd seen enough.

Guilt-stricken, Thea pulled her wrinkled black dress from the floor, forgoing shoes to make her escape unimpeded. As she crept out of the room Isaac reappeared from the bathroom, doing up his trousers, then realized with alarm that Thea was disappearing round the door.

'Where are you—?'

'I shouldn't have come back here.'

'Thea?' he said. 'Don't leave. Let's talk about this—'

'We've made a terrible mistake.'

'Please,' he said. 'I don't know what's happened – but I've wanted . . .'

She shook her head. 'Let's forget it. It's not like it meant anything.'

'Please, stop—'

'It didn't mean anything to me.' She ran from the door to the stairs, and he leaned out to watch her go, utterly confused.

'Theodora, please.'

But she was gone. He walked over to his phone to call her, to explain that it *had* meant something, that if she came back they could talk and figure things out together, like the friends they were and had always been. He lifted his phone and saw the message from Rosy.

He swiped to unlock, frowning slightly.

I'll always love you, Isa. You were right, we should get back to how we used to be, as friends. We mistook platonic love for romantic love. xx Rosy

He rang Thea again and again, but floundering in her own guilt she let his calls ring out for the rest of that week, until everyone went home for the summer, and the university was empty.

∞

Isaac and Thea land back in their own world with little drama. Isaac had sat on the glass seat, heartbroken, and Thea had leant against the side of the chamber, face pressed against the glass, to enjoy the last spectral journey of her lifetime.

'I'm sorry,' she says to him inside the glass house, and Isaac lifts his eyes from the floor to meet hers. 'I don't know what happened, but I'm sorry.'

'It's not your fault,' he says. He looks back through the glass at the night sky, the swelling lines of Earth's atmosphere the colourful sign that their home is approaching.

'Did you know it wasn't me, then? From the start?'

'What?'

'You fell in love with her. So you must have known she wasn't – me.'

Isaac puts his head in his hands. 'Thea, this is really complicated, and I don't think I can explain it right now.'

She grimaces. 'Because there's never been anything like that between us, has there? Not even after that night.'

He thinks about the impossible truth: that he built a love for a person upon his shared history with another person, though they'd both experienced the same with other versions of themselves. *Paging Dr Freud*, he says to himself, but instead he smiles at her. 'I've always loved you, Thea. And I know you love me, too – as a friend. We're friends, that's all. After the ball – we mistook platonic love for romantic love.'

He says what he thinks she'll need to hear, and because she

never read the full extent of Rosy's message, she doesn't recognize the words; she doesn't realize that, *had* she read them, she might never have soaked herself in guilt under the impression she'd slept with her friend's boyfriend.

But Isaac knows. He knows this Thea doesn't feel for him the way the other does, or did. He's left standing in this world with his friend who doesn't love him, has never loved him, while the Thea who returned his love is somewhere out there, separated by the universe.

They step from the glass house into the dark barn, and Isaac immediately notices the setup looks wrong. 'Huh?' he says, and Thea walks round, looking at the laser.

'This isn't right,' she says, moving to the control panel. 'Look how far the laser is from the glass. It's in the wrong position.'

Isaac knows this isn't Urvisha's setup, but it's not Thea's last setup, either. He walks to the door, peering out as though he could conclude from a look whether they are in his world, or the other Thea's. He remembers what they'd observed about reflective symmetry, and he searches for water on the ground to look at its vortex, but finds none.

A huge crash brings him back. He turns, horrified, to see Thea taking the largest of the firewood logs and flinging it as hard as she can into the glass house.

'Wait!' he cries, but it's too late: the log hits the glass and, in slow motion, the chamber teeters. She picks up another log, and another, throwing them at the glass house. Cracks and fractures run up and down the surface until the tension gets too much, and the prismatic glass shatters.

The noise is deafening, and both Thea and Isaac cower, covering their ears. Each surface of the glass house disintegrates with a bang into a pile of glass shards, until all that's left are fragments rolling across the barn floor.

He shuts his eyes in disbelief. If that was the portal, it's gone. All that remains are the two diamond rings with Thea in the other world, and the—

He looks to the laser as Thea focuses her attention on it.

'Oh, God,' Isaac says, as she grabs a screwdriver from the workbench and slides out the laser's vulnerable inner core. He turns away as she smashes the lens with her makeshift wooden bat, throwing up his arms to protect himself from flying debris.

'This hurts me, too,' she whispers, but she doesn't hesitate in the wanton destruction of her life's work. She pushes the laser over onto the ground and kicks it, tramples it, smashing it with the log until the casing is bent out of shape, the interior workings nothing more than detritus on a barn floor.

Thea stops, panting, and sits down on the bench as she surveys the annihilation around her.

Of course she'd be thorough – it's in her nature – but it's still agony to watch.

Isaac doesn't move from the doorway; he's too shocked. 'Are you done?' he says finally, and she nods.

'I had to. And if I didn't do it now, I'd have chickened out.'

'Fair enough,' he says, pulling himself together. 'Shall we see when, exactly, we've arrived?'

'Good idea.'

'Let's hope we're at the right point, now you've destroyed our way back.'

She grimaces, but they walk carefully past the dovecote, meeting each other's eyes before they cross the three paving slabs. At the kitchen garden, Isaac stops, taking a breath before they walk to the kitchen door, and Thea pulls it open. They walk into the farmhouse—

To find nobody there. The house is deserted; white sheets cover the furniture and hang from the light fittings, a layer of untouched dust sitting atop. Thea's boxes of belongings, her bedding and books packed hastily after her exit from Oxford, sit at the bottom of the stairs, where she discarded them after arriving here the day she'd been sent down from her DPhil.

She sighs, sitting down on the stairs. 'Remember, they're only ghosts,' she echoes, and he tilts his head.

Listening for the telltale tick-tock and not hearing it, Isaac gingerly opens the grandfather clock and pulls the pendulum to one side, settling it into a regular swing.

'We're back,' Isaac says.

'And I've been kicked out of Oxford this very morning, apparently.' She indicates her box of belongings on the stairs. 'Which doesn't bode well for my career trajectory.'

'What will you do?' he says, but as he does, they hear the noise of a car outside, and they look at each other with surprise and suspicion.

Thea opens the front door to see a very fancy car driving cautiously along the driveway, pulling up outside the house.

'That's a Rolls,' Isaac says, pointlessly.

Lady Rosalind de Glanville extracts herself elegantly from the vehicle like the Queen, holding an enormous bunch of flowers and an ancient lurcher on a well-worn lead. 'Hello, Thea!' Rosy waves with an excited shriek.

Overawed, Thea runs out onto the turning circle, grabbing hold of Rosy and not letting go. 'You're really here?' she breathes, and Rosy pulls back from the intense hug to look at her.

'Of course. I thought you could do with a friend, or two – or three. Or four,' she says, looking curiously at Isaac. 'Hello, Isaac.' Rosy leans over and kisses him on both cheeks. 'How unexpected! Lovely to see you. How was your journey?'

'Eventful,' he says eventually.

'Well, you did travel rather far,' Rosy says, walking into the house.

'If only you knew.'

But no one's listening.

'I've missed you,' Thea says quietly to Rosy, arm in arm. 'Hello, Cyril.'

'Fancy you remembering his name! You have such a good memory,' Rosy says, patting Cyril's head as he pads into the house next to them, looking for a crotch to sniff.

'Oh look,' Urvisha says, climbing from the rear of the car and breezing past them into the hall, 'our cheerleader is here. Hello, Isaac Mendelsohn.'

'Visha.' He salutes.

'How did you . . . ?' Thea stops talking as Ayo rolls down the car window and makes a face.

'Rosy, do you have the keys?' Ayo gets out of the Rolls-Royce. 'We wouldn't want a car like this to be stolen – the insurance would be a nightmare. Wow, Thea, this is quite a place you've got here – very shabby chic.'

'I like it!' Rosy calls from the kitchen, where she's broken the bouquet up into pint glasses of water. 'Very Miss Havisham.'

'Where exactly are we?' Ayo asks, walking into the house.

'Dunsop Bridge,' Rosy answers. 'We used to go hiking near here with Daddy.'

Isaac takes a deep breath, refamiliarizing himself with the time-line. He reminds himself that the last time the others saw Thea, she was being kicked out of Oxford for a failed experiment. At the point at which he and Thea have arrived back, Ayo, Urvisha and Rosy don't even know Thea recreated the Beecroft laboratory in her own barn. They can't let them see the brutal remains of the laser, or the smashed remnants of the glass house. And they can never, ever tell the others what happened to Rosy, him, or Thea.

Thea hesitates, clearly running through the same thoughts, and – he hopes – drawing the same conclusion. 'Why are you here?'

'Isn't it obvious?' Rosy says.

Thea takes a deep breath. 'You're here because . . . I was wrong.'

Isaac looks at her in astonishment. After all, she was actually right. But nobody, including her friends, will ever know.

'We're here to support you,' Rosy says warmly, putting her hand over Thea's. 'Our experimental days may be over, but perhaps we can go for some nice walks, out on the moors.'

'That would be lovely,' is all Thea says, surreptitiously picking a shard of prismatic glass from Isaac's sleeve, before the five of them begin the routine of stepping into wellies, warm jackets and borrowed coats to make their way off into the great outdoors. 'There are some amazing standing stones a few miles north, if you fancy.'

Ayo shudders. 'That sounds like quite the hike.'

'And they're really creepy,' Isaac says quietly.

They meander towards the farm's border, the village of Dunsop Bridge just beyond. 'Did you know this is technically the dead centre of Great Britain?' Rosy pipes up.

Isaac follows behind, silently wondering if grief has marked his features like a mask.

'Isn't that a bit misleading?' Urvisha says, pulling her coat around her tightly. 'Makes "the Midlands" a misnomer.'

Isaac shivers against the cold. The first leaves are falling off the trees as autumn begins to take hold in Lancashire, and he tucks his fists into his pockets to keep warm. But as they ramble towards the village and the cosy warmth of Puddleducks tearoom, Isaac feels something in the base of his coat pocket nudge against his hand.

An Alignment at Dawn

London, May 2030

It can be beautiful, seeing the planets over a city. Most people want a huge expanse of sky and spurn cityscapes for landscapes, preferring trees and heaths to squares and concrete. But Isaac wakes while it's still dark, the light from the streetlamps pouring in through his open window. He's left the blackout blind up, the curtains open, and by the light of the moon he steps into his trousers, pulling socks over his toes and finding shoes beneath his bed. He touches a hand to his chest, making sure it's still there, next to where his heart used to beat.

He had to decide where to view the ecliptic; at first he revisited all of the places with significance to him and Thea. He went to the pier in London where they had sat swinging their feet, watching the first light; he sat in the quad at Oxford, looking up at their old accommodation windows. He even went to Dunsop Bridge, and watched the dawn break behind the trees.

But it's been years now, over a decade. He's only allowed this one particular alignment, a conjunction – he promised, didn't he? – so he has to make it a good one. He has to make the memory last.

He's thought long and hard, and decided on this place.

Unhurried, Isaac walks through the city, past drunks and couples in trysts hidden down back alleys, making the most of the remaining minutes of darkness. He wanders down the main road, the theatres closed but their advertising boards still glistening in the light from the streetlamps. A bouncer stands outside a casino, and Isaac nods as he walks past, despite the bouncer's suspicious look.

He arrives in the square as the dark night begins to glimmer, the first hint of a new day on the horizon. The lions are shrouded in fog and darkness, the statues cold and black. He walks past them, and past the dormant fountains, until he finds himself at the steps outside the National Gallery, watching the sky.

'Look there.' Thea points. 'The North Star.'

'Are you sure?' Isaac squints. 'I think that's Venus.'

'Isn't it amazing that the light we're seeing is millions of years old? Anyone can be a time traveller, simply by looking at the stars.'

Isaac closes his eyes, the memory almost visceral, praying that when he opens them Thea will be lying on the steps to his right, looking to the stars as she'd done the night he'd told her he would have changed everything.

There's something between us, Thea. I know it.

They had become so distracted – did he ever tell her, in this place, that he was in love with her? He can't be sure, but he knows this is where it started, and here is where he opens his eyes.

Isaac's alone in the darkness of Trafalgar Square, the pigeons sleeping – hiding; the tourists elsewhere. None of them seem to know that a once-in-a-decade planetary alignment is about to hit its peak conjunction in the sky above at 5.09 a.m.

To the east, the first rays hit the clouds, and he catches his breath as the timid streaks of orange begin to light the sky, the moon still visible overhead.

Most people think you have to be in the darkest night to see the pooled light of the planets. But Mercury will be clearest

today while the day is embryonic, the light of the sun illuminating the universe.

And there it is.

There, like an arc of polka dots, lies the ecliptic, and he draws
a breath at the spectacular sight curving away in the sky above
him. As the blueish light of Mercury brightens to meet Venus,
Saturn, Jupiter and Mars, Isaac lies down on the steps and thinks
of Thea.

He can't believe it's been so long. He tried going back to New
York, but it didn't take; Williamsburg felt too hipster for him,
Manhattan too vacuous and empty. What good is it going to
any bar or party in the world if she's not there?

The sun cracks like an egg yolk, a round, yellow ball rising
through the buildings of the inner city, and the surrounding
clouds turn a flaming red in response. Somebody smears the
egg so the sky is coated in layers of yellow, and layers of red, as
though an impressionist painter has been dreaming of brunch.

He sighs, watching the fiery sky, the moon still visible and
the pink mark of Mars slumbering to the left. 'Red sky in the
morning,' he whispers, then glances at the square around him.
The city is foggy, and the mist swirls around the bronze lions.
He wishes it would swirl around him, maybe swallow him up
until he, too, is lost in time.

He mustn't think like this. He has everything to live for.
And yet, somehow, everything he is living for lies in his memory. Isaac touches a hand to the chain at his neck and pulls it
outside his jacket, fingering it lightly.

It had surprised him when he found Thea's ring in his pos-
session after the jump. He'd pulled it from his pocket, then
clenched his hand tight until the stone cut into his fingers, in
case the other Thea should see and realize what she had done.

He'd tried to recall her sleight of hand – the moment when Thea had both rings, and left one with him.

She had given him a lifeline, or a keepsake. He isn't quite sure which. But regardless, he wears it on a chain around his neck – he never takes it off. Isaac supposes he has one, and Thea the other.

He sighs again, his eyes still on the sky. He recalls all of the times he's dreamed she'll come back to him, or imagined – hoped – the two Theas had run a bait-and-switch, and really *his* Thea is the one who travelled back to this world in the glass house, so they could be together. But time has been unkind to such fantasies; after a decade he sits in Trafalgar Square at sunrise, alone.

'Shepherd's warning,' he murmurs at the crimson sky, the ecliptic revealing the arc of the planets tangibly close, in a familiar line-of-sight trick. Five planets lie above him on the celestial sphere, and without a shred of self-consciousness, Isaac waves as they hit their peak conjunction.

He shuts his eyes, slipping the ring over his little finger and off again, a subconscious habit he's picked up since he lost her.

Thea.

He opens his eyes.

Isaac looks through the cityscape towards the Houses of Parliament and the rose-tinted tower holding Big Ben, the dawn fog shrouding urban details like bus stops and traffic lights. His breath catches as a lone figure walks across the square, its outline hazy in the first tentative rays of daylight.

He sits up, the backs of his legs damp from the dew on the steps. Without the vista of a wide and sprawling horizon, the sunrise over the city moves in fits and starts. It takes time, and every moment is time spent alone. Not in grief – after a decade, that's dulled – but time suspended in the absence of happiness.

Isaac exhales as the dawn reveals its final bloom, announcing the arrival of today. He can no longer live in the past, or the future, or even an alternate present. The mist begins to dissipate, and the lone figure comes into focus: a woman walks towards him as the moon and the sun share the sky, and a diamond glints in the first light of a new day.

Acknowledgements

I was overwhelmed to receive a lot of support from authors, bloggers and readers for my first novel, *Hold Back the Stars*. I would really like to thank the following for shouting about the book in all manner of ways:

Thank you to world-class authors Matt Haig, Rowan Coleman, Maggie Harcourt, Samantha Shannon, Debbie Howells, Renée Knight, Laline Paull, Emma Jane Unsworth, Lisa Lueddecke, Melinda Salisbury, Anna McPartlin, Caroline Smailes, Colleen Oakley, Miranda Dickinson, Claire Douglas, and James Oswald. The way you lent your support to an unknown debut author was breathtakingly kind and I'm grateful. Thank you.

Word of mouth is everything when it comes to reading. Thanks to the book bloggers and bookstagrammers who championed my writing from the get-go, including Leah Reads Books, Stacey Woods, Sally Akins, Lia from Lost in a Story, Joanna Park, Samia Sharif, Crini and Sana, Janay Brazier, Christina from Chrikaru Reads, Lizzie Huxley-Jones, Ellen Devonport, Jana Vlogs, Beverley Has Read, Kate from For Winter Nights, The Book Haven, Kaisha from The Writing Garnet, and Ralou from the wonderfully named Collector of Book Boyfriends.

Opening the door to feedback can be double-edged and, as often happens, I found it tricky to close the door again to write this novel. When I eventually found the words, I discovered it was even more enjoyable to draft than my first! That's rare, from what I hear. So thank you to the people who helped me find my confidence again. They include Louise Dean and the KritikMe Krew, Margaret 'Kate' McQuaile, Dan Dalton, Gillian McAllister, and Craig Ainsworth, as well as my incredible family Jane Wood, Don Wood, and Jonathan Hopkins.

Thanks to my agent Juliet Mushens; I'm so honoured you believe in me. Darcy Nicholson at Transworld – thank you. So much. When I sat opposite you at breakfast and you bounced in your seat with excitement about publishing my next novel – which I hadn't written yet! – I went straight to my desk and *finally* knuckled down to it. Your enthusiasm was the push I needed, and your insight and skill at editing brought this story up beyond what I'd hoped.

Simon Taylor, Hannah Bright, Nix Wright, Deirdre O'Connell, Beci Kelly, and all of the team at Transworld – thank you. You are wonderful and I'm lucky to be published by you. Thanks also to Howie Sanders at Anonymous Content for brilliantly repping my film rights, Gemma Osei at Caskie Mushens, and Sasha Raskin for looking after my books in the United States.

Thank you to my team at Warner Bros, including Jill Benscoter, Katie MacKay, Susannah Scott, Polly Cochrane, and Jessica Turner. It's lovely to be supported in both of my jobs, and I realize how lucky I am!

My wonderful family, some of whom are mentioned above, but also Amber Wood; Ella, Finley and Sol Adamson; Sam Wood, and Liz Pearn. I adopted a very fluffy cat this year so it feels only right to add him into the acknowledgements, given rescuing him is just about the most rewarding thing I've ever done (other than writing novels). Thank you, Arthur 'Artie' Flufkin, I love you. Marley and Poppy, you are the best dogs in this universe or the next.

To Katy Pegg, to whom this novel is dedicated, for adopting me as a friend in my late twenties, when I thought the type of close friendship I'd read about was out of reach. And to Carl Sagan, for writing stories like *Contact* and reminding this non-scientific human what interests me, and why I should attempt to take risks with storytelling. Sorry if any of the physics is wrong, that's all on me.

And finally – my huge thanks to you, for reading. Authors are simply shouting ideas into the void without readers. Thank you. Always.